REVIEWS F‹

'Blackmore makes his cha␣␣␣␣␣
his depiction of postwar London is a delight, focusing
sharply on Soho life in all its tawdry and intoxicating
glamour' *The Times, Metro*

'A touching romantic book charting the relationship
between the couple over 40 years ... there's a lot more to
this Soho café than just filter coffee. A good read' *Time
Out*

'Neil Blackmore has written so convincing a novel about
fifties London that it is hard to believe he was born a dozen
years later' *Publishing News*

NEIL BLACKMORE was born in Wales in 1970. State-educated, he read history at Leeds University and went on to do a masters degree in Film and Television Studies at Westminster. He has worked in a number of fields since graduating and is currently employed full-time as a television-subtitles editor. He lives in North London and is working on his third novel.

His first book, *Soho Blues*, was published by Oriel in 1998. *Split My Heart* is his second novel.

SPLIT MY HEART

Neil Blackmore

ORIEL

An Oriel Paperback

First published in Great Britain in 1999 by Oriel
A division of Orion Books Ltd
Orion House, 5 Upper St Martin's Lane,
London WC2H 9EA

A CIP catalogue record for this book is available
from the British Library

ISBN 0 75282 134 2

Typeset at The Spartan Press Ltd,
Lymington, Hants
Printed and bound by
The Guernsey Press Co. Ltd, Guernsey, C.I.

Split My Heart was written by Ibn Hazm (tenth century) and the
translation is by Cola Franzen, © Cola Franzen 1989, from
Poems of Arab Andalusia, published by City Lights Books
(San Francisco) 1989.

An extract from *Poem of the Deep Song*, written by Federico
Garcia Lorca and translated by Cola Franzen. This version
© Herederos de Francisco Garcia Lorca and Cola Franzen.
From *Selected Poems* by Federico Garcia Lorca
Published by Penguin Books Ltd, 1997.

Special thanks to Zahid Mukhtar, for his advice and patience.

Thanks, too, to my mother and all my family,
Simon Trewin and all at Sheil Land, Cola Franzen and many
friends and colleagues, especially Zoë Fairbairns.

Palimpsest (′pælimp,sest) *n.* 1. a manuscript on which two or more texts have been written, each one being erased to make room for the next. ~ *adj.* 2. (of a text) written on a palimpsest. 3. used as a palimpsest.

THE OLD CITY

DAMASCUS, A GREAT man once observed, is nothing but a veil above veils. A palimpsest. Outer veils made of delicate cloth shimmer on the skin, revealing. Fine and delicate, yes. So much so that one can see the next veil, fluttering right below it. That cloth is also fine, delicate, maybe not quite as much. And through it, another veil is visible, and through that, another, and another, and another. This great man wrote long before the British came. Before the Ottomans, before Timur, before the Mamluks too. He was writing even before the Crusaders came. Yes, then Islam unfurled its blazing sun over the writer's known world, warming the civilised, just crisping barbarian Christian skins. Even then the great man saw veils in the stonework, he saw a shimmering skin in the architecture, a fluttering striptease in the curl of its carvings. A thousand years ago, he was writing. Even then this strange city brushed desert-dusty fingers against its many pasts. A thousand years later, it does it today, only the pasts are greater in number and the pasts of that palimpsest writer are obscured by our more recent ones. A sweeping panorama of minarets, domes, fountains, arches, swaying garden treetops. Dimashka. Dimashq. Damascus. But it's the same city, sure enough.

At the right time of day, entering the city – by car or by train or landing on its shabby airstrip – the first thing you notice, through rising heat, bare rocks and sparse brush, is the colour of the stone. The whole city is built of sandstone. And, in the first hours after dawn, or just around sunset, the sandstone is pink. Quite pink. The palest red first thing in the morning. Rouged like a lover's kiss-soft lips in the sensuality of sunset. Such redness, contrasted by the feathery green palms or the black cypresses that line the streets.

Nowadays a scientist will say, in their modern language, that this pale pink sandstone is a freak. A chemical imbalance in the rock formation. An inexplicable hint of chromium oxide – the colourant of rubies. Some bloody sediment in a billion-year-old splash of lava. But back in the forties, the Syrians liked to joke how their forefathers threw out so much illicit wine when the mullah came knocking that, as it splashed on the ground, it slowly stained the whole desert. How they used to laugh at that story! Between loud sips of tea, deep draws on the pipe, with their eyes on pink-peeling British soldiers. Long, long ago, they used to say that the stone turned pink when a single drop of Adam's blood fell, as God created Eve. A perfect scarlet tear, this drop of original blood hit the stones. When God made the whole place desert in his holy anger, a slow, shaming stain was revealed. Eve made the whole damned world pink!

Back then, Marina had loved that story best of all. And to this day, when desert winds are roaring so loud they pull the shutters in the city, the old women roll their eyes and cluck: 'That's Adam's rib snapping, I dare say.' 'By the Prophet, Eve is restless tonight,' is the reply.

Archaeologists might poke at the century after century of buried, broken pots, smashed archways, roofs torn down, petrified, turned-to-coal wood, chicken bones and black iron ladles, of Roman paraphernalia and Phoenician idols. The visiting nuns could go look at the Church of St Paul in Bab Kizan or at the Chapel of Ananias. And the Jews could hang on by the skin of their teeth in the Old City. But Marina knew that Damascus was a city of Muslims. The blazing sun up in the desert sky was Islam's sun. All other claims were pretenders'.

You could go crazy about the place. It can fill you with joy. Minarets shoot effortlessly to dizzying heights, close to God. Here and there are patterns of light and dark stone: limestone or basalt, shipped in by the old caliphs for drama. A breathtaking symmetry. A counterpoint to the rubied sandstone. Just-so, just-so, as Marina called it. A taste and restraint marks everything. Extraordinary, the old women selling on Madhat Pasha Souq cry, this extraordinary, crazy city! 'Full of devils! Full of jewels!' Soaring, needle-thin minarets, public fountains for the faithful to wash in, pillars lifted like palms into decorated domes, court-yards turned in on themselves, revealing smaller courtyards, high windows carved like flower-gardens, low doorways as old as Jericho, it was all here: the history of the known world.

Go see the Citadel, that square fortress. Yellow brick and fearsome turrets. Go see the Omayyad Mosque with its ornate treasury, that jewellery-box on stilts, all glorious decorations in gold, yellow, greens, blues. Or stare up and up at the red dome of Saladin's Mausoleum, marvelling at the great men who have come here, fought for this place, made it their own Damascus.

The Ottomans built here, too. Palaces and mosques were created for governors, soldiers, taxmen, merchants. Dreamlike memories of Istanbul, nostalgic memories of noise and smells and life on the Bosphorus. Colossal domes rising above massive square Turkish buildings. Out of gallery windows flashed the coal-black eyes of concubines and servants. Inside are dazzling decorations. Stone, marble, pottery, plaster, tile. Silver and gold, too. A palette of colours as broad as a summer garden shimmer under glazes. Rooms are cool and vast and airy. Cobalt-blue hexagons and ruby-red triangles, turquoise tulips and gilded monograms glitter, gleam. Still. You gaze up even today, with all the eyes-closed terror of Heaven those long-forgotten builders, potters, carvers, metalworkers, carpenters, dreamers intended centuries ago.

Quite literally, it is divine.

Marina Esmond, slim and pale, arrived in the Middle East during the first weeks of 1945. With the war in North Africa over, with the Mediterranean safe again, colonial wives caught in London at the start of hostilities began to drift across continents, towards their husbands. Men in cream suits smoking cigarettes waited silently with their drivers. Soon their wives would be getting out of aeroplanes, stepping off boats, in Cairo, or Algiers, or Tunis, or Port Said. Marina had sailed to Portugal, afraid that there might be submarines lurking below the cold black waves. From Portugal she flew to Tangiers, and from Tangiers she flew to Cairo. And there she was reunited with her husband, Paul. Marina Esmond, shoulder-length brown hair, glassy-blue eyes, left Egypt and went with Paul to their new life in Syria.

The Free French had reneged on their agreements about independence. Stupid buggers, Paul cried. Daft sods. When the French took over Syria in 1920, there was this kind of understanding with the Syrians. Wait your while and you'll get what's yours. Then the Free French – lost and alone in wartime Islam, with no orders coming from Nazi-occupied Paris, no grand imperial advice of what to do next – began buggering about. Damascus burst into open revolt at the end of 1944. The poor Free French. No orders from Paris, and certainly no cash. Some lunatic decided to shell the ancient city. They ended up asking the British to get them out of the bloody rebellion they had got themselves into. British troops arrived, to shoot Syrians and restore order. Paul came too, one of the clever types supposed to clear the whole sorry mess up. And Marina Esmond, long lovely hands, a freckled chest, was one of many colonial wives shifting around the globe at the end of the Second World War. Part lover. Part luggage.

Damascus, for Marina, started badly. She and Paul had been in the city just a few days, and Paul had made contact with a few old acquaintances and future colleagues. One had invited them to a party. A celebration of the expected Tory victory in the general election back home. Churchill had won Britain the war in Europe. Truman would win America the war in Japan. Marina and Paul sat in the back of a car. They were driving to a house belonging to someone called Bertie Clive-Wood. Colonial life was filled with visits to people you didn't know, in cities which were not yours. Mrs Bertie Clive-Wood would greet guests she barely knew to celebrate an election in which she hadn't dreamed of casting a vote. There'd be champagne and canapés. There'd be music, certainly a slow waltz. Rule Britannia, the trumpets would blare. When the telegrams came through, spitting and clicking news of another term for Winston, how they would laugh. How they would cheer.

The hours passed. Marina felt few nerves arriving at these parties where she knew nobody. Old money. That's what Marina was. Cultured, elegant, interested. Never the wrong word. She would put up her hair, slip into her dress, apply her make-up with a careful hand. Then the world could see – she was Old Money. And Paul, he was always so attentive, so charming, so funny. People flocked to Paul to listen to his jokes, to feel the pull of his gentle ribbing, to hear his near-the-knuckle observations about the British and whichever brown-skinned people they were ruling just then. The Esmonds were a big social success: happy, witty, tasteful, intelligent. They were the perfect party accessories for the informed colonial society entertainer.

Glasses chinked toasts. Bubbles sped through Krug and Laurent-Perrier, popping on the surface of conversations about where you had been in Egypt, had you known Charlie Woburn at school, did you see that very funny play last time you were in Cairo? Marina laughed at the jokes of men in black tie, complimented unknown women on the cut of dresses they hadn't made, turned to look at the band. More plodding versions of Noël Coward. Plod, plod, plod. Really very, very charming, she would say. Not at all bitingly dull, she would think.

Now and then, she would look through one of the French windows over on to Damascus to see a city at night. A planetarium of soft electric lights, both moving and still. The sound of the desert winds out to the east, racing across the blackness, to pour a fresh layer of dust on the city. A desert rain. Such a beautiful city. High and wide, and full of colour and noise. And silence too. Even as the minarets and towers and domes stay eternally still, the black and green and red trees sway slowly like dancers at the end of the evening. Then some voice or other would call her back, into conversations she had had a million times. This time the voice that called her was the one that she loved best.

'So what do you see?'

Marina broke into a smile. She turned to look at her husband.

'Oh, darling,' she smiled.

'So what do you think of the new posting?' he asked, nodding towards the city.

'The place or the people?' she smirked. Marina had never liked the people who lived out in the Empire. She thought it brought out the worst in people. Paul agreed. It turned the quite sane into megalomaniacs, who treated staff as slaves, and spoke to locals in a way they would never dream of speaking to Londoners.

'Place,' Paul replied.

Marina started to walk closer to the window, drawn to the lights of Damascus, the bright beacons of Old City minarets, to the glimmering starlit domes of the mosques and mausoleums. Paul followed her, lifting his fingers to gently touch her elbow.

'It looks beautiful at night.'

'Yes, it does, doesn't it?'

'Beautiful,' she repeated.

'But not as much as you do.'

Paul stretched out a hand to press the glass door's handle. The window opened outwards. A gorgeous soup of night aromas swept in. Memories of daytime heat. A scent of far-off rain somewhere in the greener west. Flowers, those rich, heady, almost decadent blooms that filled the city, of soapy palm trees, and the spicy heaviness of cypresses. Lime and yew and cedar. The salty, Mediterranean dryness.

The band dumped Noël Coward. Good riddance, Marina sighed, when Irving Berlin came along.

Cheek to Cheek.

Paul watched his wife. Her soft, wavy hair, brown, naturally highlighted with paler and darker strands, was swept up, revealing her long, slim neck and straight, bony shoulders.

'You don't mind, do you?' he asked.

'What?'

'Coming here.'

'Well, it wouldn't have been my first choice.' She smiled.

'But now that you're here, what would you say about it?'

He looked into her blue, blue eyes. Large and watery and kind. And so blue. Hers was a face, like his, quick to smile and laugh. A few slim lines edged her eyes as proof of it.

'I'd say that you were my husband and that I love you. That I love you and I will be where you are.'

For a second he was breathless.

'That's not an answer,' he murmured, when the second was passed.

'Then maybe I don't need to answer. Maybe loving you is what I need.'

'Your happiness is important, too, Mina.'

'I was away from you for three years, darling.' She stopped speaking and stared at him. Sometimes she could scarcely believe that they had been apart for so long, and that now, together again, those three years had just slipped away. Like salt through fingers. 'After that time on my own in London, my happiness is being with you, Paul. Wherever that is.'

Mina mine, he used to say, knowing it would make her face break into a happy, girlish smile. In 1945, Marina and Paul had been married for eight years. For that last three, she had lived alone and unhappy in London in a tiny flat not far from Paddington Station. Paul had gone off to war, to serve in North Africa. They had not seen each other once. Never once spoken on a telephone.

Letters came, some with sentences struck black by the censor's pen. Postcards with incongruous tourist scenery and informative epitaphs about each picturesque subject, as if the world was unscarred by bombs and bullets and battles. Leave had been impossible. Until the end of 1944, it was simply too dangerous for civilians to travel across Europe by boat or plane, and too time-consuming to give officers leave to travel between Britain and North Africa. Paul had not been back to England in the whole of his war, and Marina had not been allowed to go to him. It had been the loneliest time.

Black crows had swept down into Sussex Gardens to pick through the detritus of night bombings. Marina would pin on her green hat with the sable trim and go to her job in Whitehall, translating German and resisting old men's passes. Her parents had a house in Chelsea, to which they would summon her for chilly dinners. Such nights would always include requests-cum-instructions that she should live with them at least until 'he' got home. They felt that her living alone, just shuttling between the office and that gloomy flat, was not exactly indecent, but certainly a touch flagrant.

Paul and Marina had married one cold November. 1937. Since then, Paul had risen from his junior role in the Foreign Office, won a lot of brownie points in one hot war, and began a colder one as a well-paid mediator in the negotiations for Syrian independence. Marina, always writing letters, always dashing off intelligences. *Dear Mother* . . . Reassurances, sops, confidences. *Darling Papa* . . . To those she had left behind in England, she felt she would be able to prove that her decision to marry this 'nobody' was paying off after all. *Dear Clara* . . . *Dear Jane* . . . *Dear Alice* . . . Now she could point to a job, and a house, and a staff of white-gloved Arabs and say, I was right all along, Father, you were wrong, Mother.

But there were no children. Not yet, she used to tell her parents. But Marina was thirty and had been married for eight years. Not yet, she used to smile, feeling her smile getting weaker each time. Marina had never once been pregnant. No, she'd never even so much as suspected she was. Never once in the last eight years had she missed a period. She could not even remember a week of lateness when she'd maybe crossed her fingers as she sat on the bus. Counted the days. She was never late. If only her periods had been as unreliable as those red buses she sat on for hours, travelling from Paddington to Whitehall and back.

1945. Marina could just feel her hope starting to fade. Travelling around Damascus she could look at a pregnant woman – an Arab woman with her hands over a full bump, a social acquaintance tapping her tummy and whispering 'a month now' – and, for the first time, think, 'I'll never be you.' When she'd arrived in the Middle East from London a few months before, she'd had a short spell of thinking maybe. But Paul didn't want to raise her hopes. When she wanted him to touch her, when she tried to touch him, too often he kissed her good night and rolled over. It had been the same before, in London. No matter how much she wished otherwise – with the man she was sure she could change, who could live up to her expectations of love – things were not better in the bedroom now. They were the same. She wanted to be touched. She wanted to touch. She wanted to be fucked. She wanted to fuck. But Paul could be as cold as ice. Oh, he tried. He made the motions. Went through them. No, he never once said or did a thing that was meant to hurt her. Sometimes it only seemed when things were bad between them – when her suspicions were ripe – that he made love to her with the passion she was sure she deserved.

Mina was his pet name for her. Only he ever called her it, and when he did it was like the softest, gentlest caress on her cheek. She nuzzled into it, warmed to it, wanted it. It was a sign of his love. A reassuring intimacy. Marina loved Paul. She loved his humour, his attentiveness. The way he always said how nice she looked. The way he asked her opinion. How he came over to see what she was reading and would ask her, interestedly, what she thought of it. He would take her to functions, to dinners, and speak about her, to her, with her, in a way which was happy and proud to be her husband.

'Marina,' he would say in a small circle of laughing friends, 'tell that story about . . .' and he would let her be the centre of attention.

'Marina,' he would say over dinner, during a heated debate about the end of the empires, 'you made that point the other evening that was so true . . .'

'Marina, tell us that joke about the woman with the . . .'

When they arrived in Damascus in 1945, she loved him as much as she had ever done. But she could feel that love changing into something quieter and calmer. (She would look up at her bookcase. Proust. *Swann's Way*, in English and in French. Woolf. *To the Lighthouse*, two versions, one signed by the author. Her beloved Lorca, of course. Or a dirty-mouthed detective story from America. Maybe even the odd daft romance.) She looked at her life and found so much of it pleased her, and so much of what pleased her was to do with Paul. If her expectations of love were fading, along with her hopes for a baby, part of an older Marina thought, so what? I have so much compared to so many women I know. I have almost all of a wonderful husband. Isn't that better than all of an ordinary one?

But what of passion? What of desire and need?

The music stopped. Irving Berlin dispersed into the night air. Marina turned back from the window. Bertie Clive-Wood was standing on the bandstand, calling everyone's attention.

'I say, everyone! Beg pardon!'

The crowd chatter seeped away into amused silence. Only the sound of wine bottles hitting empty glasses remained, and that too began to die. Marina walked over to the edge of the group that was gathering below Bertie. Paul followed, and when the couple stopped, rested his hand in the small of her back.

'Thank you,' Bertie cried. He was grinning. 'As you know, Colonel Foulkes has very kindly loaned me his telegram thingy for the evening and I'm delighted to announce that the first telegram has come through from Jerusalem about the results.' Bertie was looking very pleased with himself as he read aloud. 'Now, this one is a bit dull. Says, "Estimated results coming in next minutes. Stand by."'

He looked up at the crowd, who giggled a little. Then he added, 'Is everyone's glass full?' The odd voice popped up with some comment or other. Not full enough, old boy. Where's the fizz, then? Marina could feel Paul's hand on her hip. Across her back, through her dress, she could feel the heaviness of his jacket and the warmth of his body beneath. She smiled.

Another telegram arrived. Bertie called for quiet again, and with great authority, began to read it aloud immediately. As he did so, there was a change. Or rather two changes. The first was a change in the silence of the crowd. Before, the silence had been the hush of expectation and excitement. It was actually barely contained noise, the moments before cheering and laughter and congratulations. But in no time it would be the dead, desperate silence of everything going wrong, of people not knowing what to say next. The second change was the bigger one. Because in the next moments, Britain – Britain and its whole Empire – would never be the same again.

Bertie started to read.

' "News very bad." ' He stopped, the happiness draining at once from his voice. A collective groan rose from the crowd. Bertie didn't know whether to go on. A man called to him to continue. For God's sake, to continue. ' "Labour has shock landslide. Churchill out." ' A woman could be heard clear as a bell, crying 'What?' ' "Churchill out," ' he repeated. Bertie looked devastated. Had he held up a mirror to the crowd he would have seen a room full of people similarly devastated. Bertie muttered something. 'The bastards.' And then he left the stage.

Nervously, the band began to play a lame foxtrot, but no one danced. No one even turned around to look at them. All over the British Empire, at parties just like this one, colonial society was staring at the floor and wondering what on earth would happen next.

Marina looked at Paul and shook her head, shocked. Neither of them were actually Tories, but Marina had assumed that the Conservatives would sail back in.

Churchill was a hero, after all. Paul, who did not believe much in party politics, was a little shaken. But he knew, having worked at Whitehall, that this would be a change in the management, not a change in the system. But that night the impact of change seemed enormous.

Paul's hand gently rubbed Marina's shoulder.

'Gosh,' she said slowly.

'Yes,' Paul replied.

'It's a bit of shock.' Marina laid her head back against her husband's chest. 'It changes everything, really.'

'Yes.'

'What will it mean to you, Paul, to your work, to things in Syria, with Labour in power?'

Paul put his arm a little further round her, to hold her tight.

'Consider the cat to have been duly put among the pigeons,' he said tersely, before adding: 'Come on, let's go, and leave the mourners to it.'

DAMASCUS, A HISTORY lesson.

This wasn't just a city full of Arabs on the fringe of a desert, you know. This wasn't just a name on a map, or a listing in a dictionary. Capital of Syria, population one million, et cetera, et cetera.

This is the city that Timur flattened in the thirteenth century, the very one which was rebuilt a few years later and still stands today in the twisting alleys and tiny gateways of the Old City. This is the city where Saul of Tarsus got it in the eye. In 333 BC, Alexander the Great took it. Even then he looked back three hundred years to when Nebuchadnezzar had done the same, and before that to when King David battered its walls.

Yes, this is the city that the Egyptians wrote about three thousand yeas ago, naming it Dimashka in a signature of squiggles and critters. This city is over four thousand years old, and in its time has talked more languages than anyone cares to remember or chooses to count. This is Damascus. And its name never really changes, no matter how many times its namers, in Ancient Egyptian, in Latin, in Turkish, do.

This long list of conquerors – this chorus-line of butchers and geniuses, opportunists and absolutists – was completed in 1920. At the end of the First World War, exactly four hundred years of Turkish rule came to its damp-squib end. The British marched into the city in 1918, promised the Arabs independence, then promptly gave it to the French as part of the Treaty of Sèvres. To the Egyptians, the Phoenicians, the Greeks, the Persians, the Nabataeans, the Romans, the Omayyads, the Abbasids, the

Seljuks, the Crusaders, the Mamluks and the Ottomans was added the name of the French Republic. Then, one winter, 1944, the Syrians decided that they were old enough and ugly enough to look after themselves.

And it was down to the British to step in again, to open fire on the occupants, and to whisper temptingly about independence.

Arranging flowers in the airy sitting room at the back of her house, Marina smiled to herself. She kept the windows shuttered, in the bedrooms, in the dining room, in the breakfast room all day long. But this room looked out over the lemon trees in the garden. Its French windows were ringed with pale pink irises and small white desert roses. Afternoon sunlight poured through the open windows. The heat and the perfume buoyed her. She clung to their lifebelt. Beautiful. All day she would sit by the windows, reading or writing letters to England, sketching the flowers, looking at photographs from their London days, thinking how she loved London, wondering if she could love Damascus. Or she would just sail on the sweet, heady drunkenness of the ripe lemons, listening to the singing chatter of the women in the street beyond the garden's high, white walls, the few words of Arabic she understood.

When they came to Damascus, Paul was given a house in the district where the Europeans lived. Marina disliked most of them – a mix of French-Algerian *pieds noirs*, recently arrived British administrators and their wives, and those curious well-to-do misfits who seemed to drift around North Africa and the Middle East doing very little. They warned her never to go into the city alone, never to ride there alone in her car without a driver, never to speak to the Arabs. They had cursed the Arab women for not showing enough deference, for eyeing *them* with contempt. They told her to fear the handsome brown boys for what they did to White women when they could, on dead black nights, under the cover of the cicada songs. But Marina grew to love to see those boys, dressed in white, walking the narrow city streets. She loved to see them look at her, proud, defiant, lustful.

High, white walls and a thick curtain of green cedars screened Paul and Marina from both White and Syrian Damascus. But beyond the lush cedars Marina could smell the soapy balm of high palms and the dry perfume of the pines. She could smell the city.

Each day, as Paul returned from his work, Marina would meet him in the cool, shuttered half-darkness of their hall. And each day, he would hold his arms loosely apart to greet his wife. He would remark on what she was wearing, how she had dressed her hair. Marina's hair was always immaculate. Her mother used to say, 'Even the plainest girl can be saved by a good hairdresser, my darling,' and Marina never, ever forgot her advice. Today, he said how marvellous she looked with a soft, silk scarf tied at her neck, a light yellow blouse, her arms bare and freckled. 'Even if you have to muck out, you should look right,' her mother would add. 'You never know when a nice chap will turn up.' Marina always walked into Paul's arms, her body reflected and inverted in the polished mirror-black marble floor.

After dinner, they sat on the veranda in the fading sunlight. Evenings at home were a respite from the social demands. Funny stories, anecdotes, jokes, lists of things to do, lists of things to miss. Maybe Marina would play the piano. More Irving Berlin. 'Say It Isn't So'. A little Bach. A dash of Mozart. Or maybe they played a record. Little black discs spinning shiny on a gramophone, accompanied by the cricketing of cicadas, or the maghreb wails from the minarets.

Intimacy. A hazy gold dappled the sweet, green trees. Yellow light was applied to the leaves, like tiny brushstrokes, till the naked eye couldn't tell lemon from cedar or cedar from lemon. Marina had once said that this garden in the evening was like some lost Cézanne. All you saw was light, not form. Shape. Just the play of light on colour. Paul had changed into an open shirt. Muhammad, one of their servants, came with a bottle of malt whisky, a jug of water, and glasses. He left again at once, silently. Marina let the late sun soak her. She smiled to herself, closing her eyes. Paul made the drinks, handing her one. Beside his chair was a pile of papers he should have been reading.

She turned her face to the evening sun. The pink light suffused her garden, indeed the whole of old Damascus.

'How long do you think we'll be here?'

Paul looked up.

'Pass.'

'It can't be long, can it?'

'It *could* be years.'

'Surely the French can't hang on for long. I mean, they nearly lost control just a few months ago.'

'No, you're right. I would say that London, especially Labour London, will want us out of here a bit sharpish.'

'What if the fighting fires up again?'

'I don't know, Mina. I think London would have us on the first train to Jerusalem and we'd let Paris sort it out. The war is over. Soon the French will be able to sort things out themselves.'

'The bloody French were shelling the poor buggers in Al Merjeh only a few months back. If you're shelling people in what is supposed to be your city, isn't it time to give up?'

Paul laughed.

'Marina Esmond, I think you've just solved the riddle of empire!'

She faked a cross look.

'No, but isn't it so?'

'Things aren't going well in the kitchen if you're bombing your own pantry, no.'

'So it won't be long, then?'

'Well, the bloody lefties in London aren't going to be keen to hold on for too long. They're hardly going to be big pals with de Gaulle, are they? And they've already said India can do what it damn well likes. Well, what will they care about Syria? They'll say, "Bloody Churchill has wasted far too much money on Syria. Let's spend it on some other bloody nonsense."'

Paul's cold-fish pragmatism made Marina laugh. Whenever he said the Arabs were perfectly able to run things for themselves, she smiled, because she knew, in a day or two, she would smile again when he said the Arabs didn't have the sense they were born with, thank God for the British.

Her fingers lifted to her hair, pulling out pins, letting it tumble down. The sun bleeding a hazy red into the darkening sky. Marina suddenly felt a chill, in that way skin does after sunlight. 'Paris will come up with some scheme to keep it all going until the buggers come and slit our throats in the middle of the night!'

She laughed at her own black joke.

Just at that moment a chill descended. The evenings could get cold in Damascus, especially in the areas north and west of the Old City where the desert night was unrestricted by high walls and narrow alleyways. Paul's jacket was on the back of his chair. Marina slipped it from under his weight and draped it around her shoulders.

They had been silent for a while when he asked:

'Where would you like to go next?'

She giggled a little.

'You sound like a djinni. Rub the bottle and make a wish.'

He laughed, too.

'"Oh, lady, where wouldst thou have me take thee?"'

She sucked on her lip and screwed up her eyes, in mock thought.

'Oh, ends of the earth, please!'

'And will you require a first-class ticket?'

She clapped her hands.

'I shall require a cab, Paul!'

She came over and sat on his lap, out on the veranda. Their noses and mouths were close as they spoke. Intimate.

'But you haven't told me where you want to go next,' Paul said.

She smiled broadly and happily.

'Right, Paul. I would like to go to the Savoy for breakfast. For kippers and scrambled eggs. A pot of tea. And toast going cold on their silver racks.'

'That's not much of a posting, is it?'

'I didn't know we would be posted again.'

'We don't have to be, but we could be, if you wanted.'

'All right, then. I wanted to be posted to the Savoy for breakfast. I think I would last there for a year or two, don't you?'

His hand was on the back of her head, in her hair, and pulled her face to his. He kissed her.

'I think you would.'

Their lips were touching as he spoke.

WHAT DID MARINA know? Not that much. She did not know about Paul's first time. A young man, when Paul was studying in London. A man with red hair, who smoked cigarettes in a silver-tipped holder, who claimed to know Auden. Who whispered glamorous lies as he peeled the shirt off Paul's trembling back. She did not know about chance encounters, in London, within a year of them being married. Sure, she knew what some British men came to the Middle East for. And then she found out that Paul was just one of those men. She would never forget how she found out. One day, by chance, she found a note inside his trouser pocket. It had been folded so tight that the paper was starting to disintegrate. The ink was black. Run thin, violet, as the letters looped. All it said was, '*Thank you for the little things. K.*'

That was the first time.

Yes, she thought her heart would break. She thought it would explode with grief and hurt and rejection. She screamed and shouted. 'Do you think I don't know about desire, Paul? Do you think I don't want to be loved, don't need to be made love to?' Or she went very quiet and wanted the earth to swallow her. 'Because I do, Paul . . . I do . . . ' Never ask for a name, her mother had advised her before the wedding. 'I never ask, and so I never dignify a rival by knowing her name, by recognising her in the street.' Marina would think of her mother's advice often, and so never asked, just wondering what her mother would have said if her rivals hadn't been 'that sort of girl'.

But what did Marina want? Marina wanted one thing. One

thing only. Paul. Nothing she could do, promise herself, lie to herself about, could stop her loving and wanting Paul. Sometimes she wished it was as simple as chemistry. A bit of hydrochloric acid here. A touch of manganese there. And bingo! Out of love! No, Marina wanted the whole deal Paul had once promised her. A life free of only being someone's wife, of marrying the right sort of boy, of just being pretty at cocktail parties, of holding up big hats at days at the races, of talking lightly and charmingly. That was the first hook of their love. Freedom. What kept her hooked was that he never reneged on most of that deal. He was rare, Paul. Few husbands cared what their wives thought. Few husbands wanted to hear their opinions on politics, on books, on the husband's work. So much that Paul had promised had been delivered.

But he *had* promised her love too. Mad love. The love of ages. And that's what Marina wanted from her marriage – mad love. Mad love without having to give up being a human being. And each time Paul gave her a lesson in how it was not going to happen, Marina just became more determined to work all the harder for it.

MARINA WROTE A letter to her mother.

Dear Mother,

Thank you very much for your letter, and I am so glad to hear that Papa is feeling better now. Please take care of him until I get back, dearest. Very black news, the general election, one supposes, for him. I was at a do here when they were posting us the results via Jerusalem. Lots of long faces all round, but Paul is sure that there won't be that many shocks to the system. I'm sure James must be scowling all day in that tragicomic way of his.

We arrived in Damascus safely. The city is extraordinarily old, even for someone who is used to a city like London. I do think that its great age is almost magically evident wherever you go. The layout of the city is like going back in time. There is a main street of sorts. The first part of this is really quite new, and is called An-Nasr in Arabic. I think the Syrians did most of the work. The French seem to have done bally all for the last twenty years and left it all up to the Arabs! Then it sweeps down on to this big, noisy market area called the Madhat Pasha Souq. This is terribly Middle Eastern – all stalls and shops and commotion! Of course white ladies don't really go there alone, it's the start of the Old City. But you should see some of the young Arab girls, they really are unbelievably beautiful. One almost feels envious! The last part of the main road is just as the Romans built it! It's as straight as an arrow, and that's exactly what it's called – Street Called Straight. Paul wrote down the Arabic for me but I've managed to lose it. Everyone calls it Street Called Straight, and that area of the Old City is so picaresque and tumbledown that one feels like a Crusader walking straight into the Middle Ages! Everywhere are little mosques and churches and synagogues. The Old City walls are filled with these tiny little gateways leading in and out. One could get quite lost terribly easily. Apparently there is a very big square, which is the real heart of Damascus, which is called Al Merjeh. But when the French got into trouble, a lot of Syrians got killed there, so it's something of an off-limits district for ladies. As you can understand, tensions are running quite high.

But, Mother, having said that, you must not worry at all. I am very happy here, and it still feels marvellous to be back with Paul after all that time in the Sussex Gardens flat. (I can hardly believe the rows we used to have about me living there! It all seems so distant now.) Paul has found us a beautiful house. It's large and very airy and comfortable in that Muslim way. The walls are white, but the floors are the blackest marble. Like mirrors! There is a gorgeous garden too, full of small flowers, tended roses, even lemon trees. How glorious, Mother! Next time I shall enclose some photographs of us and of the house too. Paul is going quite brown in this sunshine, and his hair is getting fairer and fairer. He is almost blond now – quite Scandinavian! His job is very responsible and everywhere one goes he is very respected and obviously listened to. I believe that when we return to London he will be quite the thing at the Foreign Office.

Indeed, I think we shan't be out here too long. From what is being said, the arrangements for independence should go ahead quite quickly, as long as the French don't get shirty. It could be as soon as next summer that we're out of here. I think that Paul will come back to London then. After all, what is there to keep him in the Middle East?

If you have the chance, do you think that you could go to Harrods and buy me some nice summer scarves? I know it's hard to get your hands on nice things at the moment in London, but anything gauzy and light would be wonderful. Pale green, light blue – you know the sort of colours that I like. It's so hot out here that one can hardly wear high necks all the time and yet the Muslims aren't very keen on one showing oneself, so a batch of nice scarves would be just the trick for getting around the city. I know some ladies couldn't give a fig for what the locals think, but if you saw how sharply they can look at you, you would want to cover up, too! They are very often a good-humoured and very welcoming people, despite all the trouble that's gone on, but they don't like you to show too much!

I think I should dash because there is still so much to do. I'm not used to running a house this size. All those years in Sussex Gardens, with me saying I didn't need a maid. Now that I've got half a dozen staff I don't know what to do with them all! If only you were here, you'd make short work of them.

All my love and affection to Papa and James. Pats for the dogs.

Fond kisses,

M

THE MAN IN the crumpled, cream linen suit, with the thinning fair hair, the wide, glowing smile was the same Paul Esmond. Nodding and grinning at the secretaries, who looked up from their typing, he cast his small, pale, alert eyes over all he saw. He felt he missed nothing. He walked with a certain *je ne sais quoi*. The most careful eye would catch the artificiality of his mannerisms – the learned etiquette, the erasure of flat vowels and dialect words from his voice – but to most, he was the perfect gentleman about town. This office was his domain, given to him for his duties as Special Deputy Envoy in Damascus. He was one of a small team of British diplomats and administrators who had come to sort out the mess the French had made of Syrian independence. Beneath Paul was Edmund Taylor-Greene, a mean bureaucrat with a box of dirty tricks. And beneath him there were researchers and clerks and secretaries, both white and Arab. Sulayman Ahmed was twenty-two years old, so not a boy at all, but even as the most serious young man he retained a youthfulness, or rather a lack of cynicism which made the secretaries treat him like one of their nephews. Eyes the colour of mocha, with gleaming black hair swept in great waves over his head, a long, bony, angular face, not exactly handsome, more poised in its stillness. Paul was slightly taller than Sulayman, but only by an inch or two.

'Hello,' Paul began on first seeing Sulayman sitting in a small side-room. 'Are you new? Or have I just not seen you before?'

'I'm new, sir, Mr Esmond,' Sulayman replied nervously.

Paul grinned.

'So you know me.' He paused, staring straight at Sulayman, then asked, 'In that case, you'd better enlighten me about you.'

'Sulayman Ahmed, sir.'

Coming into the room from the doorway, Paul sat on the edge of the desk where Sulayman was working. The younger man eyed some papers as they crumpled beneath Esmond's weight. The older man grinned, watching Sulayman. The ink on the papers was not yet dry: indigo-blue was pressing into crumpled, cream linen.

'Tell me,' Paul began coolly. Except when afraid or angry, he always spoke with the same smoothness. Clear, articulate, calm. Knowing. 'Sulayman,' he continued, 'sounds more Turkish than Arabic. Are you Turkish?'

'No,' Sulayman replied. He knew he was starting to blush, as he did on any occasion a British man addressed him. The cool gloom of the government building might conceal his purple cheeks, he thought. Or the blaze on his skin may dapple the shadowy walls in a burnished, fiery red. 'My mother's father came from Istanbul, back under the Turks. He was a sort of administrator here. It is his name,' and Sulayman paused before adding, as an embarrassed afterthought, 'Mr Esmond.'

Sulayman looked at his papers quickly. How scattered they looked, he thought, panicked, his skin on fire. Now Paul was teasing; his eyes are playing *like serpents*, Sulayman's mother might say, meaning tricksy. Sulayman was a blusher. Now he was sinking into terror. And, of course, the deeper you sink into terror, the worse your fingers-and-thumbs paralysis seems to get.

Paul's hand pressed a document about the growth of Arabic as the sole lingua franca of Syria and the decay of the older languages spoken by the Christian and Jewish minorities. Armenian. Circassian. A bit of Kurdish. Turkish too. No one speaks Aramaic or Syriac these days, but those echoes ring in the Old City too. More memories ebbing before the march of Arabic.

The veins in Paul's hand stood out large and green-blue. You could almost see the blood gushing along them. You could almost feel the blood's heat, breathe the oxygen travelling through the arteries.

Paul was in his late thirties then. Yes, it was widely held that he was an attractive man. Charming, or *soigné*, rather than handsome. He told a joke about a woman who married a horse. The consulate wives lifted their hands to their mouths and blushed, and thought him so naughty. A bluer version had already made their husbands shake with laughter. He would always remember the name of a lady's son and ask how his schoolwork was going. He'd always remember which college a colleague went to, or comment on whichever sport he remembered they followed. Both men and women liked to talk to Paul at parties. He was funny. He was happy and quick.

The consulate wives with their fat, greying husbands who talked cricket and shooting, envied Marina. Paul, they said, is so interesting, so gallant, so dapper, so just-right. Marina enjoyed their envy, their eyes as she entered a room with her husband. Green. She knew that hearts were quickening, that eyes were lifting from conversations, that thoughts were passing through heads never to be said aloud. She liked that there were women around her who wanted to sleep with her husband. But, then, she wasn't threatened by them.

'And what are you going to be doing here, Sulayman?'

Sulayman was looking at his papers, pressed beneath Paul, staining. The hesitancy in his voice was plain.

'Translation,' he said quickly. 'Sir,' he added as an afterthought.

'Oh, you're clever, then?' Paul teased. 'Which languages?'

'Arabic and Turkish, sir. And some French.'

'And what were you doing before?'

'I'm a student, sir. I'm working on a doctorate at the university, Mr Esmond.'

Paul suddenly stood up and buttoned his jacket. He had been barely listening.

'You speak English beautifully, Sulayman. One would hardly know you were not English down a telephone line.'

This was meant as a compliment, and Sulayman took it as one, though even then he was aware of its double edge.

'Thank you,' he answered blankly.

Paul smiled, then started to leave.

'You're a cleverer man than me, then. I shall keep my eyes peeled for your work, Sulayman.'

THE PIANO. FOR the refined lady about town, or the mistress of a colonial household, no matter who her husband was, the piano was a must. You had to play it. A lively dash of Cole Porter. Gershwin. Or how about 'Clair de lune'? The girl about town needed to be able to play it and listen to it. And the piano had to be a nice one. No cheap uprights. Sleek and long and black. Steinway B Grand, and no shit. Open and loud enough to fill a whole room.

Marina had been invited to an afternoon reception at the house of Mme Deschamps, one of the biggest fish in European Damascene society. The invitation had been made informally at a dinner party given a week earlier, to which Paul had gone in his official capacity. Mme Deschamps had instantly approved of Marina. Marina could speak French very well, and Deschamps resented having to talk in English to the influx of British colonial wives. Plus, of course, Marina was the real thing. She spoke in the right way on the best subjects, knew people in London that Deschamps herself had met, and looked like she had been born to sit in Deschamps' recently imported white and gold Robert Adams sitting room. Paul had let Marina borrow his driver for a couple of hours. Marina had sighed, 'I can't turn up in a bloody taxi, can I?' which had made Paul laugh.

Once there, greeted, kissed and given a glass of champagne, Marina wished she hadn't come. It was the sort of event to which her mother loved to go. Fearsome society ladies would swoop down into some perfect home in Chelsea, or Belgravia, or

Knightsbridge, to rip apart a parade of morsels, those brought in on silver trays and those brought along by black cabs.

A hired pianist was tinkling with Ravel. Marina small-talked her way around the room in the first hour, and estimated she had another hour to kill before she could reasonably leave. Mme Deschamps, quite acceptable at a small semi-official dinner thrown at someone else's home, slowly mutated into a self-absorbed monster in her Robert Adams lair.

'What do you think of my new sitting room, Marina?' she cried in French, knowing that several British women present would be hard-pressed to follow the conversation. 'I've just had it done. It's been an absolute nightmare! Do you know how difficult it still is to ship furniture from Europe? Impossible!'

'It's beautiful, simply beautiful,' Marina replied with a smile. Marina was sure she had been born without the furniture gene. She liked to be surrounded by nice things, and certainly liked to poke around the shops in London – for a coat, or a hat, or through a shelf of just-printed books, smelling of forests and chemicals – but she really couldn't get excited about *chaises-longues*. Looking at the ornate table-legs, the gilt, the plaster columns, all she felt was how difficult it must have been to pull this off. The Middle East. Months after the end of hostilities in Germany. 'You must have had a terrible time, though.'

'My dear, it is *quite* impossible to get any sense at all out of anyone in Paris at the moment. You just about manage to get what you want from London, but you need someone there to fill out nine hundred forms for you. And, well, of course, Germany is just out of the question, and just as well, given that what you'd get would be the second-hand rubbish from some Jewish banker's house!'

Deschamps lifted a dainty hand to her mouth, laughing naughtily at her own joke. Marina smiled politely and looked around at the other women present, most of whom had not followed the French conversation, let alone understood why their hostess was giggling.

Another woman suddenly arrived rather late and obviously in a flap.

Mme Deschamps turned with balletic grace and went to kiss the new guest. The two of them spoke in French, too, but Marina could hear that the newcomer was British.

'Ladies,' Mme Deschamps began in English, 'may I present Mrs George Burroughs? She's just arrived in the city but we're old friends from Algiers.' There was a brief round of hellos and introductions. The woman's name was Clementine. Marina nodded politely. She wondered desperately whether she had fifty or fifty-five minutes left before making her excuse. 'Mrs Burroughs, ladies, comes to us from Teheran. Her husband is in the oil business.'

HUSBANDS. I SOMETIMES wonder if I am anything more than my husband. I do wonder where I stop being Marina and start to become Paul. I look at my skin, touching the back of my hand or the lines on my neck, into a mirror, to examine my hairline or my eyes. But I can't see the cracks, I can't see the surgeon's needlework that sews me to him, makes me an extension of him. I could be the most educated, the most charming, the most erudite woman in Damascus. But it wouldn't matter a damn if I had an unsuitable husband. I am Paul. But he is not me. We are not a two-headed unity. Rather we are two bodies, with different functions, but, for all the world, we have only one head. Paul's.

Husbands. I married Paul against my parents' wishes. They had wanted me to marry Alfie Villiers. Alfie and his fortune. But I married a nobody who had been to grammar school and wasn't right. My mother lifted her hands to her face as if she was about to cry. My father shook his fist. Husbands, he shouted angrily, women are *nothing* but their husbands. But I had wanted more than just to be someone's wife. I had wanted a life that I could call my own, and a man who would let me live it. And yet, somehow, as the years have passed, alone in London, or flying out here, in a way I haven't even noticed, I have accepted the life I never wanted. Paul has never forced me into that role, into the role of extension and prop, but he hasn't exactly complained when he saw me change from the fire-breather he married.

Wives. That's what we are all forced to become. It is wrong for me to blame Paul. He took nothing from me. And I gave up nothing for him. Paul and Marina, we're just cogs in the wheel. We could kick and scream and demand a better, fairer world. And we would not get it.

CLEMENTINE BURROUGHS WAS ten years older than Marina. A short, round, doctor's daughter from Surrey, she had been visiting an old schoolfriend in Spain when she had fallen in love with an American oil speculator, who went on to dig a fortune in the wastelands of Persia and Arabia in the thirties. She became Marina's first friend in Damascus almost by accident. A week later, Paul was invited to a concert being given by the chairman of the Mandate Economic Committee.

A string quartet played Mozart. Violins, a viola and a cello. Breathed, bowed, sawed through a slow, beautiful recital. Shifting textures were woven together into a dreamlike whole. Notes ran out like little waves over sand. Rippling and warm. Sparkling and detailed. The fingers of a larger, more magnificent whole. Marina sat transfixed by the playing. The careful synchronisation between the musicians, the way they manipulated the audience through moments of silence, sudden bursts of energy, through the sheer revelatory nature of interpretation of wonderful music. She watched their careful hands draw and turn the bows. Fingers, she watched them too, as they went white, then pink again, as they pressed and released on the bridges. All to create that marvellous, spellbinding, spine-tingling sound.

Sleep. It was like sleep, she thought. All your senses were occupied. She was cut off from the real world.

'Hello, we've met, haven't we?'

Her rapture was broken open. A voice spoke up loud and clear behind her and a hand touched her shoulder.

Startled, woken so unceremoniously, Marina jumped slightly, then started to laugh nervously.

'I'm sorry,' she cried, 'I was absolutely miles away!'

Clementine was standing behind her, grinning back, cheerfully extending a hand. Marina grasped it and shook it.

'Oh, sorry!'

'No, no, it's fine,' Marina lied.

'Clem Burroughs, in case you didn't remember.' There was a brief silence. 'Which, I'm afraid, I don't. Remember, that is.'

Marina smiled and shook her head.

'Oh! Marina Esmond. How do you do, Mrs Burroughs?'

'Oh, Clem, please. I don't like all that Mrs business.'

Marina smiled again and relaxed.

'I'm Marina, then.'

'You look like you were enjoying the music,' Clem said brightly.

'I was. I thought it was quite beautiful.' Marina paused to watch the musicians turn their sheets, whisper to one another about the next piece. The change in music caused a sudden upsurge in activity and conversation. White-coated waiters skimmed the surface of society. Champagne and martini made the rounds. Marina returned to her companion. 'And what about you?'

'I can't say that I do love it, Marina. I'm a terrible philistine. The worst sort!'

They both laughed.

'And what do you think of Damascus, Clem?'

'I think the city is beautiful. Quite beautiful. Teheran is an awful place. It looks like it was built last week, most of it. But Damascus is quite lovely. Have you been here long?'

'Hardly.' Marina shook her head as if to say, oh, no. 'Weeks, really.'

Clem mock-arched her eyebrow.

'And you know old Deschamps already?'

'Well, not *know*. Mme Deschamps adopted me. How do you know her?'

A waiter whisked by. Clem turned lightly and quickly, lifting champagne from his silver tray. Marina watched her give the young man a wink. Clem was a one-off among the dutiful, dull or desperate Europeans of the Middle East.

'She claimed me about nine years ago in Algiers. My husband is an oil speculator and we were living there for a while. He's a crook, really, but, hell, I love him.'

'And you've been friends ever since?'

Clem took her lips from the champagne and stared dramatically at Marina.

'She is not my friend. She just has the knack of turning up in cities before George and I arrive. But Deschamps is an old horror. The worst sort!'

'She seems to take a lot of pleasure in throwing her weight around.'

'Right,' Clem trilled, 'and she's got a hell of a lot of weight to throw around.'

Happy cackles. Each woman takes a sip of champagne. Bubbles race through their blood.

Clem looked around the large reception hall with its dim chandeliers and tall, feathery palms. The warmth of the evening slid down their necks, along the insides of their arms.

'Where's your husband?' Marina asked.

Clem peered through a sea of cigar smoke towards a tall, thin, bald man being circled by government officials.

'You see that one over there with the shiny head and the vultures starting to descend?' Marina nodded. 'That's George.'

Marina watched George talk animatedly for a second. How curious, she thought, to see husbands and wives for the first time. To match up the woman with the man and to wonder how on earth they ever got together. Clem was round and George was long. What about her and Paul? Surely people looked at them too, and wondered why.

'It looks like a lot of people want to be George's friend,' Marina said.

'He's as rich as Standard Oil, my dear.' Clem adopted her best

Lady Bracknell voice. 'It makes one *terribly* popular, cash wealth.'

'I see,' Marina laughed. Clem had the brightest smile, like she was filled with happiness. A happiness which couldn't help but burst out of her.

'Which one is yours, then?'

Marina looked around for a moment, without spotting Paul. Then she clocked him standing in the corner of the room, cigarette between his lips, being talked at by a prominent member of the old Free French regime. Marina nodded in his direction.

'That one. Cigarette. Fair hair. Frenchman getting upset about something.'

Clem pursed her lips and nodded in confirmation.

'He's not a bad one, Marina! You'll be the envy of the ladies tonight.'

Marina was looking at Paul as Clem said the words. You'll be the envy of the ladies tonight. It struck her hard, right in the heart. What Clem said was true. Compared to their bald, old, fat, boring husbands, Paul was quite the catch. And yet there was that part of him – that chemical imbalance – which none of them would have ever envied. She smiled at Marina as if to say thank you. Clem watched Marina's eyes return to her husband. A red raw moment. But Marina thanked her all the same.

Throughout the rest of the evening, the two women kept bumping into one another until each realised they had spent most of the evening as a pair. Clem spoke with such a freedom that Marina felt pulled into her orbit. Among the staid, subservient ladies of the Empire, never discussing anything more substantial than the difficulties of shipping couture and why Arab servants were surlier than African or Indian, Clem was a joy. She was loud and funny and didn't really care who disapproved of her. Marina would grow to like her more and more. At one point that night she said to Marina:

'Look at them, these dreadful drudges!'

She nodded towards a gaggle of women hovering around the hostess.

'Which ones?' Marina asked.

'Why, all of them. All of the bloody women here. Except you and me, of course.'

'Oh, of course, Clem!'

'They're like those little caged parrots you used to see everywhere. No one keeps them now. Too Hollywood. Parrots preening and trying to be pretty, but no use to anyone. Just slightly shabby ornaments.'

Marina turned to look at her. There was an honesty in what Clem had said. Not just that what she had said was true, but in that Clem really thought it. And yet, Marina thought, look at us, Clem and Marina. The only reason we're here is because we've followed our husbands.

'Maybe they think the same about us,' Marina said quietly. Then she brightened up. 'Maybe they're having the very same conversation about us right now.'

Clem hooted out loud. A couple of bow-tied crustaceans turned around. Girlish laughter sprung from the two women. That laughter which echoes memories of girlhood. Topped up with a lot of alcohol.

'They don't have the brain to think that, Marina. Not a one of them has that many thoughts in a row!'

'So it's just you and me who have a brain each?'

'Just you and me, kid,' Clem replied in a gangster-flick drawl. 'Just me and you are the only sane women left alive in Damascus.'

They were both laughing now, laughing as they were speaking.

'Just Clementine, Marina and a whole army of lobotomised society ladies!' Marina laughed. 'We're a danger to society!'

'We'd better stick together. Or else they might get to us too.'

The women strode off into the room together, in a warm, fuzzy glow of new friendship and flat champagne.

MODERN SOUNDS HAVE appeared in Damascus. The scratch of pen-nibs on paper, the click of receivers on to telephones. High heels tap against the black marble of office floors like morse code. But above the *au courant* frenzy of information passed, the flat, painted past watches the sinister, silent future. The curling Arabic script, gilded and inscrutable to Western eyes, whispers. 1945: the scribes, clerks, counters of coins, scribblers are blue-eyed. They speak English and never attend mosque. Blue eyes lift to the decorated ceilings under which they work, wondering what those wave-like words conceal, what the gestures of the figures mean. Pink skin blushes. Hot thighs press hard.

Paul arrived at work. Stopping for a second outside the door to Sulayman's office, Paul listened to an electric fan whirr inside. Opening the door, Sulayman Ahmed was sitting back in his chair. Feet up on the desk, he was reading a book. A cigarette smouldered between his raised fingers. Falling light from an open window was glinting on reading-glasses. It was late morning. The bright, fresh yellow light seemed like a canvas for the curling blue smoke.

'Mr Ahmed?' Paul called loudly, unable to stop himself smirking.

Glancing up, Sulayman's face fell. Horrified, he stopped himself falling from his seat, scrambling to his feet, dropping his book.

'Mr-Mr Esmond!' he squealed. The book's hardback spine loudly smacked against the marble floor.

Paul began to laugh, watching the young man panic.

'What *are* you reading there?'

Sulayman glanced at the book on the floor. His eyes flashed with terror but he dared not look at Paul:

'Oh, nothing! Background reading!'

Paul looked at the electric fan. The room was not warm yet.

'It's quite cool in here, Sulayman. May I call you Sulayman?'

'Yes, of course, Mr Esmond.'

'It's quite cool in here, Sulayman, but you keep the fan on.'

Sulayman's ears had already become accustomed to the fan's drone.

'If the room is kept cool from the start of the day, the heat does not build in the afternoon, Mr Esmond.'

'I see,' Paul whispered. 'That's very clever.' He paused. 'I shall have to tell my wife.'

Neither man spoke. Paul stared intently at Sulayman. Loving Marina – what Paul called love (always on Paul's terms, Marina would reflect) – had not prevented a series of affairs with young men. At moments like these, Paul was not thinking of Marina. Loving Marina – at moments like these, the cruellest deception men perform is not the act itself. It's that they are not thinking of their wives at all. That emotion is temporarily shut off. No, they are only thinking of what is before them for the taking. Yes, about sex. And for Paul, the Arab world offered these young men up for the taking. To him, they were little more than tender morsels, brown-skinned, lithe, exciting. He hated the encounters to be had in London – hurried, breathless sex in public parks, in lavatories, snatched moments close to the footsteps of shoppers, dog-walkers, people watching brass bands on sunny afternoons. Here, there was no shame and little secrecy in the pleasant diversions the young men invented in that womanless youth that preceded marriage. And if a small exchange of money was all Paul had to worry about here, that was no problem. He believed that almost any proud-eyed youth on the city streets would fuck you, wash and quietly leave. That price was no higher than a late-night taxi fare or a round of drinks at the Empire Club. But Paul, like all those white men who trawled the Middle East for sex, was wrong. It's just that Paul was the one who learned hard.

Paul was suddenly curious to see what book Sulayman had been reading and had dropped. He slowly walked around Sulayman's desk. The marble floor was so magnificently polished. An inverted, impressionistic Paul was reflected in it. Huge feet and legs receded into strange, mirrored angles. Slim shoulders and an obscured face loomed into reflection as he stretched down to pick the book up.

With its spine between his fingers, Paul read the title aloud: '*Collected English Poems 1890–1930*, edited by Dorothy Nicholas.'

Paul suddenly turned and walked away, the book still in his hand. The ball of terror was ballooning inside Sulayman. He was sure to be sacked, yes.

He would have to return home, tell his father that the British had sacked him. Oh, and now too, with the marriage negotiations, when they needed all the money they could get.

His father would strike him, call him an idiot, an ingrate. Dr Siddiqi would be angry when he returned to the university. The other students would mock and berate him, accusing him of confirming what the French had always said about Arabs. Good-for-nothings! Layabouts! Fools!

Sulayman watched Paul turn back to look at him.

'You like poetry, then?' he asked slowly.

Sulayman rose to his feet. The fan was whirring. A shaft of light hit the black marble floor. A golden haze.

'Yes, Mr Esmond.' Sulayman was nervous.

'My wife – Mrs Esmond – likes poetry very much. Has volumes of the stuff at home. She insisted on taking them, even when we trooped off here.'

'Yes, I like it very much.'

Paul grinned broadly at Sulayman's understatement. He clapped his hands.

'Good! You shall come to dinner at my house tonight. Dinner

with Mrs Esmond and me! She shall bore you with poetry and I shall bore you about work. What do you say?'

'But, Mr Esmond –'

'I shan't take no for an answer, Sulayman.' Paul grimaced mockingly.

And Sulayman could not refuse. He would telephone his father to let him know what was happening. His father would instruct him how to behave, to be polite, to make a good impression. His father would tell him he was proud of him, with this job, impressing the British. Paul looked at Sulayman and grinned charmingly again. Serpents. 'Cat got your tongue, Mr Ahmed?'

'Pardon, Mr Esmond?' Sulayman did not understand the phrase.

Paul pushed the book of poems under his arm. 'Will you come, man?'

Sulayman could not refuse. He could barely breathe, with nerves and terror. He was looking at Paul, watching him smile knowingly, seeing the book under his arm, and suddenly heard himself saying:

'Yes . . . Yes, thank you, Mr Esmond.'

'Excellent! I shall call for you here at six sharp.' Clapping his hands, an echo rang loudly in the high emptiness of the room. 'Don't worry about dressing. Mrs Esmond is not your average sort of English girl!'

And he breezed out, taking the book with him. Sulayman looked down at his cotton shirt, his navy-blue trousers, beige sandals. And beyond, in the mirror-like black marble, an inverted Sulayman, was wondering how he should be dressed.

Clark Gable in a tuxedo?

Sulayman finished the translation. He popped the poem into an envelope and marked it for Siddiqi's attention. He slipped out of the office. It was four thirty. A little over an hour to go.

The next day, Siddiqi, his old tutor, would open the envelope and read the poem four times. It was a beautiful translation and a tear of pride crept into the old man's sentimental eye. Sulayman had written a note above the ancient lines. 'Once you said to me, "Let the pen kiss the paper, let the poet's voice enter yours." I think I've finally understood what you meant. I've understood what it means to be taught.'

> How I wish I could split my heart
> with a knife
> put you inside
> then close up my chest
>
> So that you would be in my heart
> and not another's
> until the resurrection
> and the day of judgement
>
> There you would stay while I lived
> and after my death
> you would remain buried deep in my heart
> in the darkness of the tomb.

The poem stayed with Sulayman, in his head, in his bones, in his mouth.

The poet's voice stayed too.

HEARTS ARE NOT made of stern stuff, you know. They're as soft as ripe fruit. Paul Esmond was a charmer. His hair was neatly groomed. His eyes were pale, but could muster such an intensity it would take your breath away. His smile was wide, almost magical in its easy happiness. He played games and wanted to win them.

Marina was waiting, as usual. She played with cut flowers, discussed the menu with the cook, flicked the pages of a book, a magazine, watched the hands of the clocks in her house, and awaited Paul's return. Sometimes she hated being here, without any friends, or rather without anyone she wanted to befriend. But Paul was the centre of her world. Her mother had raised her to love a man to whom she could devote her life, no matter what. And if Paul wasn't the man her mother had planned for, her training was every bit as effective.

An afternoon breeze danced with the diaphanous window-nets in her bedroom. In a wide, clear mirror, Marina applied her mascara. In the glass, the weightless nets blurred like ballerinas mid-movement. The hush of the lemon-scented wind calmed her.

Marina clipped on a pair of pearl earrings. Paul had bought them for her just before he left London to come out to the Middle East, she remembered. They had walked Regent Street, Jermyn Street, into Mayfair. Paul wanted to buy his wife a gift. For no special reason. 'Because I love you,' she remembered Paul saying. The warmth of her happiness was so strong just then. At last, Marina's hands had pressed against one shop-window. Reflected in the shining glass, Paul had watched her sparkling, delighted smile. Those ones, Paul, those ones. Paul kissed her neck in the street as he handed her the box. Wrapped in red silk, tied with a bow. Each told the other how much they loved them. The first drops of rain were splashing the street. Such memories had a strong pull on Marina.

The Arab driver nodded courteously at Sulayman as he held the door to Paul's car. Sulayman climbed into the back; his eyes were watching the windows of the government buildings, watching for eyes behind screens. Paul was sitting beside him and told him not to look so nervous. Paul talked idly as they drove through the city. The driver was silent, nudging the silver-grey Daimler through its dusty streets. Six sharp, more or less. Damascus was swapping masks. Old men in fezzes stepped into the road, carrying folded newspapers, cursing drivers in their big, black, rusty cars. Tanned soldiers smoked cigarettes in their parked jeeps, eyeing small groups of pretty girls. High bundles of kindling, or aubergines, or purple-and-gold rugs, dried fish, lentils, lemons, coffee beans teetered on the backs of mules, as market traders struggled home. Women in their veils moved among the mules, the cars, the jeeps, the old men in fezzes, hauling their shopping and their children along. Their daughters – hair piled high Paris-style, in floral print dresses – swung their university books as they teased the boys in front of them. Others pressed pamphlets into hands, nervously eyeing the soldiers, who lustfully eyed them back. Grandfathers held grandsons' hands as they walked in the fading sun, the old men brown and bow-legged, the boys lifting huge, dark eyes up to fantastic stories. Men and women running food stalls were wiping the grease off their sleeves or swilling down their trays. Shawerma, they shouted. Lamb cooked under fat and served between bread. Imagine it, one hot Damascus evening. Shish kebab or shish tawouq – dinner on sticks. Or how about a cold aseer juice, the sellers cried? Cold and sweet, lime, orange, mango, with a splash of milk in. Wives and mothers smiled down from high windows, their arms bare in the evening sunlight, their tired calling to friends in windows across the narrow street. Sulayman, only half-listening to Paul speak, wondered if White people saw Damascus in the same way as him. Or was it as mysterious to them as the black or white veils the old women wore? Concealing and secretive. Below that veil, Sulayman knew, was the greatest mystery of all: the people who made up this crazy, ancient city. 'This city,' his mother would shriek, 'is crazy! What a crazy place! It's on fire with life and full of nothing-at-all!'

THE SERVANT OPENS the gates slowly. He gives Paul a shallow bow as the car pulls into the drive. Staring up at the neat white house, shrouded by high cedars, I shiver. Gable is out of his tuxedo.

Paul turns to me and says:

'Well, Sulayman, this is it. The ranch.'

Paul is like most Englishmen. He assumes that anyone who speaks the language understands its idioms, its colloquialisms, its slang. But I do not. And now, here in the world of Arab servants, white gloves, pretty Europeans in pretty clothes, now I feel like an interloper. Or an assassin.

'It's very nice,' I say, feeling sick.

An Arab in his work-clothes, coming to dinner with his boss and his wife, talking poetry. 'Think of such a thing!' the women of the city would cry, 'think of the shame! Just thinking of *your* shame cripples *us*!'

Oh, ululations!

Father purred with pride when I telephoned him at the shop. In the background I could hear English voices talking loudly. I had felt ashamed of him and of me, like we were parasites, little bugs in the body, feeding on the misfortune of the whole.

'You make me proud now, my son! Make me proud!'

My university friends would scoff at me, or call me a fool, even as they asked if his wife wore a low-cut dress, if I could see her breasts.

*

49

A glorious evening sunlight streams through an open door into the Esmonds' dark hallway. The servant – Paul calls him Muhammad – bows again and motions for our jackets. The coolness of the marble through my sandals is wonderful. Nervously I hand my jacket to Muhammad.

Suddenly Paul shouts out: 'Here she is! Hello, old girl.'

In sweeps Marina, in a light violet sundress, a white, silk shawl patterned with pink roses, and her brown hair pinned up high. A light, quick step. She smiles brightly.

For the briefest moment she rests in Paul's arms. He kisses her cheek. Seeing him there, with his nose pressing flat against her cheek, with his wide, handsome smile breaking, even as his lips are against her skin, I feel my heart go boom. I feel myself pulled deeper.

Marina's large blue eyes sparkle as Paul introduces me to her. No beauty, my mother would have shrugged, not the stuff of dancing girls. But I think she dresses like a movie star and talks like a queen. I watch the two of them – Paul and Marina Esmond – in their finery.

I do not understand the idioms. But I want them, Paul and Marina. I do not understand the slang. But I want to be them, Paul and Marina. And a part of them too.

AND HEARTS, THEY'RE nothing at all. Soft, ripe fruit, nothing more. Charmers like Paul can easily burrow deep inside them, like little white worms, and make themselves at home.

'So, Sulayman, what is it that you're studying?' Marina asked.

He was listening to her voice, low and light. She spoke quickly and with much humour, listening attentively to answers, putting in questions, adding anecdotes where she thought she should.

'Well, the lecturer with whom I'm studying is a specialist in classical Arabic poetry. I concentrate on Arab Spain's poetry, but he's undertaking a broad anthology of the poetry of the western Arabic world of what the West calls the Middle Ages.'

'Only the West?' she asked.

'Well, yes. During the Middle Ages, Christian Europe was of course . . .' Sulayman was going to say backward but stopped himself. Such large blue eyes staring so intently on him might flinch at so harsh a word. 'It was not concerned with art or science very much.'

'But you Arabs, you were just beavering away, eh?' Paul grinned.

Sulayman laughed a little. Because he did not understand what 'beavering' meant. Such confusion. The servant brought in plates, on top of which were what looked like a bright pink fish, a dollop of half-boiled potatoes and hardly any sauce. Wine was poured. Sulayman didn't drink but took some all the same. He held his knife at a different angle to Marina and Paul, and this began to concern him.

'And you're a translator, Paul tells me?'

'Oh, yes. Well, I speak Arabic and Turkish. Well, a lot of people do here, but not many Syrians speak English, so . . .'

Talk.

Marina watched the young man speak. He was careful in which words he chose, careful not to offend these two British people, careful not to offend his boss. Nervous too as he told her about poetry, or the city, or his life at the university. Marina nodded and smiled. Nodding and smiling, these were her fortes, she often joked to Paul. Turn up, nod, smile. 'It's not much,' she used to cry, 'but no one does nodding and smiling better than me!'

But as the dinner progressed, Paul was jovial, charming and irritatingly attentive to him. Sulayman relaxed a little, even as he felt Marina watching his every move. Truth was, she quite liked him. He was a nice boy, she thought. He shared her interest in books and poems. Sweet and serious, polite and intelligent. She even dashed off upstairs to find a book of poems she said she wanted to give Sulayman as a gift. *An Anthology of Modern British Verse*. But all the same Marina was wondering, 'Why are you here?' Or rather, 'Why has he brought you here?'

Suspicion. It lasted no time. It was almost gone in the morning. But, despite compliments about women being envious of Marina, despite Paul's hand in the small of her back at social occasions, despite happy conversations in the evening sun on the veranda, this was what Paul had given her. Suspicion.

Lucky old Marina, she was thinking. Lucky old me.

NIGHT AIR, COLD. The sky, such a ferocious and beautiful black.

A drop of blue in the painter's enamel, you could say, just softening the purity of a midnight sky. Marina stood in the doorway as I walked Sulayman to the car. Cedars rained down like frankincense, glorious, intoxicating. Sulayman later told me that he was tipsy on our few glasses of wine. My driver nodded as he opened the car's back door for Sulayman. The night was deliciously close, loud with the breeze, the hoot of owls, the movement of the trees. A blue-black heat, buzzing with passion. With desire, the uncontrollable need for skin to touch skin.

'You see, Sulayman,' I whispered, suddenly moving closer to him, 'I brought you here to show you it's all right.' I paused, staring straight into Sulayman's eyes. I barely knew what I was saying. I had not known I was going to say it. And yet here I was. Saying it. 'I wanted to show you how things are and that it's all right.'

Sulayman's head was swimming. I could tell it was, even then. Swimming with the end of the evening, with the wine, with cedars, and frankincense, and Damascus at midnight. And with my words.

'Sorry, sir?' A terrified reply.

'I brought you here to show you it's all right.'

Sulayman blushed deeply, sweetly and innocently. I thought I wouldn't be able to stop myself. I could see the future then.

'I see,' he replied. Then he stepped into the car.

I closed the door behind him and raised a hand. But my head

53

was filled with noise and panic and fear, and all that swimming, narcotic desire. Cheerfully I waved as the car pulled away, feeling like I was an actor running through a part.

'Thanks for being a trooper, Mina,' I said as I turned round to face my wife. But I could see a look in her eyes, which I had seen before. And it frightened me.

That night she and I made love.

THE STREET
CALLED STRAIGHT

THE CITY IS a spook, Sulayman. Spectral. A phantom. A neon glow in night-black. A djinni, you might say. From shadows, from corners, out of sewers, out of the very stone itself, the city throws things at you. Flashing in the darkness, scary, eerie, it forces you to see things anew. Suddenly, violently, without mercy. Your spine tingles. The hair in the nape of your neck goes rigid. You see anew.

Morning: the air was cool and fresh in Suli's bedroom. Light: a clear, white light fell through the shutter-slats. It hovered in space, the light. Diffuse, pale, shimmering. Blinking as he stretched, Sulayman turned on his side. Facing the clock on the floor beside his bed, he screwed up his eyes, checking the hands. Seven o'clock.

From the street he could hear the rattle of cartwheels. Traders' voices sailed on the lightest of breezes. They called to recalcitrant mules. To old friends. 'Salaam aleikum, Ali!' A laugh, cut with cigarettes and the sparse air of the hills. 'Wa-aleikum asalaam, Abbas! Is that pig you call a mule still troubling you?' Ha, ha, the voices cackle, crackle. Ha, ha, ha. The wind sweeps up each greeting, every word, the laughter, like the waves on the sea carry seaweed or bobbing gulls.

Sulayman could hear the doves on the roof flap their wings and coo gently. Courting and dancing in the morning sunlight, the birds made low noises, scratched their feet on the flat roof. They had scratched and flapped up there every day of Suli's life. They were eternals, the locals said. The doves had even been here as long as ancient Damascus. They had flown over Jericho and heard the bugles. They had touched the hand of Moses. Their wings had ridden the wind and skimmed the waves back when the world was all water, they said.

Suli stretched and climbed out of bed. Below him, his father was barking orders at Fatma, their servant. Fatma would be preparing their breakfasts, taking the force of his father's indignation at the day's news, as if she was his wife, like she was supposed to care. She would have put the coffee on by now. It'd be bubbling and spitting on the stove. And the aroma! Now that Sulayman's mother never got out of bed, now that her body was racked with mystery illnesses and minutely detailed complaints, the family was split in two. Fatma would move between the two, carrying trays of food, coffee, perfumes, as she moved from the mother's bedroom at the back to the rest of the house, the father's territory. 'Let me out! Let me out!' Sulayman's mother would screech when the doctor came to dole out the pills and potions. 'Let me out and see this damn crazy city first thing in the morning!' she would shriek, hearing the doves flap.

It was a long, long time since Sulayman's father had ventured into that enemy camp at the back of his house. Sulayman went for filial visits and for his mother's blackly absurd jokes and stories, for inventories of disease and treatment, for her part-stoical, part-outraged version of her own life. But, even this early, with the coffee spitting on the stove and the rooftop doves shaking out their feathers like dance-club flirts, Sulayman and Fatma were expected to negotiate the minute intricacies of Muammar and Diniz Ahmed's war. Sulayman stood in the middle of his room, naked and stretching. How Fatma knew how to make coffee! What a delight it was to smell it brewing! An aroma like no other. Like chocolate, like preserved roses, like tobacco, like the smell of cedar freshly cut, like, oh, like nothing else. Sulayman's mother, who never had a good word for any Arab's coffee, would take a cup from Fatma. 'I don't know where you learned to make it, Fatma, but, woman, you make coffee like a Turk!' Sulayman listened to the house's sounds. To the slow, soft spread of warm sunlight on stone. To the scuttle of a lizard on a window-ledge. To his father's voice, raised, raging unintelligible through a stone floor and the orchestra of cicadas.

Such heaviness. Such light.

Standing before a full-length mirror Suli idly examined his naked body. He was thinking about last night, about Paul and Marina, about a dinner of fish and potatoes with soft white bread. Drinking the wine they offered, it made him dizzy. Moving his hand across his flat stomach, Sulayman thought about Marina, how beautiful she looked. He thought of her fine clothes, how they might feel between fingertips or pressed beneath a palm. He thought of her freckled arms and chest, her slim, white throat. Fingers lingered on the little pouch of fat on his hips. He remembered their talk of poetry, of Browning, of Byron, of Shakespeare. Marina nodded as he briefly explained the basics of Arabic poetry. She had this knack of not making you feel what you said was boring. She nodded, smiled, asked questions, rushed upstairs to get a book of English poems. His eyes flashed across the mirror. There the book was, beside his bed on the floor. It sat beneath the book that Paul had returned to him at the end of the evening. Suli felt each of his ribs, dragging his fingertips across his chest, up to his throat. Curling black hair caught against hard skin on his palms. Paul had grinned at him the whole evening long. Giddy with the unfamiliar taste of wine on his lips, Sulayman had let his eyes rise to Paul's and laughed slightly. Before the mirror, Sulayman let a hand fall, brushing his penis, his testicles, the inside of a thigh. He smiled. Marina had written in one book, in pencil: *To Sulayman, do enjoy this. With best wishes, Marina Esmond.* Paul had shaken his hand at the end of the evening, as Sulayman had leaned forward, only feet away from his wife, and whispered, It's all right. When Paul had said that, a tightness grasped Sulayman. In his throat. In his brain. Dizziness translates into excitement. Newness. Now, in the morning, the words, the secrecy, yes, even the deception exuded a sensuality. An eroticism. Sure, there was guilt and shame in store, too, but first – and strongest – there was desire.

'Sulayman! Sulayman!' His father was shouting from downstairs. Sulayman jumped. Padding across the bare floor, he pressed his face to the bedroom door, which he held ajar, as he called:

'Father?'

'Get yourself down here, boy, and tell me about last night!'

'Yes, Father.'

Sulayman said he did not understand his father's fascination with the British. He preferred them to the French, whom he in turn preferred to the Turks. The British were great. That's what he said, attempting to make a joke. As Sulayman sat with his father, sipping Fatma's coffee, describing the Esmonds' home and what had been discussed, he could only be amazed at his father's subservience. The coffee's strong, bitter taste tingled on the inside of his lips.

'Oh, son, this will lead to great things, let me tell you! To have the favour of the British is such a good thing.'

Sulayman shrugged, staring at the black coffee in his cup. Swirling it around and around, he thought of how Paul and Marina had been so ordinary, yet at the same time so alien. Nowadays the young boys could buy comic books on the city's paper stalls: the stories about green Martians had pictures drawn in New York City and words translated into Arabic in Cairo. Sulayman realised that his father didn't understand the modern world, even as he wore Western clothes, tried to speak English, and think of cultural similarities, not differences. In the modern world, Sulayman was sure, he should be able to look Paul or Marina in the eye. And lose the kowtow. And yet, somehow, Sulayman had spotted the magic of Paul and Marina – their very difference, the crystal sparkle. It was an alien magic to Sulayman, you see, that was the source of its charm and beauty. In Paul there was that easy, attractive laziness: his smile would break slowly, happily; there was the slightly ruffled elegance of his clothes, his hair, offset by the clean shirt and the manicured nails. There was stillness, the unhurried, graceful way he moved; the way he talked of work, as if it were a time-consuming hobby that had been thrust upon him, but which he enjoyed in small doses. There was that joke about the woman who had fallen in love with a horse. As he told it, Marina, a little tipsy, had put her hand on her forehead, and cried, 'Not again!' Marina, she was Paul's matching half. At least that's what Sulayman thought. Elegant, charming, educated, easy. The charmer and his charming wife: these were the observations of an outsider. Sulayman, the outsider. The Damascene lost in a Damascus that was not his.

'Oh, Father, it's not really so much. Mr Esmond is just a garrulous sort and his wife, gracious though she was, probably didn't really want me there.'

With a loud crack, Sulayman's father banged their cedar-wood table with his fist.

'Nonsense! They sound like perfectly nice and sensible people to me! It is very progressive of them to invite you to eat with them, very . . . condescending!'

'But, Father, Mr Esmond will forget about it in a day or two.'

'Don't talk such foolishness!'

Sulayman's father took so much nonsense from some and none at all from others. Heh, Suli's mother would croak, always the sign of a coward.

'Yes, he will, Father. He'll probably look straight through me when he passes me in the corridor.'

'Great things are afoot.'

Muammar Ahmed's eyes were twinkling brightly as he spoke. They were near-black, like his son's. His face was Suli's: long, slim, bony angles, a too-big nose, too-big lips, pleasant as opposed to handsome, composed rather than elegant.

'Whatever, Father, whatever! Anyway, I have to go. I have to meet Haroun. Salaam, Father. Salaam, Fatma.'

Fatma never replies. Half-turning her old head and nodding at him, Sulayman knows she despises his parents, their house, probably him too. He knows she would prefer to be with her family. But with her two sons interned by the British and nine grandchildren to feed, she can only dream of an old age spent sitting on a sunny doorstep, spinning and sewing.

Father – Muammar – had to go, too. Collecting his newspaper and asking Fatma to find his cane, the one he had imported from Scotland, Muammar drained his coffee cup, then fiddled with the radio dial. The newsreader's voice crackled. A story about detected bombs, brave police, arrests made. About the threat to the peace the British had brought with them. (Like it was a Christmas present or an eid gift, Sulayman thought to himself.)

'Independence fuckers,' Muammar murmured to himself. Fatma returned with the cane, handing it to her employer. 'Fatma, those independence fuckers will ruin this country, you just see if they don't.' Fatma said nothing, privately remembering the independence fuckers who threw bombs at the Turks, who welcomed the British in their armoured cars, who then courted the Germans too. To them, one oppressor was as good (or bad) as the other. And these great British, hadn't they killed Syrians? Hadn't they come into Damascus to save the Free French regime? Everyone knew the facts of the matter. The Free French had actually shelled the city in the first weeks of 1945. Shelled it! All those men and women were killed. Al Merjeh! The square was ankle-deep in blood!

If the nationalists lobbed bombs at the British, she thought, lightly brushing fluff from Muammar's cream linen jacket, so what? 'Yes, ruination! Ruination!' her employer trilled as he headed for the front door. Fatma whispered as she closed the door after him, so what?

Muammar worried about Sulayman. Fathers do. Especially ambitious ones. He wanted his only son to do well in life, and so indulged his academic ability, although he doubted its real value. What he really wanted was for Sulayman to join that small, powerful group of Arab Damascenes who had one way or another – contacts, crime, culture, commerce – made themselves indispensable to the French, then the British. The Husseini family, with whom they had been in marriage negotiations, were connected, respected, sophisticated. They were flat broke too, due to the extravagance of Mother Husseini. Firdaus, patron, puller of strings, gourmande and, finally, grandmother of Sulayman's near-fiancée Leilah, had a fail-safe nose. Firdaus's remarkable nose had smelled the future on Sulayman Ahmed the first time she clapped eyes on him. She remembered his mother Diniz from the days when Old Erbakan, Sulayman's grandfather, was as big a fish as fishes come and Diniz was one of the most sought-after girls in Damascus. Inexplicably she had been allowed to marry for love to a nobody who (all the world could see) did not love her. But beyond the machinations of Muammar and Firdaus, what did Sulayman want? Well, he had poetry. Ibn Hazm or Robert Browning. New political poems from Egyptian radicals, from Harlem. The first Celan in a tiny, French-published journal. No, maybe what Sulayman wanted was love. He hadn't known he wanted it, of course. No one ever does. He knew the Husseini negotiations were going well, that Mother Firdaus did nothing without a good reason. He could be married in a year, even less. Sulayman wanted, just once, to fall in love. Oh, he knew men like Paul Esmond. They filled this city at times, on the prowl. So, love was not what he was expecting from Paul. But soon enough he would start to find that Paul was what he wanted, for reasons he could not always pinpoint.

Haroun was standing on a crowded pavement of the Street Called Straight. He watched his old friend, Sulayman, approaching, bobbing in a sea of heads.

Sulayman was late. He was almost running. Waving and smiling, he could see the short, full-faced Haroun shrug mockingly. Haroun's background was not dissimilar to Sulayman's: that mix of administrators, merchants and fixers who spoke grandly of Turkish forefathers. Haroun's family owned a business and lived affluently, too. Like Muammar, Haroun's father hated the independence fuckers. 'Heh, what a bunch of country rubbish and bloody university Marxist sister-fuckers! Spouting the Quran! Spouting their bloody pamphlets, and all! Independence fuckers, all!' In the morning sunshine, Haroun finally broke into a grin, as Suli – which he, and a few others, called him – breathlessly rushed up. Every morning they bought a glass of tea from a stall here on the Street Called Straight. This was the start of that twisting, turning, chopping, changing thoroughfare leading from the innards of the Old City out into the new city, to a big grand avenue called An-Nasr, up past the bloodstained square of that last winter's martyrs, Al Merjeh, and on into the north-west suburbs. Every morning, mingling in the teeming tide of people, they stood for a minute or two, loudly slurping the hot black tea and breathing the petrol fumes.

Syrians like their tea hot, hot, hot. Hot enough to make you wince, boy! So hot you have to share a story with a friend to let your tongue stop burning, boy! (But the Syrians like their coffee too, though. That strong, black coffee the Turks had brought and not taken with them when they went. You get three ways to drink coffee in Damascus. *Qahwa*: you get the strong, muddy black coffee with a mountain of sugar in. *Mazboota*: you get less sugar. *Sada* – plain. *Sada* got you more loud moans from your friends, who cried 'crazy, crazy' at you, for all to hear. But in Damascus they like their coffee one way. *Qahwa!*) The boy who worked the tea stall was eleven, maybe twelve. All day he stood behind his counter. The washed glasses sparkled like diamonds in the sunlight. The dirty ones all had a half-inch of the cooled black brew at the bottom. Sweating in the rising steam, the tea-boy's hands moved like lightning, pulling levers, switching pots, yanking off tea-tin lids, sloshing the soup-like tea into glass cups. Penny, please, was his million-times-a-day cry. It greeted Suli and Haroun each morning as they approached and bade them farewell too.

'Heh, you never guess what my father said last night,' Haroun began excitedly.

'What?'

'He said,' Haroun laughed, slipping into his father's voice,

' "that Sulayman is a very fine boy indeed, son, heh? Do you think that his family would indulge the idea that we may find some mutual satisfaction of the marital sort?" '

Suli turned to take the tea from the serving-boy, laughing as he moved. Haroun was already sucking loudly on the cup's rim. Sulayman knew the way men like his and Haroun's father talked. Haroun mimicked again, 'Heh, son?' The two friends winced and laughed.

'Oh, God, what did you say to that?'

'I tried to play so dumb, Suli. I said, "*In the name of Allah*, what are you talking about, Father?" Oh, he hates it when I say that. He lifts his hands and cries, "What are you, some rubbish up from the country to be going, 'In the name of Allah'? Didn't I teach you to speak like a gentleman, heh? You bastard!" and slaps me round the head!

'He goes, "Now, this family has two daughters. Very nice girls, going to high school, never a day's trouble in their lives. I hear that Muammar Ahmed is talking about marrying Sulayman off to some *girl*, and I wondered whether one of my two little doves would be better. You know, it would be a good match. Very suitable." '

When his tongue stopped burning, Sulayman took a shot of tea, screwed up his eyes and cried, 'Oh, God!'

Haroun was laughing right out loud, bent double and cackling.

'Heh, but not to worry, man.'

'Why?'

'I told him that you were a communist!'

'What happened then, man?'

'He shook his head, got up and said no more about it!'

'I think old Firdaus Husseini is more than a match for your father, anyway, Haroun. I think she'd say she had first claim on me!'

'Aw, wouldn't she see him off, heh? Like an old terrier.'

Haroun yapped and howled, making Sulayman laugh out loud. One or two other drinkers turned and smiled. Then the two friends knocked back their glasses. The last of the tea is the thickest and bitterest. Banging the glasses on the counter, Haroun threw an extra penny on to the counter for the serving-boy. Penny, please, penny, please, came the boy's cry to the early-morning rush of customers. 'Too busy for a thank-you?'

The Street Called Straight, what a place, what a goddamn place! Cars, mules, buses, bicycles, carts all crowd the long, narrow road, braying, tooting, revving, ringing bells, honking horns. Thousands of city-dwellers get all pressed up close between the high, shuttered shops, houses, offices. What were all their names, back in 1949? Who knows? You only know that they *were* Damascus. More than minarets or domes, they were the reason the mountains of sandstone had been cut. They were the audience for the drama created by centuries of architects and patrons. Office workers, shop assistants, tailors, bakers, butchers, secretaries, teachers, factory workers, journalists and judges. Husbands, wives, mothers, fathers, sons, lovers, enemies. Some nodded at friends or colleagues. Some spat and shook fists if they were pushed too hard in the throng of people, elbowed in the ribs, stamped on the foot. Ach, they were city-dwellers all right: rude, uptight, indignant, pushy, selfish. And Sulayman loved this crazy city. Walk it, cry the tour guides, you've got to walk it. Know every inch, every tiny detail, the names of the streets – Baroudi Street, Al-Amin Street – which road leads on to which road – Souq Saroujah, Souq al-Hamidiyyeh – how to find such a square, know where you get the best tea, the best coffee, the best pastry. Get to know the people too. These million men and women. And then you too can be part of the audience of a drama of Damascus.

A clutch of schoolboys were throwing coins in the street. Whoever threw the furthest won the lot. How they laughed, as copper flew, span, glinted, in mid-air. Coins landed on the pavement with a crack. Crack! An old man sallied into the group, outraged to see them gamble. Smacking their heads, he shrieked: 'You pigs! Don't you ever read your Quran, heh? Don't

you know it's forbidden to gamble, heh? What are your parents –
goats?' The sound of the boys as they ran off, sore-headed but
laughing, lifted above the crowd, ringing in the stone, the
shutters, the rooftops. Sulayman could see them running off,
satchels bouncing on their backs, fists clenching the coins they
had won. 'Devils! Pigs!' the old man shouted after them, as they,
like everyone else, merged back into the banks of people up and
down the Street Called Straight.

'You'll never guess what happened to me last night, Haroun.'
Sulayman had thought it best not to tell anyone about the
Esmonds. The Old City, though, was so alive with excitement.
He wanted to share his bit of it.

'You met a girl?' Haroun replied, teasing.

'Yes, but that's not it.'

Haroun's face fell in disbelief.

'You didn't screw a girl . . . ?'

'No, of course not,' Suli cried.

Imagine the confusion felt by the poor British on their arrival
in the city in 1918, the French in 1920. On one hand, it was one
of the most liberal and secular cities in all Islam. Men showed
off their bareheaded wives at social events. Occasionally, you
saw a woman in a street café, sitting alone, usually unhassled.
Even before 1918 some women went out to work, suspending
for a few hours their Muslim responsibilities as mothers and
wives. But somehow men and women, especially before marriage, lived in parallel worlds, too. If those worlds were not
quite separate, they touched only briefly and insubstantially. So,
to young men, girls were a mystery. A picture of a naked woman
– even if she was made out of white marble, had no arms and
was torn from an art history book in a library – was like gold
dust. Yet this was a liberal city. Everyone turned a blind eye –
sometimes not such a blind one – to the fumblings and flirtations
between the city's virgin males that so relieved the tensions of
bachelorhood. Then, imagine the surprise of the White colonial
élite, on its arrival after the First World War, to find that certain
schoolday pleasures weren't as much a thing of the past as

they'd thought. Sulayman said to Haroun, 'I went to eat in my boss's house.'

Saying nothing, Haroun stopped dead. They were only a few yards from where they went their separate ways – Sulayman to the government buildings, Haroun to his job as an accounting clerk.

'That Esmond fellow I told you about. He caught me reading a book of English poems at work.' Sulayman was now laughing. Haroun detected his nervousness. 'Shit, man, I thought he would throw me out there and then but he said that his wife liked poetry and if I wanted to, I could come to dinner.'

'And you said yes?'

'Well, he didn't actually ask me, he sort of told me. You know, we talked about poetry. They were very nice.' Sulayman's voice was light and breathless. 'His wife was a real knockout, let me tell you. She was dressed in the slightest of dresses, with her arms bare to her bloody shoulders. And her skin was all freckled with big, pink spots. And her eyes, boy, they were like –'

Sulayman's voice fell away. Haroun was staring at him. He whispered, so as not to be heard by passers-by.

'God, man, you're going to turn out as big a bastard as either of our fathers if you carry on!' He was shaking his head, staring in disbelief at his friend. 'What kind of bollocks is this? Dinner with some British sister-fucker and his wife? Going on like you never saw a white woman before, heh? Like her skin was fucking silver!'

Haroun tsked out loud, then stormed off. Sulayman could only stare after him.

White men are white men. Full stop. That's what they used to say. Sulayman should have listened up.

THE NOTE CLINCHED it.

Sulayman's hotel room was small and clean. Just a bed, a table, a pot. Sulayman wondered how he was supposed to wash himself. There was no basin, no soap. He could feel that un-Muslim dirt building up on him already. He sat down on the bed, there being no chair or stool, and looked at his watch. Five o'clock.

Paul had written, '*If you wish, we can talk some more. Meet me at the Alhambra Hotel at five o'clock today. You will have permission to leave work at four. Go to the hotel and give my name. I have a room booked. Yours, P.*' An envelope had been left inside the folder on Sulayman's desk, secreted away from secretarial eyes, between sheaths of paper written on in the Arabic script. And when Sulayman had arrived at work and opened his folder, out fell the envelope with his name on. Out fell the future, he later thought. Slitting it open and reading it over and over again, Sulayman traced the words for possible meanings. Possible meanings of meetings, of explanations of the night before, of getting sacked for having the temerity to understand what Paul wanted, and of love. Love, that weird, wonderful, seasick word. Sulayman looked up from the note after its fifth reading and knew he had to go.

Ach, the thrill! New skin! Desire!

The half-length shutters had been left open to air the rented room. Voices rose from a kitchen below. The banging of ladles, pans, hammers, spoons, the chopping of knives. Arabic fizzing and jumping in the afternoon heat. Street-vendor sassiness and cab-driver curses sashaying in the warm air. Sulayman could hear men talking about sport, about business, about pleasures to be had. Laughter. Honking horns. Scratchy 78s playing jazz-tinged Cairo crooning from a quiet café down the road. The Alhambra Hotel, on the edge of the Old City, with the late-afternoon stink of the Barada River not too far away. Sulayman waited for a knock or a key in the door.

Paul's footsteps were quiet on the cool terracotta tiles as he walked up Sulayman's corridor. He stopped in front of the door, composing himself, hiding his last-minute nerves. This was the scary moment: just before the kill. There was always the chance that there had been misread signals, that the other man would jump up, smack him in the teeth, cry rape.

Paul rapped on the door once, and softly called: 'Sulayman?' Silence, terror. And desire. 'Sulayman, it's Paul.' Not Mr Esmond any more.

Sulayman's watch counted out the four, five minutes they sat quietly in the still-dark hotel room. Outside Sulayman could hear foul mouths from the kitchen, the teasing banter of café drinkers. Damascus, at the end of hot afternoons, is a twitchy place. Strange, diaphanous light fell through the shutter-slats. It was soft as the sleeper's breathing. Golden, hushed, hazy, dreamlike. Sulayman dared not look up from his hands, as he sat on his bed. Paul's forced-carefree and stop-start sentences lurched awkwardly from subject to subject.

'So you came? Did you manage to get away from work without any problems?'

'Yes, sir.'

'Paul, please.'

'Paul.'

'Did you enjoy yourself the other night?'

'Very much, Paul.'

'And Mrs Esmond? Is there anything you want to ask about Mrs Esmond?'

Yes, yes, of course there was. There was how and why Paul could do that, bring his latest conquest-to-be to her house, talk to him in front of her, encourage her to like him, just to deceive her. There was how and why Marina could put up with this. Or maybe she didn't know, and their whole marriage was a lie. There was how and why Sulayman was here, sitting on a bed, now sure of what must be coming.

'No. Though she was very nice.'

'Yes, she is.'

And then silence. Paul wanted to explain why he had brought Sulayman to his house, dangled him in front of Marina, as if to say, look, nothing's wrong, I'm a good boy, the jig ain't up. Paul said to himself that he was bound to hurt Marina this way, that this was the way it was. Better for her mind to be at rest. Better for her not to suspect, let alone know. You hear it time and time again, Paul said to himself. I'd rather not know. And so he justified what he was doing to her, and to Sulayman too.

'You understand this, then, Sulayman?'

Sulayman looked up, into pale blue eyes.

'Yes,' he whispered.

'Good.'

Paul's cold fingers touched Sulayman's warm skin, his hand, then his cheek. Sulayman watched Paul walk to the door, turning the key in its lock. Returning, the older man kissed the younger on the lips, craning down, falling to his knees. Paul's scary moment passed.

Paul was not a bad man. He was certainly weak. He was trapped too. Trapped by the time he was born in, the life he had chosen, the society in which he lived. But Paul had managed his life quite well so far. Legally, at least. Never any trouble with the police. Never any trouble with blackmail (when so many men woke up one day to find a note demanding cash from the man they thought was their new love). But Paul had two things he couldn't

71

manage. The first was Marina. Marina, whom he loved and wanted to love. And the second was Sulayman, whom he never expected to love.

As boys, in the city, Sulayman and his schoolfriends sniggered when a white soldier would furtively call from his jeep, 'Heh! Hal tatakallam faransi?' They were just boys – fourteen, fifteen – but so were the soldiers – eighteen, nineteen. But they knew the city, they knew its ways. You knew because soldiers never usually asked a question that way. They shouted. They pointed guns. They smacked you across the head. If a soldier held out a coin or a bar of milky, sweet European chocolate, you knew. The soldiers, far from home, had come to this weird and wonderful place. Everything seemed back-to-front. Things that were easy to get at home – a pint of beer, a kiss from a pretty girl – were off-limits here. But here, other pleasures – forbidden at home – were readily available. 'No faransi,' the schoolboys would shriek, 'no French!!'

'What happens now?' Paul asked when it was over.

Sulayman shook his head.

'Et maintenant?' he laughed, remembering conversations he had never had.

'What?' Paul frowned. He was obviously nervous, unsure of what to do or say.

'Nothing,' Sulayman replied quietly, starting to smile.

Only those who have been lovers seem able to look one another steadily, unflinchingly in the eye. An act of intimacy, no matter how quick or brutal or impersonal, permits one to stare, to strip back masks. Sulayman had built a fantasy of what Paul was: carefree, sophisticated, charming, witty. And otherness too: that wild, intoxicating drug – otherness – which made everyone else frown, shriek, disown. But now Sulayman had seen Paul as being real: nervous, lustful, needing. Paul had become whole, not just a collage of things Sulayman wanted to be or to have. And, for Paul, there was that brief, scary moment when Sulayman had held his stare and received a kiss on the lips. In the suddenness of the afternoon light, he saw Sulayman as more than the slim outline, black eyes, a proud, brown face his predecessors had been. Wholeness again. Not the collage. For Paul, that was something which he had only previously found in Marina. And, however much he loved his wife, Sulayman provided an extra, powerful thing. Raw, narcotic desire.

'Well, the future,' Paul said.

'I won't make any trouble for you, Paul. You can forget I ever existed, without any worries about my discretion.'

'And what if I don't want to forget about you?'

'Then, don't, Paul,' Sulayman replied softly. 'Then don't.'

They were choosing the road straight into the heart of madness.

REMEMBERING

MARINA WROTE A letter to a friend.

Darling Mona,

Here's hoping you and David are on top form and that the little ones are rosy, too.

Trying to settle down into life in Damascus, but it's not easy. It's not like Berlin or Paris. It's very different and very strange. One looks around to touch the familiar, in the way one would, say, in the shops on Boulevard Haussmann, but can't. What's sold on the street is so alien. Sizzling meats fry on open-air stalls. The veiled women look up at you as if you are some kind of thief. I feel like a robber! Even when one comes upon a European-style store – the French have a couple here – you breeze in and out, feeling so grand, then see that the doorman isn't looking at you in a certain way, or some urchin on the street looks at you as if you are such a horror.

But then you see the city itself. The colours, the buildings, the spires, the domes! It is so beautiful! I can hardly describe how beautiful it can be here. You look out of a window and see some unearthly minaret shooting up like a rocket, or some huge mausoleum, which is literally encrusted with works of art! Venice has nothing on this!

I was reading some Lorca the other night, waiting for Paul to come home, and it captured perfectly the scents, the colours, the quality of the evening, even how the warm breeze feels in this part of the world.

Dry land,
quiet land

of immense
nights.

(Wind in the olive grove,
wind in the sierra.)

Old
land
of oil lamps
and sorrow.
Land
of deep cisterns.
Land
of death without eyes
and arrows.

(Wind along the roadways.
Breeze in the poplars.)

I was reading the book because I met this Syrian boy who told me
Lorca's style came from the old Moors, who were of course Arabs. Little
things like this seem to turn everything you thought was true on its
damn head! The Arabs are such a puzzle. They seem so old and we seem
like interlopers.

Paul is well and enjoying his job, but sometimes I think he forgets
about me. Forgets about us.

Sorry, darling. Feeling blue. Send me a lovely long letter with lots of
gossip and a nice little present. Something gorgeous and pointless you
can only get on the black market! Listen to me, Mona. I never thought
I'd miss the ration book!

Love, love, love,
Marina XX

P.S. I've got the most glorious piano, though. It sounds an absolute gem!
And the whole city is filled with the most odd white people. Like the
refugees of the *ancien régime*. It's like a history lesson here!

SALMON AND POTATOES. Marina had asked the cook to use dill, not coriander, but Sulayman didn't notice the error. How could he have? Earlier Paul had rung her from his office to tell her they had a guest for dinner. She did not question why. The ringing, happy tones of his voice filled the wires, singing in the receiver. She smiled as he joked with her. She was pleased, even for this unexpected phone call, just to hear him happy.

Love, she could have sighed, plays tricks on the eyes and the mind. Because, in 1945, she was coming to accept that what she had wanted for herself as a twenty-two-year-old bride – a house in England, children, a husband, easy, faithful pleasure – had failed to turn up. These were the precious moments between unhappiness. These were the times to which she could refer when asked how or why she could accept what Paul did to her.

On her instructions, Muhammad had gone to fetch a cab. He always accompanied Marina into the city. Paul insisted on it, despite her mild protestations.

'I'm a big girl, you know, Paul,' she said, holding her head to one side, affecting a pout. 'I can look after myself.'

'Oh, I know you are, Mina. A regular fire-breathing demon!'

'Then, let me get a taxi and pop into town!'

He lifted a finger to her chin. Just the warmth of his skin on hers could still thrill her. After all he had done, after all he was capable of doing, she still moved into his touch, wanting to occupy it, be him. She could barely explain it, not even to herself. Theirs had not been an easy marriage. Through their eight years together, she knew he had been unfaithful. She knew he had been unfaithful several times. With men.

Marina was forever pressing her suspicions into her gut, closing off her mind to its own whispers. The strength of love, she sometimes thought. Self-deception, she said at other times. But to Marina, her inability to fall out of love with Paul was the most shocking thing of all. She had given up a lot for Paul: the consent of her parents, the approval of her friends, a lonely war spent in unhappy solitude whilst he was abroad, finally her home in London to come to a new life in Syria. Marina had made such a heavy investment in Paul.

And yet she had few real choices. This was 1945. She was not prepared for the life of the divorcée then – that lonely, ostracised world where escaping from the end of love could only result in further, perhaps permanent, lovelessness. You see, part of Marina knew that she was stuck with Paul, and that he was a better man than most to be stuck with. He was kind and thoughtful and charming and attentive. Except . . . He was able to make her laugh, he always said how nice she looked, he always asked her opinion. But . . . You see, Marina knew she only had to change this one thing to be happy. This *one* thing.

Turning serious, Paul said:

'Things are never going to be safe here, Mina, not until the Syrians get what they want. You know that. Damascus has been crazy this last year – there's a craziness beneath all this old-world charm. There are still bloodstains in the street in Al Merjeh, for God's sake . . . No, I'd prefer Muhammad to be with you.'

Paul was right, she knew. Things would never be safe, not really, in Damascus until there was independence. She was always being warned. Don't go out in the sun. It will turn you funny. Don't go out in the city alone. You'll go native. Black-eyed and brown-skinned. Stark raving mad. But that wasn't what Marina meant. More than once, she had begged Paul to change, to stop, to be nice, to be good, to love her, to show her she could trust him. Marina didn't know how tired she was of begging just then. Things *were* starting to turn. When she had written a letter to her great friend Mona, it was like a mirror was lifted to her face. She could see her life as it was, not as she imagined it to be.

Marina and Muhammad sat in the back of the taxi, waiting in the clogged traffic, en route to the British shops on An-Nasr. A piece of paper – a shopping list, its details scrawled in blunt pencil – was in her hand. The heat was oppressive. She lifted the folded list to her chin and fanned herself. She wound down a window. The rich, heady, weird, stale smells drifting out of the city were high and dizzying. Watching her in his mirror, the driver called:

'Hot! No, miss?'

Marina smiled and nodded. The man's broken English possessed a handful of well-worn phrases. *Traffic bad, Jesus. An-Nasr allays bad, sir.* For purposes of back-of-the-taxi communication. *These bludi roads, heh? Thin as mountain passes and twice as smelly with goat shit, no?* Muhammad spoke to him in Arabic about the traffic, probably warding off the goat-shit talk. The taxi-driver's response was bookended in heavy sighs.

'What did he say, Muhammad?' Marina asked, aware she was being excluded from the conversation.

'Oh, nothing of consequence, madam,' Muhammad replied, composing himself.

'Was it about me?' She tried a little laugh, to win some trust, to show she could take a joke.

'No, madam, not at all,' he replied, ruffled, almost breathless. 'It was about the traffic. I'm sorry, his tone was unnecessarily tragic.'

Muhammad had been with the Esmonds since they arrived in Damascus. Marina knew nothing about him. Not where he came from. Not if he had any family to speak of. His past. His attitude to the British or the French. Whether he liked being in service. Whether he liked her. Once, none of it had mattered to her. She would tell herself that she was fair, she paid reasonably, not excessively, that staff were staff and everyone should know where they stood. But she remembered being at a party in Regent's Park in 1944. The bombings had stopped but Paul was still in Egypt and it was not yet safe to travel. Marina had stood on a balcony, looking out over the huge, round and beautiful park in blackness, aware that the world was spinning. The war was ending. Soon she would, pray God, be back with Paul. Soon all her dreams would come true, and it scared her. Beneath her high heels, she could feel the planet spin. She could feel the movement through four inches of leather and wood.

Recently, in Damascus, through dry, hot afternoon winds, the drifting scent of lemons, cicada songs, the blackest nights she had ever known, she could feel it again. The sensation of her feet on the ground moving at great speed. The strange, colourless moonlight danced on the high, bleached-pale buildings, but you could hear the whistle of radios behind shutters or penny-pushed jukeboxes in cafés. Music travelled the evening skies – imported jazz bands. Scratchy vinyl or radio wires. Miss Billie Holiday singing sad and slow, groups of men in a house singing 'The Internationale' or some devotional song. It all signalled change. Muhammad still kept his eyes down when he spoke to her. He did what he was told, skilfully dodging the few, wary personal questions she dared ask. Marina knew the world was starting to change. And so *her* attitude had changed, too. At first, in 1945, Winston Churchill being left face down in the water had shocked her. The prospect of change was starting to excite her.

On a street corner, a scuffle broke out. Two men – one in Islamic dress, one in open-necked shirt and plus-fours – threw punches. A crowd was drawn. The rising heat, the petrol fumes, the heavy gold of a late afternoon ladled the scene with a feeling of drunkenness, adding to its craziness. Men and women pressed around, shaking their fists, shoving their hands forward to pull the men apart, cheering them on, clucking, cursing. Old women called out to the Prophet for some sanity. Young men pointed and shouted, 'Kick him in the balls!' But the two men threw each other nervous looks, suggesting that maybe they'd lost their taste for battle. As the taxi pulled away, as the traffic jerked forward, Marina saw one of the men, the one in Islamic dress, had a cut lip. Spots of blood were slowly spreading on his white, cotton tunic. For a moment, the man's eyes met Marina's. There was the briefest connection. Embarrassed, she looked away. The taxi moved forward.

She turned to Muhammad.

'I do hope the shops have something left, or else I will have to ask Cook to make us Arab food!' she joked. He did not smile. He did not enjoy her crass joke, even though he knew her intentions were good in a shallow way.

'Madam,' he replied blankly, as mere acknowledgement. Marina blushed, recognising her insult, but she could only stare at the freckles on her hands. Change aside, to apologise was still unthinkable back then.

Henri Leyfeau was a French-owned shop on the nicest part of An-Nasr, that imported jars and boxes and bottles, crockery, silver and linen from fine Paris and London stores, that bought in Krug and Bollinger when it could. But M. Leyfeau was growing sick of bombs on the railway tracks costing him his profits, and scared of the proud-eyed Arab youths who theatrically caused a fuss nowadays when they were refused service. One of them – a bloody girl, too – had thrown a stone at his window, smashing it into a million glittering pieces.

Marina and Muhammad stood and stared at the beady-eyed fish lying on cut ice. Muhammad asked the boy behind the stall if he could clean and fillet the salmon Marina wanted. But the boy directed his answers to Marina. 1945: Marina could feel it again, the speed beneath her feet, the dizzying, orbiting, changing world beneath her imported, mid-height shoes.

Sulayman's mother had memories, too. Down the years, doctors had told Diniz Ahmed that she had high blood pressure, low blood pressure, angina, asthma, eczema, psoriasis, measles, chickenpox, diphtheria, scarlet fever, sleeping sickness, water on the knee, water on the brain, arthritis, a low libido (*ach!*), hypothermia, hyperthermia, pneumonia, breast cancer (*ach!* she had cried, clapping her hands over her ears, thinking such a young doctor had no business saying that word to a woman of her age, even if it was 1943 and things were different now), stomach cancer, cervical cancer (*ach, ach, ach!* she had shrieked, smacking the doctor around the head and calling him a devil), a twisted intestine, a pierced liver, brittle bones, a clot on the brain, spots on the lungs, nothing wrong at all, a medical mystery, in her forty-six years of life. Ailments, infections, diseases, conditions, imaginings, phantoms, fears, phobias, fevers, agues and suspicions: some of them she had had, some of them she had not. With all the skill, elegance, stomach, fire, intelligence and downright pink-stone brilliance of one of those great American film actresses (who were no better than whores, in her opinion, no better, mind you!), Diniz Ahmed had enjoyed every day, every hour, every minute and second of her deathbed existence. Nothing in life had given her more pleasure, more to think about and consider, more conversation and more to curse, decry, detest, mourn and detail than decades of imminent death. Nothing except Sulayman.

You know that Diniz's father was a big man in the city back in the Turkish days. You know that the British took him, one dark night, back in 1918, out into the desert. Diniz remembers the rattle of guns. Her fingers had curled on the window-screens as her brown eyes watched horse-drawn carts pull out of the city and into the night.

Death had electrified the blackness. One empire had fallen and others had spread. Casualties, the report typed out, were inevitable. The British promised independence but didn't keep their promises. People said that they had lied. Just a year earlier, Muammar said he was marrying Diniz for her beauty. She had been quite the prize, and should have married much better than an Arab merchant on the make. But Old Erbakan could never refuse his precious one, the likes of Firdaus Husseini remembered, and for some strange reason (unfathomable, people said), Diniz had fallen head over heels in love with Muammar.

But then the Turks lost the Great War, scurrying off north. It was then that the depths of Muammar's real feelings had been revealed. How he had torn his hair, Diniz remembered. Gritted his teeth. *A goddamn Turk!* That's what he had called her when the British had ordered all Turks and their spouses to report to the forecourt of the black-and-white Azem Palace. There, amid piles of smouldering furniture, screaming soldiers, well-respected men of the city with their papers all in order being thrown to the floor, Muammar told Diniz that he wished he had never married her. 'Ach, I wish I'd never married you, woman!' That if he had known all this would happen, he'd have married a nice Arab girl. Diniz was eighteen and six months' pregnant. She looked at herself in a long mirror, hands on her bump, her child, and she cried.

For six years, Muammar tolerated her snooty Turkish accent, her cursing of first the British, then the French, and her constantly expanding-receding stomach. Eight pregnancies in only six years. Eight little lives grew within her but seven had not stayed in her for more than six months. Four tiny girls, three tiny boys came into the world without a breath or a heartbeat in their bodies. A litany of heartbreak! Ululation upon ululation! But then came her sweetest angel. Little Suli, eighth of eight, emerged into the world at full term, kicking and screaming. Muammar had burst into Diniz's confinement room, shouting and shrieking at that sweet sound – a healthy baby's loud cry – making the old midwife nearly faint at the indecency of it. 'You modern couples!' she had cried. 'This is too much! Never have I seen such a thing!'

A month later, Muammar sent Diniz from his bed once and for all. She sulked and rotted in a gloomy back bedroom. With nothing else to do, she took to her sickbed, and at last found an art to hone. She was only allowed to see Suli every Friday, after mosque. His voice was sweet to her and she adored him, even though his birth had ensured her banishment.

Now her son was twenty-two. His hair was still thick, oh-so-dark, the whites of his eyes were like pearl, his irises impenetrably dark.

'Mother?' he would call from behind her bedroom door. The curves of his voice pierced the half-lit silence. Diniz had been lying on her bed, as she nearly always was. A book lay open but unread. The room was filled with hush. Her eyes flickered, but she had not been asleep. Sulayman had never quite outgrown the fearful wonder he felt on entering his mother's room. Unable to remember his parents as a couple other than on paper, the child Sulayman was kept away from Diniz. Nurses were hired by Muammar for the cleaning and feeding and smacking and walking of the cherished infant. Diniz was allowed to have him on Fridays, between mosque and bedtime. And so, for Suli, Diniz was more like a favourite aunt, doting but distant.

Only when he went to university did Sulayman want to rediscover his mother. Innumerable winters had passed into uncountable summers since the eighth of eight had been born kicking and screaming. His proud mother was then twenty-six. When he nervously returned to the back of the house, to find Diniz where she had always been, propped up in bed, Sulayman encountered a fatter, greyer, sadder, forty-six-year-old. She told him slow stories. The stories of her memories of life. That there had been seven tragedies before the eighth miracle. How she had thrilled at the sound of her baby's first cry. How it was when the Turks were in charge. How her father kept a vast house in the Turkish Quarter, with a hundred servants.

1945.

'Oh, God,' she cried, 'you've come to see your old mother, have you, heh? That whore's dog has stopped bending your ear about communists and the like, heh?'

Sulayman sniggered as his mother comically railed against her husband. Diniz's coruscating tongue rained fire on everyone except him, her son.

'Oh, he's going on about independence, and the fighting

86

through the winter. On and on,' Sulayman moaned, rolling his eyes.

The mother clapped her hands together and a loud smack rang in the high, still bedroom. ' "Ha!" ' she mimicked Muammar's voice. ' "Those buggers! Those bastards, they'll take my business off me, those independence fuckers, and then where will we be, heh?" '

'Oh, Mother . . . !'

Loud laughter crashed and tinkled around their heads. Diniz knew Muammar would be able to hear it. He would moan about it to Fatma. 'Listen to them, heh, listen to them . . .' Diniz flung open her arms and smiled the widest of smiles. Her son came towards her. Drawing him into her, she held him tightly, then slowly, softly, put her hand on his forehead to bless him in the Muslim fashion.

Safe in his mother's arms, feeling the warmth of her heaviness, smelling the closeness of her life in bed, Sulayman's eyes roamed around her room. All of it was both so immediately familiar and so strangely alien. One tiny window cast a grainy evening light across her bed. For years, though, she had kept the room shuttered, except when Fatma pushed them open in the early morning, to let the songs of next-door's caged nightingales in. Ornate wardrobes and tables, in the Ottoman style, lined the room's walls. All of them had seen better days. Rubbed-thin gilt; chipped and flaking paint, cobalt blue, ruby red, lacquer black. Here and there, a table-leg was coming loose, the odd handle on the odd drawer was missing. Great swathes of fabric covered every surface, the crumpled folds covered in dust, made dull by age. Old dresses, both Western and Islamic, unworn for years, had been pulled to one seat or other, been left on a tabletop and never put away, over a dressing-screen, so Diniz could consider the colour, or check whether the moths had got to them. Shawls, wraps, kaftans. Now and then the eye caught books. She could not decipher Atatürk's Roman letters, only the old Arabic script. The local Turkish-language rag went over to the new style in 1930, so she had not read a paper since. So, almost alone in the gloom, she burned incense, dressed herself with perfumes, arranged the flowers and aromatic herbs Fatma brought every day. She lived the life of her grandmothers: shut-up, pampered, useless art objects, shuttered away in the cool grandeur of the harem, many years from the rather undemanding chore of tempting their man to get it up. As a boy, Sulayman had now and then thought of her as a potion-brewing, spell-casting witch and of her room as a dark, gem-encrusted lair. Those thoughts had never entirely receded.

Diniz released her son from her grasp. He pulled himself upright, on the bed's edge.

'What did the doctor say, Mother?'

'Oh,' she began. 'All I'm good for is the grave, you know? Every little bit of me is gone to ruin, son, every bit! It's amazing that I'm not dead already, heh?' Diniz fell back theatrically against her piled cushions, arms outstretched, palms upturned, sighing. A smiling Sulayman placed his own palm flat against hers.

'You've got a hundred years in you, Mother.'

From the bed, Sulayman stared up at the ceiling's decoration. Little stars and roses were dotted at regular intervals. Each dot – star, rose, whatever – was gilded. The leaf had grown thin and dull. Azure paint distinguished the golden webs. Even that had grown faded. But Diniz could remember the stories her old Arab nurses had told her in such ceilings. Up there you'd find sailing boats (Heh! Is that you, Sinbad? Up to mischief, heh? they used to cry, wagging a finger, making the child Diniz shriek with delight), princesses waved from olive groves to handsome suitors, sorceresses turned themselves into ruby-red snakes or into giant, diamond-spitting rocs.

'The marriage negotiations are going well?' Diniz asked.

'I think so, Mother, but it's still early days.'

The one thing Diniz and Muammar Ahmed agreed upon was that Leilah Husseini was quite a catch. Nothing had been finalised but Muammar kept talking as if it had. Diniz said to Fatma, 'That Firdaus has got more tricks than a magician with a snake. If that crafty old witch wants Suli, she has sniffed the future on him.' Indeed, the Husseinis did seem keen, sending polite letters and intimately small gifts. The families had exchanged not one but three sets of photographs. Sulayman did think Leilah was pretty. Muammar heard only good reports of her character and education. She spoke and wrote English and French, played tennis and piano, and had been accepted for a university place. Suli reminded his family that he still had to meet the girl, that they all knew so many negotiations collapsed at that stage. But Muammar's brother, Rashid, insisted the pair were as good as married. 'The deal is in the bag,' Muammar would declare, making Uncle Rashid grin, though the old man had no idea what the phrase meant, even in Arabic.

'Ach! Early days?' Diniz cried out loud, mischief twinkling in her eye. 'We've exchanged three sets of photographs and I've received two letters from Firdaus! And a tray of pastries, heh? You scoff down all that honey and pistacchio and you say, "early days"?'

'It's only two letters in three months, Mother.'

'Two letters in three months is a lot to me!' she shrieked theatrically. 'I've only seen your father once in the last two years! I know more about the Husseini clan than I do about my own!' Cackling loudly, rolling her head, slapping her hand on her thigh, Diniz was never happier.

A knock at the door silenced them.

Mother and son swung their heads around, peering through the gloom as the bedroom door slowly opened. It was Fatma, carrying a bowl of water for Diniz to wash in.

As she came close, Sulayman could smell the water's subtle perfumes. This was Fatma's genius (well, this and her wonderful coffee). She kept bottles of salts, herbs, oils, scents, flower-heads and ground stones. With these she brewed bathing fragrances of high drama, dizzy eroticism, decadent splendour. Tiny purple flowers bobbed on the surface of the water. Diniz recognised the scent as mountain lilac. Fatma's slow, heavy steps shot glinting concentric ripples across the water. The lilacs bobbed like fishing boats in a harbour.

'Almost time to pray,' Fatma murmured.

'Already?' Diniz yelled. 'Great God, woman, you pester me and drive me spare with your fussing and your bloody five-times-a-day godliness! What business is it of yours if I pray or not, heh? Send me to the lowest parts of heaven, I say! It must be better than the hell I've got now!'

LONDON. WINTER. THE first, birth-wet moments of 1945. A world away.

A telephone call is something to be cherished, it's true, she thought, with her head back against the aeroplane seat. But it's not a sudden, light kiss across a dinner table. It doesn't make other diners smile, or their eyes glint in candlelight. Kicking off her shoes, Marina's gaze fell out of the aeroplane window. Down, down, deep into the crystal-blue. Sun-glittered waves rolled across the Mediterranean far below. A letter is lovely, she thought, but it's not a hand held tight on a cold winter's day. And it's not the familiar warmth of his legs moving between yours, his ruffled hair beneath your chin, in your old bed, on Sunday morning. Marina closed her eyes, letting them flicker for a moment. *American Vogue* slipped slowly from her lap. How many months, weeks, days, hours had it been since she had seen him? Three years, nine months and eight days.

Arriving at the airport in Alexandria, her heart was beating so fast. The excitement had been rising inside her for the last week. It had been in her when she watched the clock all through her last day at her job. Excitement – no, barely concealed terror, the panic of love – gripped her. It made her feel like a fool, like when she went shopping with her mother, dropped her bags in the middle of Harrods, spilling lipstick and paper tissues. She had burst into tears, to the astonishment of the well-heeled shoppers. Even in the back of the car to the airport in London, she had rolled and fidgeted and bitten her nails like a child. Three years, nine months and eight days, it had been. A lost three years, nine months and eight days.

In the queue to disembark from the plane, she straightened her skirt, adjusted her hair. But inside, she was absolutely terrified. Her knees shook. Her ankles were going, she was sure. But, in the line that filed past the stewardesses, she smiled politely and said goodbye.

On the steps, she thought her heart might explode. She didn't want to cry. Marina gripped the rail, terrified she would faint. The still-fierce Egyptian winter sun met the vast expanse of tarmac, which didn't help. Distant figures were reduced to impressionistic daubs of colour and shape, hazy through the banks of rising heat. Perspiration between her shoulder-blades. A man asked if she needed a hand with her bags. He smiled and tipped his hat when she replied no, with her customary smile. She added she was being met by her husband, and she felt proud at the sound of the word.

Paul had not been called up. He had been with the Foreign Office for several years, and his transfer to the North African army was more a secondment than an enlistment. Alone with the falling bombs, the night fires, a leaking sink, a solitary mouse under her cooker, Marina resisted her parents' demands that she move back into their house in Chelsea. She stayed in the flat in Sussex Gardens. 'He left me here, and when he comes back, he'll find me here, too.' A small, frayed photograph was tucked away in her purse, and she took it out every morning and night to kiss him hello and good night. That's my girl, he would have said, you're as daft as a brush and I wouldn't change you one bit.

Her father had found her the job in Whitehall. Good German and good breeding were the only requirements of the post. Through the interview, she talked about going to Berlin before the Anschluss, shopping at KaDeWe, a family fishing trip to Schleswig. On the bus home after she was offered the job, she remembered how her mother's friend Zita had cooked the salmon on a makeshift barbecue, and how her father got badly bitten by the midges.

So, she waited for Paul to return, an internal exile of her own making. One morning, she woke up, went to brew the coffee and found her under-the-cooker mouse dead on the kitchen floor. Tipping the shiny brown beans into the mill, scared to look at the stiff, tiny corpse, Marina cried and cried and cried. Her investment in Paul was so heavy. Now she just wanted him back.

Sod the Nazis, she thought. Sod the Japs.

The saddest, most threadbare production of *Così Fan Tutte* the war could muster was no competition for her mother's soaring voice that night at the opera. In the dead silence of a pitifully female auditorium, her cut-glass tones pierced the lonely blackness. 'If you had had children, dear, you wouldn't be so resiliently proud. You would have had to come home and let us look after you.' Lying awake in the early hours, watching the sky ablaze, the bombers having poured fire into the black night, killing off Mozart after an hour, Marina imagined her life with Paul after the war. A house in the country, dogs, children. Children, she murmured. She named them, too. In the loneliness of her big, cold bed, she pretended her pillow was a darling little girl – Olivia – or her very own soldier – Marcus. Alone, with a pillow for a future, Marina pushed the war away, wishing that Paul was with her.

She stopped. He was there. Through all the sun and heat of an Egyptian airport. Like he had never been anywhere. Oh, Paul, she whispered to herself. Oh, Paul. He opened his arms to her. She could see him mouth, 'Hello, you,' across the tarmac. Two such madly happy smiles! 'Hello, you.' The lost years flew away. She stepped towards him, lightly at first. Her hands let go of her bags. 'Oh, Paul.'

The bags hit the floor. She was running.

She was running. Madly happy.

To him. Madly happy.

And when their bodies met, made contact, she thrilled to feel that chest, those thighs, those hips. His lean, slim body, wiry from the war, warm from his suntan. He kissed her. He called her Mina, as only he did. 'Oh, Paul, Paul.'

The brilliant sunsets over Paddington were forgotten. The past was forgotten. She fell deaf to messages in the scarlet and crimson evening sky. She could not hear the screams of gassed babies, of children left to wander a brutalised, bleeding continent, of flattened cities, and the whole world gone murderously mad for five years. The feel of his fingers in the small of her back, the strength of his arms around her, were powerful anaesthetics.

As the war in Europe was coming to an end, he rang her from Cairo. He said that he would not be back for some time. Maybe not at all, he added, as if it was a confession. The Foreign Office, he explained, might have some work for him to do. But knowing that he was safe, that it was over and he had been kept safe for her, she sat down and cried. Sitting at her desk at work, she put her face in her hands, and cried. Going to her mother's for dinner, she cried. When his new posting in Syria was finally confirmed, Marina put the house in the country and the dogs to the back of her mind. Marina had been in love with Paul from the moment she met him, that rainy lunchtime in Whitehall. Maybe he was the wrong class. Maybe he was not the perfect husband. Maybe the bedroom wasn't everything it could be. But he didn't care which school she had been to, which families she knew, how much she had in the bank. She made him laugh. He thought she was funny and smart. He told her so. They read books and newspapers. He asked her opinion on politics and cared what she thought. He always told her how beautiful she looked and always meant it. And once a week he wrote her a letter from North Africa. Once a week, every week, for three years, nine months and eight days. Enough time for absence to do its stuff with hearts that might not otherwise have stayed quite as loyal.

She had looked Syria up in an atlas in her father's library. Pink for Britain. Blue for France. She got out a ruler and worked out, in miles, how far it was from London. Her fingers tracked the entries in an encyclopaedia, looking for Damascus. '*Liberated by the British from the Turkish sultan, 1918. French mandate, 1920. Syrian self-government suspended by French, 1928. Attempts to restore self-government through League of Nations, 1934–6, opposed by French. Ruled by Vichy collaborators, 1940–41. Country liberated by British and Free French forces, 1941.*'

The Empire Office paid for her one-way plane ticket. Her father loaned her his car to drive her to the airport. Her mother kissed her goodbye and told her to write. Marina stepped across the gravel path and into the old blue Rolls. The driver tipped his cap as he closed her door. And the two of them, not speaking, drove off into her future in the Middle East.

London in the rain, that last day. A grey, cold drizzle painted the streets with the finest sheen of silver. That would be how she remembered the city in the long, hot, dry summers ahead.

An Egyptian airport, not long before noon, the first moments of 1945. Birth-wet in the brand-new world. Feel the rising heat on your legs. Paul was cradling Marina in his arms, telling her that he loved her. How much he loved her. They walked to the car. It would take them straight to the boat, that would in turn take them to their new life in Syria.

All around them was change. Paul had picked up Marina's bags and said she hadn't changed one bit. It wasn't true: she had turned thirty during his absence. As they walked slowly through the airport, Marina rested her head on Paul's chest, enjoying the heaviness of his arm across her shoulders, listening not to what he said, but to the sound of his voice, and how it felt as it echoed in her body, her bones.

NOVEMBER 1937. The clock reads quarter to seven.

Marina stands in her dressing gown, wrapped in a pink velvet curtain, ten feet long rail to floor. The hotel is silent. No feet press the floorboards in the corridor. No doorknobs turn. Snow flurries in the Mayfair air. The skies are grey again. Grey and icy cold. A drama of clouds is played out above her. There is a little snow on the ground. Like icing powder shaken through a sieve, it lines the early-morning streets. Pigeons, black against the white, hop and flap, searching for something to peck at.

Marina turns away from the window, letting the heavy curtain sweep back into position. Slipping back into the bed, under the warm heaviness of the sheets, she snuggles close to her new husband and kisses him once. At the touch of her lips on his cheek, Paul purrs contentedly. Turning towards her, opening his eyes, blinking in the half-light his feet stick out from the end of the bed. They are cold.

Curling under the sheets, pulling her body towards his, Paul plants a kiss in the centre of her chest. Her skin is warm. It smells of weddings, of flowers in the hair, of silk and cologne, of champagne and cake. And of their lovemaking too. He even smells himself on her skin. It makes him happy. November 1937 and newly wed.

'What is today?' she murmurs to him.

This will become their code over the years. *Theirs*. She will ask many times, 'What is today?' but will mean 'I still love you.' And he will reply – giving the correct day, Monday, Tuesday, Friday – but will mean 'Whatever the day is, I still love you, too.' They will say it so many times down the years that one year, when they stop to question if they really do mean it, it will have become so commonplace that they will be unsure whether they ever meant it at all.

Today is Sunday. At ten o'clock, a taxi will come to take them to Waterloo Station. From the bed, Marina can see the sable coat her father bought her in Stockholm. And she loves it, its feel, its warmth, its pure, distilled luxury. Marina and Paul will snuggle together under the sable coat in the freezing cold carriage, as the train carries them to a boat which will sail them to France. One friend told her she was mad to go to Paris for a winter honeymoon. She should have gone to Egypt, to the Middle East. The heat would be nice, the friend said. Years later, Marina would remember this advice. Sometimes she would laugh at the irony. Only sometimes, though.

Paul drifts back to sleep, his head against Marina's breast. They have been married eighteen hours. She is happy.

And her mother hadn't approved, she knew it. Her father shook Paul's hand when they first met, but frowned when Paul came to ask for Marina's hand. They hated it when he called her Mina. So familiar. Didn't like it when his hand slipped loosely around her waist. Hardly appropriate. Late summer. Autumn sweeps in again. If it's not a problem, why have you kept him a secret for three months, Marina? At a party, they remember, there was a faux pas. Couldn't remember what it was. Nothing as crass as wrong-fork wrong-knife, no. But Mother and Papa remembered an arched eyebrow or two. Maybe a smirk. The not-our-kind look they all understood. Marina understood it, too.

No, her mother didn't like it one bit. After all, Marina was virtually engaged to Alfie Villiers. Poor Alfie, her mother had cried when Paul had left their house, one engagement ring lighter, what will Alfie say? What will his father say? And his uncle goes to your father's club! Your picture was in the *Tatler*. The caption told everyone in the world that you danced with him all night. All night! Poor Alfie has a baronetcy coming and twenty thousand a year. Poor Alfie is so suitable! This Paul, her father spluttered, this Paul, who is he? An accountant's son? No, Marina replied, almost in tears, a teacher's son. A teacher! Her mother throws up her hands. What is to be done with you, Marina? Her father growls and grimaces. A bally teacher! Scowling, her brother sulks in an armchair, nursing a cognac, watching this little family tragedy, feeling a little responsible.

Paul married Marina for a number of reasons. First of all, she was everything he wanted in a wife, everything someone on the way up in the world would want his wife to be. Secondly, she wanted to marry him. Can't explain why, she must have thought, and, well, love doesn't have a knack for explanations. Put simply, Marina had wanted to marry Paul and said yes as soon as he asked her. Thirdly, he was sure that if the right girl – a girl like Marina – came along, he could solve his problem. The man with red hair – the one who said he was a friend of Auden – the one who smoked a cigarette through a silver-tipped holder – had said that Paul had to accept the way he was made. But looking at Marina, seeing how beautiful she was, hearing the low melody of her voice, talking to her about, oh, politics, or books, or the theatre, Paul was sure he could change.

And there was a fourth reason why Paul married Marina. If he was not in love with her, he did love her. He loved her and he wanted to be with her. And for Marina, that was the worst thing of all. Knowing that – despite everything – Paul loved her, that Paul wanted and needed her, trapped her all the more.

1937 had been a long, wet summer. Through May and June, the rain fell fast and hard. Pools, not puddles, filled London's streets. Silver circles rippled, splashed. Concentric circles of light trembled and spread on the water's surface, glinting. Friends rushed into cafés and restaurants, laughing, flapping their umbrellas. Lovers sat in smoky pubs, raincoats dripping on the backs of chairs, wet hair curling. The heavens opened time and again, without warning. Sun showers painted the sky with rainbows. High, wide, pale clouds rolled across the domes and roofs of the city. In the parks, among the litter of curling green leaves, still-blind fledgelings, baby squirrels had been flushed from their nests. Their tiny bodies lay drowned. Walkers stepped over them. Their dogs sniffed at the frozen wings and tails, then ran off, towards their owners' calls. The cricket was cancelled. Wimbledon ran very late. Marina wanted to go to Ascot but didn't in the end. She holed herself up in London and wondered whether Alfie's friend with the house on the Côte d'Azur would invite her too.

All over Whitehall, the lunchtime crowd was rushing through sun-silver rain. Hands, newspapers and hats were pressed to heads, brollies were held high. Men and women were laughing or cursing, caught yet again by the summer storms. Rushing down the steps of his office in Great George Street, Paul Esmond, en route to a dull meeting, spied a black cab. Its wheels cut the water-glassy road. Paul gasped with excitement. Its fare flag showed it was free.

On the other side of the street, Marina Russell could see the cab, too. Feeling bored with the rainy summer, she had met her brother for lunch opposite St James's Park. Walking arm-in-arm with him towards his office, she saw the cab, quickly kissed him on the cheek and cried a happy goodbye. Paul Esmond and Marina Russell stood on different edges of Parliament Square, thrusting out their hands, shouting for the single spare taxi in all of Westminster. Marina's brother didn't wait to see her get it. He was late and a little tipsy from lunch. He didn't even think to turn back to see if she was all right.

Paul's heart sank when he saw the pretty girl also running for his cab. He would have to give it to her, of course, then wait for another to take him to his meeting. That was in Belgrave Square and he was nearly late now, he thought. Through the driver's-side window, then the other, Marina saw Paul. She could see his hand on the door handle. Poor chap will have to give it up, she thought, and then he'll be drenched.

Large rain-drops splashed on the glass. Paul could see her big blue eyes and her wide, happy smile. He thought she was so pretty. Suddenly her head popped over the taxi's roof and she started to speak.

'Hello,' she said. 'This is yours really, isn't it?'

Paul was shaking his head, grappling with his armfuls of papers, wincing at the pelting rainspots.

'No, no, you take it. I'll wait for another,.'

She laughed at his miserable courtesy.

'You going far?' she asked.

'Just Belgravia,' he replied.

Lifting her eyes up to the thundery clouds, she called:

'Come on, we'll share. I'm only going as far as Sloane Street.'

Paul was about to say no when suddenly, in his panic and confusion, his bundle of papers fell from his arms, flapping and fluttering in all directions, all over the street.

'Oh, Christ!' he cried, dashing backwards. Another taxi almost hit him. It had to swerve. Jumping around, he tried to stop the papers blowing away.

Marina started to rush around, too, to help him out. Soon they were both happily shouting and laughing.

'Oh, my!' she was crying. 'Oh, my!' The two of them danced, hopped, jumped and span around, chasing Paul's windswept paperwork.

One rainy lunchtime in Westminster, summer 1937. Two people meet quite by chance. Taxis are furiously honking their horns. The two of them are standing in the middle of the road, roaring with laughter. Sheets of soaked paper stuck to their clothes.

They don't know it yet, but they are falling in love.

Or, at least, into love.

WAKING

THREE SOLDIERS ARE killed in one day. Two British, blue-eyed. One Arabic, black, maybe brown. Damascus groaned. It had only been months since the Free French had shelled the city, since the squares and streets hid snipers and bomb-makers. The Syrians longed for their freedom. But their experience was a harsh one. No one welcomes bloodshed less than those who have had to shed their own.

Boys – not much more than fourteen, claimed one eyewitness – jumped on the Arab and, in the blink of an eye, slit his throat. A meat cleaver flashed in the sunlight. Dark red blood pumped on to the pavement, glistening and quick in the hot afternoon sun. The first British soldier to die was shot in the back of the neck in a café on Madhat Pasha Souq. *The Old City!* shrieked the English-language paper. The second British soldier did not see a steel-black pistol lifted from a basket full of lemons. The gunshots rang around the city. Windows, walls, pipes, roofs, telephone wires, the city rattled in the recoil. People looked up from their coffee, their glass of tea.

Killings in broad daylight, they tutted up in Henri Feydeau, whilst they pondered which confiture or caviar to buy. Railways and proper government, the voices groaned in the Whites-only bars of the Empire Club and the Grand Hotel. And this is how they repay us! Marina started to fidget. One afternoon, she turned suddenly and saw Muhammad standing behind her. She yelled out, even as he said he was only there to tell her Mr Esmond was on the telephone. You see, Damascus was getting the heebie-jeebies.

A man selling tin bowls was shot dead on Al-Bakry Street. The British soldier lifted his gun, hearing a report about an attempted rape of a Frenchwoman off Hassan Kharat. He had shouted out, frightening the bowl-seller. The Arab, who probably spoke no English and almost no French, started to back away. Resisted arrest, the report said. The wound in the bowl-seller's throat was the body of a cactus, round, pert, shiny, dotted with fine, hard fibres. Except it was deep and dark and red. The crowd stood in silence as his blood gushed into a dry gutter.

Soldiers raided a café near the East Gate. The customers panicked at the sight of the guns. Men and boys scattered, toppling chairs. Cups fell from tables. A symphony of tinkling glass and cracking china rang around the room. A percussion of shouts and shrieks. A boy of sixteen got accused. The soldier holding him was barely nineteen. His sister had just had a baby girl at home in Bradford. Their mother sent him a violet-scented letter, enclosing one photograph of the family, taken in front of their terraced house. But now he was thinking only of two dead British boys – the murdered soldiers – who ain't ever going home, except maybe in a box. 'A young boy was one of the killers!' the young soldier shrieked. But the accused boy did not speak English. 'La afham!' shouts the boy. 'I don't understand,' replies the soldier. If only they'd known they had said the same thing. 'He knows who it is! He knows! He must know!' Hot coffee was pulled from the plate. The soldier held the boy over the counter. The black liquid was steaming, scalding. Men were shouting. Both Arab and British. Arabs tried to speak French but the British soldiers did not understand. The nineteen-year-old soldier was shouting uncontrollably. Slowly he poured the boiling coffee over the boy's face. And that soldier would never forget the boy's deafening screams, the maddening way in which his legs squirmed in agony, until the soldier's own weight, not the Arab boy's legs, was holding the Arab boy up.

A woman got searched right in the middle of the Street Called Straight, during the busiest time. She was old, wearing a white veil. The young soldier lifted her veil, accidentally touched her throat. Not since she was a girl, not since she was married, had any man touched her like that. She started to scream. Sometimes it seemed like the whole city was starting to scream. He shouted at her to stop. A stunned silence gripped the Street Called Straight. Voices rose in protest, then in damnation. Stones were thrown at the young soldier. The soldier fired his pistol into the air to make the crowd back off, and was pulled into an army jeep, which sped away. A lone voice shouted, 'British out!' For many of those that crowded round the distraught old woman it was the first time they heard what would become a familiar cry. The British had been friends rather than enemies till now. They were not the French, no. They were the ones who had come and pushed out the Turks. They had complained to the League of Nations when France reneged on its agreements on independence. And back during the winter revolt, even when the British marched into the city again, many welcomed the return of order, and many said that the Free French shells would have killed everybody before they gave up. But now people were starting to mutter: these white men, they're all the same.

Fatma would come to Diniz, to tell her half-stories of the world beyond the high walls, the dim shutters, the next-door nightingale songs. Diniz shook her head slowly, picking at the baklawah tray, and whispered:

'There's a new craziness, Fatma. There will be blood in the streets long before there is rain to wash it clean.'

Fatma thought that November and December – with their street-washing showers – were a long way off. She shrugged and replied blankly:

'Seems like there is blood now, madam.'

DAMASCUS EMITS A heavy, weary eroticism – the sensuality of dry heat, of summer gardens, of ancient stone – in the hot afternoon, drugging lovers throughout the city. Shutters are pulled closed. Husbands and wives make silent, hurried love, so as not to alert the children rolling fire trucks or dressing dolls out on balconies or landings. Lovers hurry to the souafa gardens, to sit under magnolia trees to kiss and touch quickly. White men pass ten or twenty piastres in change to nearly handsome youths or heavily made-up women for a few moments of ecstasy. The whole city, it seems, meets up to celebrate desire, to share passions.

Paul had started to meet Sulayman at the Alhambra Hotel regularly, just beyond the Old City's North Gate. The hotel owner had been convicted for gross indecency in Britain. Fleeing to the Middle East on release, he had set up a tacky hotel in Damascus. Here, in safety and without a single prying question, the visiting white men could bring the Arab street-boys for an hour, or two, of paid-for pleasure. Paul, as with all local dignitaries, especially those who were not strangers to Alhambra etiquette, would be ushered in through the kitchen door, so as not to be seen. But Sulayman had to muster the front to walk through the lobby door. They left separately too. But today they had met in a dusty black cab. Sulayman had waited, as arranged, on the corner of Al-Amin Street, down in the Old City. A cab drove up close to him, with Paul grinning inside it.

Raw, drowning, scented with desire. The heat in the Alhambra was stifling. From other rooms, noises. Cockroaches and fans, clicking and whirring. Slow, slow creak of plaster and wall joints. And other sounds too. All these sounds – ecstatic, sinister, insect, electric – were marked by their hush. Shutters kept the rented rooms dark. They asserted a level of privacy, though hardly ensured it. Occupants knew a pair of eyes could easily check who was coming in and going out. But sometimes desire, with its intoxicating drive to be satisfied, is too strong. You become possessed by it. And so you almost willingly take missteps.

Madness, passion, desire. By the time they got to the room they were laughing out loud. A carefree insanity. Maybe it was the aroma of magnolia in souafa gardens. Maybe it was the intoxication of the high-summer heat, the smells, the steam and, yes, the sweat of the city. Or maybe it was just the sight of one another's skin, it was looking into eyes dark, eyes pale, it was remembering the rawness of what they had once felt. And hadn't they thrilled when their hands had accidentally touched in the back of the taxi, and then when Paul touched Sulayman again deliberately? The driver's eyes stayed on the road, undisturbed. Sulayman wondered how the driver did not notice. White light was exploding. Electricity. Like live wires lashing like snakes, sparking in a storm. How could the driver not feel what they felt right then? How could he bear not to be them, swimming in that glorious moment?

CLEM BURROUGHS HAD invited Paul and Marina to dinner. Marina dressed herself slowly and with great care. Stepping into knee-length green silk, she felt the smooth, luxuriant rustle along her skin, even with her stockings on. Careful hands brushed the dress out until it hung from her hips and stomach. Still and glorious, silk.

Marina loved her green silk dress. Back in London during the war she had very little money and would not accept more from her parents. Their offers came with a catch. Obedience. But one time, during the late autumnm of 1943, she suddenly found she had about ten pounds surplus. Sure, the sink was leaking. And the gas stove in her kitchen was beginning to flicker. But Marina had this ten pounds and it felt like a fortune. She had got a bus from Paddington to Mayfair. Her excitement almost made her faint as she skipped along Bond Street in a light, chill rain. London, grey and autumnal, one bleak October. Large rainspots spread in her old coat as she turned down Bruton Street and reached the dressmaker she used to go to all the time when she had money. Barney's of London, with its army of mannequins looking blankly at the customers, with its swirling sea of satin and silk, those glorious, iridescent rainbows. Mr Barney pinned the pattern to her hips and made her smile as he murmured, 'The green, Mrs Esmond?'

Clem's house looked like a Spanish villa. Big and white with a touch of the *paysan* about it, it was enclosed in a breathtaking lime-tree garden. The moment that Marina stepped out of the car she thought she would faint again. That same pure sensual pleasure she had got from once having ten pounds to spare. Not the green silk this time, but a garden of lime trees, where the very air seemed ripe with the aroma of blossoming fruit. That swimming, sensuous green. The sky was just blushing red into blue, like a counterpoint. A summer night coming on, and warm waves of lime, the green leaves, and flowers swam around Marina, lifting her skyward.

Clem came to the door herself and grabbed Marina by the shoulders to kiss her cheek.

'Oh, darling, I'm so glad that you've come!'

Marina giggled. Their lips smacked loudly and happily as their cheeks touched.

'Clem, this is my husband Paul.'

Clem's smile gleamed brightly in the dimness of the evening light, as she looked Paul straight in the eye and offered him a hand.

'It's wonderful to meet you, Paul. Marina has told me a great deal about you.'

Paul laughed and replied:

'Same here. It seems we're quite the matching pair of mysteries!'

George Burroughs stepped to the door as well and Clem introduced him. The quartet rode on a tide of happy, nervous conversation into a huge, beautiful Moroccan drawing room. Clem was asking Marina about her dress, who told her the story of its making. George and Paul were discussing one another's jobs, having already received their wives' briefings. An American maid entered the room and began to fix drinks.

'Everyone loves martini,' Clem boomed, declaring a fact rather than asking for preferences.

'Oh, certainly,' Marina replied.

'But no one is quite as passionate about it as Clem,' George joked in a stripped, clear Boston accent.

Clem laughed out loud, as she passed the glasses from the maid to Paul and Marina.

'When I'm dead and gone, they'd better rename it after me! I keep three separate vermouth empires in business, you know.'

Marina lifted her glass and made a toast.

'At the funeral, we'll all drink clems till dawn.'

'And dip an olive in,' George added.

The green silk dress always brought luck. It always signalled a good night ahead. The evening with the Burroughs was no different. Once everyone was dizzy on martini, Clem marched Marina around the house to show it off, leaving the men to talk about Paul's work and the effects of independence on the oil business.

Each room in the house was decorated differently, so that this Spanish villa in the Middle East started to resemble a pop-up gazetteer. Red silk walls in a Chinese library. A high wood fire – unlit – in an English kitchen. No hares hanging, though, not in this heat. There was a sitting room in high French rococo. And that drawing room, of course, with its cool blue height, mosaic floor and feathery palms, looking for all the world like downtown Casablanca. As they walked back to the ritzy Fifth Avenue dining room, their heels clicking lightly on the green-sea marble floor, Marina said:

'It's marvellous, Clem.'

Clem shook her head.

'Oh, I can't claim any credit,' she sighed. 'I already told you, I'm the worst sort of philistine. George's secretary in New York picked it for us. Can you imagine?'

Marina laughed.

'Yes, I can, actually! I don't know two things about furniture. Put me in a dress, or a coat, and I'm quite the expert. Ask me to fill a room with chairs and I can't even pretend to care, quite frankly.'

'And you said such nice things to Deschamps about her Robert Adams showroom.'

'Could you believe what she said about Jewish bankers?'

Clem shook her head.

'It's a bit much. Really it is. But she hates everyone, you know. Jews. Arabs. Spaniards. Americans. British.'

'I wish she'd hate me. At least then she'd leave me alone,' Marina groaned.

'Oh, don't worry, darling. One day she'll hate you, all right.' Marina grinned.

'But what could I ever do?'

'Don't worry about that. She'll sniff out the dirt.'

Clem laughed out loud, missing the flash across Marina's eyes. They were at the door to the dining room. Inside they could hear George and Paul already chatting. Suddenly Clem touched Marina's arm and stopped her.

'Isn't Paul quite the catch, dear?'

Marina felt shocked that Clem should say it. Not because of what she said – Clem had spoken what was on her mind from the word go. Not because of Paul. He was charming and good-looking, always well turned out, always lively and intelligent company. When another woman reminded her, she would always blush and then fill with pride. She started to do both right then, too.

'Well, like you said, I can't claim any credit really.'

Clem arched an eyebrow.

'Oh, come on! You and I both know you have to whittle them away to get them as you want them.'

'Well, yes,' Marina replied.

Marina's stomach churned because even if she didn't think about Paul's infidelities every waking moment, there was a part of her brain on to which they had been branded. And whenever someone complimented him, after she blushed, after she felt full of pride, that part of her brain would flick its own switch, and she would remember that Paul was not at all perfect. Charming, so what? Lively and intelligent company, so what? For God's sake, this part of the brain would shriek, your husband sleeps with men.

Clem went to open the dining-room door.

'They don't come out of the box like Paul, you know. They aren't just made handsome, charming and – more to the point – clean.' Clem pulled a face. 'They come out of the box *like George* . . .'

Then they walked into the dining room. George and Paul were standing, smiling. Both men turned as their wives entered.

George said:

'I think the food is pretty much ready to go, Clem. You wanna come to the table?'

Clem sighed comically.

'Bloody Americans! They can't wait to sit down and gobble their meals. If you go to New York, you'd swear they were charged less if they didn't sit at the table too long. Their table manners are the worst!'

George raised his eyebrows in mock shock. This was clearly an old routine.

George sat down, and the other three followed him. The same maid came in with the first course. Paul looked up at Clem. His warm, open smile, his twinkling pale blue eyes made him look so handsome right then. The way he stared directly into the eyes – into the soul, a romantic might say – of whomever he was speaking to made him seem so much more attractive than perhaps he really was.

'And so, Clem, what were you two chattering about out there?' Back then, when men and women would spend time apart at any function, this was the standard dinner-table icebreaker. It was the cue for flirtation.

'Why, Paul, what goes on between us girls is top-secret stuff!'

'Oh . . .' Paul gasped mockingly.

'Isn't that right, Marina? Trying to figure it out would be like rocket science to you boys!'

Marina smiled weakly, thinking only of her churning stomach.

George interjected, 'It can't possibly have been of interest to tough guys like us. We're businessmen. Professionals.'

Clem was laughing, pink-cheeked, and shaking her head.

'You're so wrong! Right, I'll tell you what I said, just to shut you up!' Clem looked over at Marina. 'Why, I was just saying how handsome Paul is, and then I was wondering about how I ended up with an old warhorse from Boston.'

George replied, 'I guess you just got lucky, old girl.'

'Lucky, lucky, that's me!'

Paul turned to look at Marina. She was smiling weakly, obviously uninvolved in the game in front of them. Her eyes lifted to his. Large and glassy blue, they rested on him for a second, then moved away. Paul knew that look from before.

Suspicions.

PAUL WISHED HE wasn't this way. He wished he was different. He wished he could give her everything. A soul is not enough.

You need the body too, she said. I need the body too, she cried. But so did Paul.

Marina woke to the singing of birds and the sight of Paul at the end of their bed with a tray of coffee and bread rolls. A plump green lime had been sliced in two. Its light tartness filled the room.

'I've got a whole day planned for us,' Paul said quietly.

Marina rubbed her eyes, smiled a little and took the tray for him.

'What do you mean?'

Paul laughed and climbed close beside her. He kissed her cheek.

'We're going to go for a drive, Mina, out into the country.'

'What?' she said, turning to look at him.

'Come on, we'll go for a drive. See if we can get to the sea in a couple of hours.'

'But it's all desert.'

Paul shook his head, still laughing at her. Sleepyhead, he used to call her when he was trying to wake her, when, bleary-eyed and confused, she would try to make sense of his early-morning sprightliness.

'Don't you have the iron grip on geography!'

'What?' she repeated, in the same, senseless tone.

'Not if we drive west, silly. If we drive west to the sea, it'll be beautiful.'

Marina took a sip of coffee.

'Which sea?' she croaked. 'The Mediterranean?'

'No, Galilee. There's a place called Fiq on the Sea of Galilee. We could head that way.'

He kissed her cheek again, making her smile.

'You're so daft,' she murmured.

'Come on, then, lazybones. Get up, get dressed. We have to get a move on, old girl.'

A light breeze. Palms. Pines. In the distance, yew and lime trees, heady and spicy. Garden flowers, hanging, climbing, blooming, dropped a million perfumes into the air. Some smelled sharp like lemons. Some sweet, almost sugary. Roses bore a chocolate heaviness. The colour of the light – it was a hundred shades of green, orange, gold, white, silver, blue too. The feel of the light – clean, clear, silky, steely, cold, white-hot. Everywhere, gentle sounds. Treetops swayed in these gentle, aromatic waves of air. Birds cried and cooed in the green, heavy branches. Nightingales in cages. Doves up on the roof, waiting for Noah to come back and rescue them from this desert isolation. The first muezzin was calling out in the distance for the faithful to come to the asr prayer. Marina stood for a moment and just breathed the morning in. Muhammad closed the door behind her and she slipped on her sunglasses. The car horn honked once. Paul was already sitting in the car, grinning.

Driving out of the city, past the crowded bus station at Bab Mousalla, the two of them talked, laughed, pointed at the sights in the south of the city. Old men in fezzes and gabbadiyeh, women in veils or on heels, kids with toy guns or tightly wound packages waited for the battered buses that would head off south to Suweida, Quneitra, Izra, even as far as Amman. The road out of the city was baked yellow. The dry dust of the desert to the east had rained down each night for years, moulding into French-laid tarmac. Fresher dust lifted under the car's spinning wheels. Leaving Damascus, with her head falling back to her seat's headrest and listening to her husband's idle, happy talk, Marina's cares seemed to drift far away. Now and then she would let her head tilt to the left so that she could watch him joke, discuss, explain. And she loved him then. She loved him very much.

The desert has a shore, just like the sea. There is a space where the dry, yellow rock and sand gives way to almost green pasture, to threadbare groves of olives, oranges, yews and limes, to hibiscus, lilac and cork trees. You smell the Mediterranean on the breeze. Fingers of moisture seep thirty miles inland, sculpting the salt and the starfish into sparse trees and windswept flowers.

An hour or more passed. The sky was blue. Impossibly blue. After a while, Marina noticed the impossible blue was glinting iridescently, like the sun had melted into the whole sky. Then she realised that she was not looking at the sky any more but at the wide, flat expanse of the Sea of Galilee. The whole world – sky, sea, sun – was swimming together in that magical cobalt blue.

'Isn't this glorious?' Paul said, squinting.

'Glorious,' Marina replied quietly.

'You can't get that in England, can you?'

'No. Brighton, it's not,' Marina joked. 'Where are we going to stop?'

'I read in that guidebook I bought that there were some Roman ruins just before you get to Fiq. There's a beach there too.'

Marina shrieked in horror:

'I can't swim, Paul, you know that!'

'Oh, yes, you can swim! I've seen you swim!'

'Well, I haven't got a costume with me. Plus, you've never really seen me swimming. Not properly! You've seen me waddling like a pooch in a rock pool!'

'But it was *so* wonderful to me, Mina!' Paul giggled.

'Sod off!'

'You could always go in the buff, darling.'

'Forget that! Forget that! I'm not a burlesque act!' she cried in mock disgust.

He put his hand on her thigh and laughed out loud.

'You could flash at the Arab boys!'

'Frighten them off, more like!'

'And I was only thinking of a way to get you out of those clothes, too!'

'I think the world could live without the sight of my thighs, Paul.'

'Oh, you're right . . . It's probably too cruel to other bathers, you swimming naked!'

'Think of the fish.'

'I'd have to call the RSPCA!'

'You're such a bastard!' she laughed.

Then suddenly, Paul leaned over, there in broad daylight, on the open road, to kiss Marina on the mouth. He sort of missed, more catching the corner of her lips.

Daylit. An open road.

Marina thought her heart would stop.

They stood in the middle of the ruins at Fiq. They had parked the car over on the sandy beach-track. It was getting on for midday. The sun had grown strong. A heat crisped the skin. All around them stood ancient pillars, collapsing walls. They were cut from the same yellow-pink sandstone as Damascus. In the bright light, without shade, the stones were bleached dazzlingly white. Patches of green sprouted from cracks, fissures, erosions. Sparrows, salt sparkling on their sea-battered feathers, hopped among the rubble of the ages.

The ruins at Fiq recalled two things. Firstly, that this was all built hundreds of years before the Prophet, before one word of the Quran had ever been written. When older languages were spoken here. Secondly, the men – the Romans – who built Fiq, or at least designed it, were European. Maybe not like Paul and Marina. They were conquerors too, just like the British. This was not a place of Arabs or Islam. It was older than that. Prehistoric, Marina thought to herself as she stepped through snapped columns and tumbledown yellow-pink houses. In an odd way, the Roman Empire forged a common cultural bond between Britain and Syria. Both were old Romans, historically speaking. Marina found this sudden sisterhood with the Syrians bizarre, not a little unsettling.

'In England,' Paul said suddenly, 'there's Stonehenge.'

Marina woke suddenly from her thoughts. She had not quite heard what Paul had said.

'Sorry?'

'Stonehenge, in England. It reminds me of this. Doesn't it remind you of it?'

Marina looked at him for a moment, wondering why he was talking about Stonehenge.

'I've never been, Paul.'

'Really?' Paul replied, genuinely surprised.

'No, never. Don't sound so shocked.'

They were walking in little circles round and round the age-old rubble, like the way people wander around museums. Aimless, a touch bored, but oddly fascinated too. 'It's old,' she murmured to herself.

In cities, architecture is history. To read a palimpsest, you must understand each layer, every veil. Culture after culture, era after era, adds a new layer. Carvings, paintings, a fountain or a garden, a tower. In the end, the buildings, their interiors and decorations belonged to none of the layers and to all of them too. Damascus's multicultural history was writ large, but so too was the inevitability of Islam, of Arabic. Sulayman, or Muhammad, or any gaggle of local schoolgirls on an outing, could look at each and every stone and see the Prophet's thumbprint, and see themselves too. Marina could look at what the Romans had left behind, what the French had tacked on, but knew the city would never be hers. It was theirs. Always theirs. But here, only the hot and salty maritime climate had changed the Romans. A single moment from the past leapt out like a spook. Marina felt that she had stepped out of history in any urban sense.

Paul was still talking about Stonehenge.

'They reckon it's thousands of years old, the bods do. And the men who made it – it's far more weird when you get up close – must have been bloody geniuses to manage it.' Paul scratched his head. 'Odd, really, because I think they were Welsh.'

'What are you gibbering on about?'

Paul looked surprised.

'Stonehenge.'

Marina smiled.

'Come here.' Paul came closer and she kissed him on the cheek.

It was quite hot. Looking at his watch, Paul said it was just after midday. Mad dogs and Englishmen, he joked.

'And women,' Marina said, smiling. 'I'm quite thirsty, actually.'

Paul bounded over to a kitbag he had brought with him, producing a plump orange from inside. Standing very close to his wife, Paul began to peel the fruit.

Marina watched Paul's long, pale fingers work. Immaculate nails pierced the gorgeous, pitted orange skin. A spray of golden liquid burst out from the puncture. Nectar. Its aroma – sweet, pure, dizzying – swamped Marina's senses. Saliva filled her mouth. The fresh, strong smell – inimitable orange – wrapped her up.

Paul peeled off the first of the zest. Creamy white pulp, soft and acidic, fell away, revealing the delicate, golden-red fruit beneath.

Paul could see the sweat glistening along Marina's hairline. He could smell the first, fresh perspiration building under her cotton blouse.

'Are you hot?' Paul whispered.

'Yes, Paul.'

There was a nervous silence. Suddenly, out of nowhere, a moment had appeared. A moment of desire and tension. Paul leaned forward and kissed his wife, his tongue just brushing her lips.

The orange peel fell from Paul's fingers, bouncing as it hit the ground. Zest tumbled into lizard-filled crevices, over sun-bleached stones. Like Marina's thirst, it was forgotten. Paul slowly split the fruit's segments, pushing his thumb into the small, soft hole at its top. Paul slowly placed a single segment into Marina's mouth. It was sweet, delicious, quenching.

Paul kissed Marina again. Harder. The taste of orange was breathtaking, heart-stopping. Moving his hands across Marina's shoulders, feeling how warm her body was, Paul's lips went to her chin, nuzzled into her neck. Marina said no, terrified of getting caught, of being found like this, here. But the ruins were deserted. And Paul's kisses drowned her protests. The heat, the orange, and the kisses stopped her. As they made love on bare rock, no one was near, no one could see. Her blouse was unbuttoned, her skirt pushed up to her waist. Paul's trousers and underwear were pulled down to his knees. The sun was almost impossibly hot on exposed, private skin. Freckles appeared as they moved on one another, pressed hard against the scattered, broken stone. And when they were close, their breathing hard and heavy, Paul yelped into Marina's ear:

'I love you. I love you.'

In a moment it was over. Done. Paul collapsed on top of his wife. Marina stared into the blue sky with him still inside her and she thought about how untypical of Paul it was to say that, and of the slightly desperate way in which he had said it. She remembered back to other times when Paul had said he loved her during sex. They were very few. It was not something he did. That was fine, it didn't mean he didn't love her. She didn't need – or want – Paul to tell her he loved her if it was just a stage in a sexual act. But for him to say it then – I love you – was so unusual that she could remember quite clearly the occasions when he had said those words during sex.

It was only a few days before she found the first note in London. The one that read, '*Thanks for the little things. K.*' She sifted through her memories of life before she knew about Paul's infidelity. That happy, easy, certain time of trust. He had taken her for a proper tea in a café on the Brompton Road. They had talked idly and lovingly for hours, then taken a taxi back to their flat in Sussex Gardens to make love like they hadn't done in, oh, months. A few days later, she found K's note.

I love you, he had said again now. She remembered the

desperate, yet almost dispassionate way in which he had said it. I love you. That was the hardest thing of all, because her heart sank to hear him say it again.

The night-black sky cracked and crashed thunderously, split with white forks, purple flashes, deafening thunder. Holding herself, the lightness of her cotton nightdress was soft between her fingertips. Turning to watch Paul sleep, seeing his face in the moonlight and lightning, Marina knew there was something wrong. At first she tried not to think about it. She could not sleep, though. No, she stared emptily out into the darkness of her bedroom. A wash of moonlight did not quell her feeling of emptiness. She could do nothing but think about it. Because she knew something was wrong. Paul woke briefly. Sleepily, he could tell she was awake.

'What's wrong, Mina?'

The drive back from Fiq had been a little quiet. He had been conscious of her distraction and wondered whether she felt silly or embarrassed about making love in the open. He had even asked if something was wrong. She had complained about a thread that had come loose from the hem of her skirt. He couldn't see any loose threads.

'I can't sleep, that's all,' she replied.

Paul moved closer to her, and put an arm around her. But she did not move into him to cuddle. She remained in his loose grasp until he was starting to fall back asleep.

It was then she asked:

'You didn't say why you brought that boy home, Paul.'

Marina was wide awake. Her eyes were staring at her husband through the moon darkness. She saw his breathing change. She felt his muscles contract.

'What . . . ?' he whispered, croaking.

'That boy. Sulayman. I don't see why you brought him home that night.'

Paul opened his eyes. He smiled at his wife.

'I just liked him. I thought you might like him.'

Marina started to pull herself up on to her elbow.

'How strange.'

'Marina, it is rather late.'

'What a strange thing to think! That I would want to meet this young man. I mean, why would I want to meet this young man? I mean, he's very nice, yes, but . . .' She stopped herself. She could see that Paul was not going to budge. He kept his eyes closed. He pretended that he was not waking up when she knew he was.

'There's no mystery, Marina,' Paul replied sleepily. 'Let's go to sleep.'

No more was said. Lying awake for most of the night, she watched the darkness turn meek, black go to blue, then blue into gauzy white-gold. But the pale yellow light of morning did not clear her mind. In the pit of her stomach, that old terror was back. No, this was not the first time. Nor the second. Nor the third. Each time Marina had fooled herself into thinking things could be all right. Only when her sixth sense started to prick like this did she admit that things would never change, unless *she* changed them. Her instincts were pricking again now.

IN WINTER, IN these parts, it is dry. In summer, too. Only spring
and autumn bring rain. Out in the desert or up in the hills, the
rain refreshes the sandy scrub. Slow waters seep into the rock,
the sand, the holes, filling wadis, trickling over dead wood.
Suddenly life is renewed. A million flowers burst forth. The
yellow expanse is engulfed with exploding colour. Green, white,
red, pink, a little blue here, a touch of purple there. Bees buzz.
Birds fly up from the coast, to harvest this flood of nectar,
carrying it home on salty thermals, to feed. As the last of the rain
blows off, you can still smell the sea in the air, taste its salt, see its
sparkle. You feel those Mediterranean waves rippling over your
feet. Gorgeous colours, glorious scents, delicate brushstrokes, no
longer just shades of yellow, but a whole rainbow of red through
to violet, and all in between. It's a magical place then. Like
Matisse.

It lasts no time. A week or two and it is all gone. The sea of
flowers is reduced to dry, colourless straw, drifting with the wind
across the desert. The French were delighted when first they
encountered this unique hiccough in the desert climate. The Arab
girls shook their heads as they watched white ladies stepping out
of cars to look at the myriad colours sway and blend. The Arab
girls get out of the bus in the middle of nowhere to pick as much
as they can carry. Their idle chatter, their light work-songs carry
on the clear desert air. They will sell the flowers later in the souq.
Some will be sold to the very white women they quietly watch
out in the desert. Poppies, hibiscus, lilac, tulips, whatever seeds
have drifted this way.

That freak tempest – the one which had kept Marina awake, alone with her terrors – came in the rainless heat of summer. Unexpected, sudden, torrential, unseasonal. It was so out of the blue that the women in the city had not bolted the shutters, men had not rolled tarpaulins over their cars and motorbikes, no one brought in their goats, their washing, or the fruit they'd laid out in the sun. With the first crack of thunder, an atomic-bomb flash of electricity, every last soul in the city shot out of bed. Out in the desert, the herders' rough animals sped off in all directions, charging through the tents. A party at the Governor's house came to a standstill as the guests rushed out on to the lit-up verandas. Cool rainspots fell on all of these faces, white and brown.

A whole night of sky-high explosions caused rivers in the streets. Shutters banged, left-out café chairs toppled over, old brick came loose, smashing to the ground. Cats screeched, birds squawked, goats bleated. The old sewers filled and burst. Drowned rats floated in the rain pools that greeted the dawn.

Sulayman lay in bed, with the covers pulled up around him, and, in between the white explosions, thought about Paul. Marina lay in her bed, watching the sky flash silver or purple, and thought about the same thing.

The next day, the city cleared up. Driving to work, Paul watched the people on the Street Called Straight. Long faces, palms upturned, complaints. Puddles as big as horses filled holes in the roads. Buses charged through these mirror-pools, splashing pedestrians. How the curses rose! By the Prophet, such language! All around, men and women opened their shops and cafés, pressed their hands to their foreheads in consternation, murmuring God's name to themselves, looking bleak. Outside cafés, the left-out chairs were tipped up. Rainwater poured to the ground.

Paul leaned forward in his seat to speak to the driver:

'Sa'id, will there be flowers in the desert?'

'Flowers, sir?'

'Yes,' Paul continued. 'Like in the spring or autumn, will there be flowers after all this rain? Out in the desert.'

Sa'id smiled into his mirror.

'Oh, yes, sir. The girls will be on the buses as soon as they can, off to pick them for the market.'

'Already, Sa'id?'

'Oh, yes, it only take a few hours for the first flowers to show. The girls like to pick them the best, because they have the longest lives. The old women say it's lucky to pick the first desert tulip.'

'But how did tulips get out there, Sa'id?'

Sa'id rolled his eyes.

'Those Turks, sir, they were tulip-crazy. God knows how they got there but the desert is full of damned tulip seeds.'

Early-evening light dappled the room. A little like moonlight. Falling through the nets, diamonds and pearls of gold and white shimmered across walls, tables, chairs and floor. Tiny movements – zipping up the back of a dress, lipstick being applied – brushed the stillness. He turned from the mirror to look at her, and she wanted to cry. Silently he mouthed her name. Marina, on his lips. He had been fixing his bow-tie. She had been watching him do it, in her dressing-mirror. And all the while she remembered how he had been telling her unconvincing stories, how he had been disappearing off at odd times, for too long, conflicting with the schedule he had given her two days earlier. Does it always have to be this way? she wondered. Why does it have to be this way, when we could so easily be so very happy, Paul?

What drove her to ask then, just as they were dressing for the reception, she couldn't say. Except that, having been bitten more than once in the past, her anger and disappointment were just burning to be proved right.

'You're seeing someone again, aren't you?' she suddenly asked.

'Marina . . .' he whispered, with slow lips.

Like lightning, a strange, black look flashed across his face. It was then that she knew for sure. She had seen the look before. The look of Paul getting caught out. That mix of anger, fright, embarrassment, queasiness, guilt. No, this was not the first time. Nor was it the second, nor the third. That black look was terrible in its growing familiarity.

Then he just stared at her across the room. The bow-tie limply unravelled.

'Paul,' she began firmly, 'I asked you a question.' But she was choking back her tears.

'No, Marina. How can you ask me such a thing?'

Standing up angrily, Marina's gown fell in pleats around her legs. He was too quick to deny and bluster. The sound of falling, rustling silk electrified the room.

'Don't lie to me, Paul!' she shouted, immediately furious. 'I know the signs, Paul! I know only too well!'

'What are you talking about, Mina?' he spluttered.

'I can see the signs!' she cried. 'I can bloody well smell them!' Then she slapped her fist against her stomach. 'I can feel them here!'

'You are imagining it, Marina.'

All his promises of the past, all the happiness he could give her, except when he went and did this, evaporated into thin air. Because she knew what he was.

They were almost ready. It was almost time to go.

'Come on,' Paul said quietly.

She looked at him hard.

'I don't believe you, Paul.'

'Marina . . .'

'You said you loved me.'

'What?'

'That day at Fiq, when we did it. We did it on the bloody ground.'

'Marina, don't be silly . . .'

'You said you loved me.'

'So?'

'Well, you don't, do you,' she snapped, then turned away.

'Of course I do!'

Marina ignored him, and left the bedroom.

'Marina . . . ?' he called, starting to feel sick. 'Marina . . . ?'

They sat in the back of the car, en route to another reception at the Governor's residence. The sky was going dark blue, but the city was still full of people and traffic and noise. Paul and Marina sat silently staring out of the windows for the longest time. She lit a cigarette. Lazy blue smoke swirled. Paul turned to look at her.

'Don't get ash on your dress!' he said blankly.

'I don't plan to, Paul,' she snapped.

Paul gasped, then pushed his hand through his hair. It fell from his fingers messily ruffled. She could see him starting to go red. It was always the same.

'I don't know why you're being like this, Marina! I don't know where these ideas come from!' he declared.

'It comes from you, Paul! From you! From the smell in your hair, Paul. From the way you scurry around, trying to deceive me. From the way you sleep so soundly, cos you've had your fucking fill!'

'Marina!'

'Because I just know, Paul. Because I know! You're like a child in a damned sweet-shop here! I know what goes on here.'

Paul yanked closed the driver's screen. His voice was high, sharp, angry.

'Why don't you just wind down the window, Marina, and shout it out? Why don't you ask Sa'id to pull over so he can listen, too?'

'Maybe I will,' she sneered thinly. 'After all, your driver knows better than me what you've been up to!'

'Stop it!'

And then she drew out her big guns. She was staring at him intently, making him squirm. Coolly, deliberately, she said: 'You're having an affair with that boy, aren't you? That Sulayman.'

Paul stared at her, stunned, then looked down at his hands.

His plan had been to avoid this suspicion. By parading him in front of her, he could deceive her and pursue Sulayman. She would never have suspected such flagrancy.

Suddenly he was engulfed in shame. At times like these he wondered what he was doing, what was going on in his head. He loved Marina more than anything else in the world. But he also knew that he was like so many other men. Men who loved their wives, wanted their wives, but just couldn't resist. And then, after the tears and the name-calling, when the wife had let life go on, they felt that maybe it had been worthwhile after all.

'Aren't you?' she repeated, in response to Paul's silence.

There was still a bit of her which wanted to hear him say no. She feared the undertow of him saying yes. His silence fuelled that tide of dread.

'Marina . . .'he whispered eventually.

She thought she was going to choke.

'Is that a yes?'

He did not reply.

'I asked if that was a yes, Paul!' she said sharply.

Every inch of her skin was on fire. Every cell in her body was throbbing with the fear of what she was about to hear.

Paul looked up into her eyes.

'Marina . . .' he began. 'I'm sorry . . . I'm so very sorry . . .'

A part of her could not believe it.

A part of her had wanted him to defy her suspicions, to say 'I've changed', 'You're so wrong'. But when he looked at her, then at his hands and could not even try to think of a lie, she could feel her heart sinking. Fast and hard. Free fall.

She had wanted to be tough. To be brave. And here she was, yet again, being told that her husband was sleeping with some man. Here she was, yet again, horribly wounded, thinking she was going to cry.

'I'm sorry . . .' he repeated, afraid of her silence.

Fight back the tears, girl. Don't let yourself go now.

Marina could feel herself trembling with rage. Was she really that easy to pacify? Did Paul really regard her with such contempt? The hook was not that easy to slip off, Paul.

'You're sorry . . . ?' she sneered.

'Yes, of course I am. Terribly.'

Only the wind, high in the treetops, could ever bother that moment. That still and horrible time, when she watched her husband trying to wriggle out of what he had done to her. Of the life he had made for her. One of deception and rejection and pain.

She could feel her anger in her throat, rasping and dry and burning.

Watching him there, so apologetic, so ashamed, she wished she could break every bone in his body, smash his teeth, crack open his skull.

To give him a taste of how it felt to be so irrevocably wounded.

And when he said, 'Of course, I'll stop seeing him. I'll get rid of him,' she turned and felt able to speak at last.

'You what?'

'I'll get rid of him. Whatever you want, Mina. I'll do whatever it takes.'

'It's so easy, Paul, isn't it? It's so easy to please me, to keep me happy. You just say that you're sorry, say you won't do it again, dump the poor sod you've been fucking and pretend life can go on.'

Paul's eyes nervously flicked to the driver.

'Please . . .'

Marina drew closer to Paul, her face right up to his. The dread she had feared was turning into a whole, fiery anger. Slowly, steadily, in a whisper, she mustered all her strength to tell Paul that she couldn't pretend any more. Life could not go on this way.

'Things can't go on like this, Paul! I won't let them!'

'I know. I'm sorry. I'll do whatever you want. Anything.'

'I don't want to hear that, Paul.'

'What?'

130

'I know you'll do whatever I want, Paul.'

'Yes.'

'Things are different this time, Paul.'

He looked scared.

'What do you mean?'

'The old rules no longer apply, Paul. I've had enough of this. That old game is over.

'This is your last chance, Paul! Your last. You do this to me again and I will leave you, Paul.'

Paul could not believe she was making such a threat. It terrified him.

'Mina . . .'

'Don't call me that,' she snapped bitterly. 'Do this again and I will leave you, Paul. Leave you to explain to the Foreign Office, to whoever the fuck you like, why I've gone and why I'm not coming back.'

'Marina, how can you say that –?'

'Very easily,' she interjected, with a low hiss. 'Very easily. I just look at what a fool you've made of me time and time again and I'm able to say pretty much anything.'

'But I love you!'

'That's the worst thing of all,' she cried. 'You think that by saying you love me that we can get through anything. We can't! We can't, Paul! Life is not simple, Paul. It's hard, too hard to be explained away by platitudes about love!'

He was shaking his head, desperate and upset.

'Don't, Marina.'

'I need more than that, Paul! I need more than to hear that you love me!'

Paul could barely process her words, fit them into coherent sentences.

'How can I say more than that? How can I say more than I love you?'

She was shouting.

'Because they're cheap words, Paul! Fucking cheap!'

'No, they're not!'

'Those are the words that you say to him, I'll bet, words about love.'

'No, Marina.'

'Well, they're dirty words to me! Dirty!'

Paul was watching her fury, afraid.

'But what other words could I say, Marina?'

Marina was close to him. Her big blue eyes were splashing, stormy seas. He was transfixed by their anger. He could barely breathe as she replied:

'I want actions now, Paul! Actions! Words are gone from me! They're gone! From now on, you have to show me you love me, or I have to leave you!'

PAUL LOVED MARINA, it's true. He loved her intelligence, her acceptance, her humour. Loved the way she looked, the way she looked at him, the way she moved, the way she laughed. And Paul loved Sulayman too. But that love was more basic, more primal. To say that Marina was Paul's life was no idle romantic cliché. The life that Paul had achieved (the life that Paul expected to achieve, too) was propped up by the social kudos and respectability brought to him by having a wife like Marina. So Marina had more power than either one of them had ever consciously recognised before. And now she was making one simple demand. Paul had to concede but even as he did so he knew too that life is not simple.

And hearts? Soft, ripe fruit, that's what they are. Nothing more. Removing Sulayman from his heart, like the life that he and Marina had spoken about, would not be simple.

DO WE SPEND our lives waiting for a kind of love we'll never get? That was Marina's question to herself. It was the next day. Marina had called Clem and had asked whether she wanted to meet to go shopping.

'What's the matter with you, then?' Clem had trilled down the phone. Marina heard that happy voice echoing in the wires and felt so very, very empty.

'Nothing. Look, I'll drive round to you if you like.'

'No,' Clem replied. 'I've got George's driver for the day. I'll pick you up and we'll go to Feydeau's to buy something extravagant.'

Marina laughed a little, then said goodbye.

By the time Clem arrived, Marina had put on her face. Pinned on a little blue cloche hat. Was ready for the day.

She got into the back of George's car. She could see the look on Clem's face.

'What's the matter with you, Clem?'

Clem shook her head. 'You look like death warmed up. What on earth is wrong?'

Once or twice Clem had caught a look in Marina's eyes which suggested things were not all as they should be. Hollow. That was the word. A hollowness. At that moment she saw it again. It was chilling.

'Oh, thank you very much,' Marina replied. 'Remind me to dish out the compliments next time!'

Clem touched Marina's arm lightly.

'Tell me what's wrong.'

Marina liked Clem very much. Clem was so easy to like. But there was a part of Marina that could trust no one. How could she ever turn to a social friend and say, my husband is a homosexual? Says he loves me, but he goes off and sleeps with men all the same. She could never even form the words, let alone release them.

'Really, I'm fine.' Marina scooped up a few wisps of brown hair from her cheek, into a loose pin above her left ear.

'You would tell me, wouldn't you?' Clem asked, sounding genuinely concerned. Marina half-knew the concern was genuine, but even the idea of a whisper to Deschamps, or any of the other old witches of Damascus, terrified her.

'Honestly, Clem,' Marina said again, starting to sound irritated, 'I would tell you. Now, let's get this tank moving. I feel the urge to spend some money on things that I don't need!'

Clem laughed and tapped the driver's window. 'Feydeau,' she boomed. 'Foot to the pedal, too.'

Same hour, same moment. Paul was sitting in the smaller bar at the Empire Club. A wide, long room, patterned entirely in green and gold. Curtains, carpets, upholstery, marble-top tables, gilded rococo chair-legs, overly ornate mirrors, all green and gold. Paul looked up from his seat beside a large, bright window, over into a ten-foot-high mirror. Paul was getting drunk very deliberately.

A British waiter brought over another large whisky and a fresh jug of iced water. Even his uniform was green and gold. Paul watched the waiter move away in the mirror, and then looked at his reflection again and groaned. You're a damned fool, Paul. You're a damned fool to sit here, getting drunk, just to punish yourself. You're a damned fool to be missing him so much already.

Green and gold, mirrors and whisky. And a damned fool.

TAYLOR-GREENE, PAUL'S deputy, was waiting for Sulayman when he arrived at work. Sitting low in Sulayman's chair, he was smiling. He was a small, spiteful man, who had spent weeks with his eye (and suspicions) on Sulayman. He'd seen the way he and Paul looked at one another. And there was something about Paul. The way he spoke. Maybe the way he dressed. Too much care, he thought to himself. Too much. Once he'd even gone so far as to put Sulayman's name on a list. A list of suspected independence activists in Paul's small office. Another name was on it too. Fathia Sadawi.

But it was Paul that Taylor-Greene really resented. For years he had worked in different parts of the Empire for different government departments. Never got him anywhere, either. Not when he kept his head down and did his job well. Not when he schemed against colleagues and snooped on his superiors. Taylor-Greene, put simply, was too suburban for Whitehall. He had been paying for the wrong accent, the wrong intonations for the last twenty years. To see Paul, halfway through his thirties, arrive in Damascus to desks full of important papers and to secretaries with their fingers poised on typewriters was too much for Taylor-Greene.

A single lamp was lit, though enough daylight was filtering through the high, screened windows. And so there was a sense of swirling darkness, even at nine in the morning. Confusion flashed on Sulayman's face. Taylor-Greene saw it.

'Is everything all right, sir?'

Taylor-Greene pulled himself up in the chair and coughed sharply.

'Besides you being very nearly late, everything is fine.' Sulayman could see the self-satisfaction on Taylor-Greene's face. 'Although I must say that I have myself noticed your perpetual lateness, and had you been under my direct supervision, would have pulled you up about it before now.'

Taylor-Greene held a small, white envelope between his thumb and forefinger. Gripping it by the corner, he swung it gently in mid-air. Back and forth. He watched Sulayman's attention draw slowly towards its pendulum motion. 'No, Sulayman, I am here to talk to you on a more serious matter.' He motioned that the door should be closed. 'Come in and sit down.'

Pressing the door shut, Sulayman picked up a rickety cane chair, and took it over to the desk.

'What is the matter, sir?' he asked quietly, just as he sat down. The cane chair creaked.

Taylor-Greene was breathing heavily and steadily through his nose.

'Well, I'm afraid, Sulayman, that the department is forced to let you go.'

Sulayman looked up in amazement. For a moment, he couldn't believe what he was hearing.

'What, sir?'

'The department is having to let you go. You understand the phrase? Has to sack you.'

'I understand the phrase, sir,' Sulayman replied in disbelief. 'What I don't understand, Mr Taylor-Greene, is why.'

Taylor-Greene watched Sulayman. He knew the sort. Jumped-up little black shits with some piss-easy Arab degree and an eager-to-please mouth. Fuckers. After twenty years serving the Empire – Malaya, Gold Coast, Transjordan, here – Taylor-Greene knew boys like this were both scratches to itch and nothings to squash. Never trust a black in colonial buildings, he knew. Never trust a black, full stop. What sort of empire, he thought, uses its blacks to run it? He had hated Sulayman since they had first met. His flawless, careful English. That quiet, unrevealing manner. Taylor-Greene tightly smiled, putting the envelope he was holding flat to the table and laying his hand on top. He was one of those little boys who burned ants with a magnifying glass. Taylor-Green even saw himself as such.

'Mr Esmond has requested that you be dismissed. Apparently –'

'Mr Esmond?' Sulayman cried. Nausea shot through Sulayman's chest and throat. Horror ran through his spine, into his legs.

'Yes! Yes – Mr Esmond!' Taylor-Greene snapped, shifting in his seat.

Taylor-Greene paused to breathe and finger his collar. Sulayman was staring first at Taylor-Greene, then dropped his eyes to the floor.

He could not believe it. He knew what was happening. Someone had got to Paul too. Someone had noticed, found out. Only Paul wasn't quite as committed as Sulayman was. Taylor-Greene was speaking again. 'Mr Esmond has instructed me to tell you that your employ here is no longer required.'

'May I ask why?' Sulayman asked quietly.

Taylor-Greene laughed abruptly.

'Sulayman, I'm afraid that you are not expected to question Mr Esmond's decisions. After all, yours is not a long-term position here. You were employed solely for the current project.'

Sulayman looked up. His throat was dry.

'Mr Esmond has not complained about me, has he?'

'Sulayman, I will not be questioned by you!' Taylor-Greene yelled, his hand slamming the tabletop. The echo in the wood, the loud crack silenced Sulayman. It was futile to continue his protest. He knew now that it was over.

Paul had quietly, efficiently got rid of him.

Taylor-Greene slid the envelope across the table. 'This is a reference, Sulayman. It says that your work here has been good and that your dismissal was not caused by any deficiency in your work.'

Sulayman stared at the flat, white shape. 'You can give this to your teachers at the university or use it to find other employment. Mr Esmond instructs you to forward any requests for references to me, not to him. Similarly, should you have any reason to contact the Cultural Department again, you will approach me and not Mr Esmond.'

There was a brief pause. 'You are not in any circumstances to contact Mr Esmond.' Taylor-Greene paused and tapped the table once with his finger. He drew Sulayman's gaze to his. 'If you do, there will be big trouble for you, Sulayman.'

Taylor-Greene watched Sulayman pick up the envelope and hold it loosely in his hands. 'Do you understand, Sulayman?'

'I understand,' he sighed.

Taylor-Greene stood up.

'You may clear your desk and leave at once. Then go to my secretary. She will give you a credit note which you can cash in the Finance Office.'

'Yes.'

Taylor-Greene was prickling with the moment. This was his last opportunity to take a swipe. Spoiling references was out of the question. Paul was going to have a standard one written.

'If it was anything to do with me, Sulayman, you wouldn't even get paid. If it was up to me, I'd throw you out now, without a penny. I mean, I'm sure Paul Esmond has made your being here well worth your while, hasn't he?' Taylor-Greene rubbed his fingers and thumbs together, meaning 'lots of money'.

Sulayman's shame engulfed him. His skin burned purple. He could not look Taylor-Greene in the eye. Not only was Taylor-Greene referring to him sleeping with Paul, he was assuming he had done it for ready cash. Sulayman got up and left, too ashamed, too disappointed in Paul to attempt a protest.

Sulayman was walking home only an hour after he had arrived at work. Clutching two brown envelopes, one containing a few papers from his desk, the other the money he was owed, and the third, white one containing his reference, he strolled along the city's streets.

Sacked, he thought, shaking his head. He didn't mind losing the job so much as the way Paul had unceremoniously, unkindly dumped him. Bastard, he hissed under his breath. Then Sulayman shook his head, marvelling at his own stupidity. In this crazy city, Arab boys learn from a very young age what White men want. Sulayman, who liked to think himself pretty damn smart, had been well and truly duped. The Alhambra afternoons, the days since, the way that Paul spoke to him, touched him, the way Paul had used that little 'l' word. Sulayman had been taken in by all of it. He had convinced himself he was more than a convenience to Paul, and he had been wrong.

Sulayman hadn't seen any of it coming.

'Sacked?'

Muammar looked up from his evening newspaper. A story inside detailed the arrest of the celebrated political agitator Mubarak. For two years Mubarak had been trying to set up a trade union in a textile factory. Lately he had become something of a hero. So, following his arrest on a charge of disorder, there had been disturbances in the run-down Shadah district, a poky little warren of one-storey hovels and sweatshops. A single grainy photograph showed a mad-eyed crowd of young men throwing rocks at the police. Such smart uniforms, the British. That's what Muammar said. Pressed and clean. His eyes rose to his son, who stood there, trembling.

'Yes, Father,' Sulayman murmured. Fatma brought in lemon water and cumin-spiced almonds. Hearing the word rumble in Muammar's throat – *sacked?* – she hurried from the room again, at quite a pace.

Muammar let the newspaper fall. One page after another slipped softly from his lap.

'What do you mean, sacked?'

'Just that, Father. I went to work today and Mr Taylor-Greene told me that they were no longer employing me.' Sulayman pulled a few green notes from his pocket. 'They paid me off too.'

Muammar stayed calm. He eyed Sulayman slowly.

'But why, boy?'

'I don't know, Father.'

'Did you do something wrong, boy?'

'No, Father.'

A steely glint flashed in the father's eyes. He put a finger on the plate of almonds but did not pick a nut up.

'But you must have done something for them to sack you.'

Sulayman shook his head and showed his palms.

'Honestly, Father, I did nothing wrong. I've been doing whatever they told me to.'

Muammar stroked his chin. He narrowed his coal-black eye on his son.

'Nothing, heh?'

Oh, Sulayman, he was thinking, you're a dead loss, you. You've got no more brains than that Turkish goat's arse of a mother of yours, no more! Getting yourself sacked like some country-rubbish cleaner caught with his hand in the petty cash, heh? Sharp, coal-black, his eyes grew fierce, frightening. Poor Sulayman felt he had swum through the sea and come eye-to-eye with a big, mean old shark.

The father spoke, his suspicion deliberately obvious.

'Something is fishy here, boy. Very fishy indeed.'

'Nothing's fishy,' Sulayman replid urgently, 'nothing at all. I went to see Dr Siddiqi and he said that he needed someone to come and do some research for him –'

'Oh, Great God!' Muammar yelled, clapping his hands to the side of his face. A whining whistle slipped through his lips. 'The last bloody thing I want you to be is an academic!'

Muammar stood up. He was flailing his arms around, shrieking and jabbing his finger in the air. 'A bloody teacher up at that crackpot university, yakking on about bloody Islam and all that commie bollocks? Do you want me to die of starvation in my old age, heh? Whilst you get paid a pittance for writing dreary books and filling the heads of students with leftie nonsense, heh?'

'But, Father, it's only a bit of work and surely you want me to finish my doctorate?'

'Finish it?' his father shrieked. 'The only reason I let you go on with these bloody interminable studies is so that you could get a nice Doctor in front of your name and then go off and do something useful! I never wanted you to sit on your arse day and night with nothing better to do than read the Quran and bloody Karl Marx!'

'But, Father . . . !'

Now Muammar was walking around and around and around. Round and round, his footsteps traced a small circle of tension. Hands on the top of his head, he groaned and hissed. Sulayman could feel his own muscles screwing tight, awaiting the inevitable blow.

'When was an academic any use to man or beast, heh? What a bunch of degenerates and tarted-up whores! I had planned so much for you and now this!'

'But,' Sulayman was stammering, 'I've only lost a temporary job in the Cultural Department, Father –'

'Heh?' Muammar shrieked.

'Father!' Sulayman cried in exasperation. 'It's not a tragedy!' (But, in Sulayman's heart, that's exactly what it seemed like.)

'Oh, you little bastard,' his father screamed, 'you're as fucked-up as your crazy mother! I had planned so much for you! This was such a big step, working with the British. You could've made something of yourself. Do you really think that the British will ever re-employ you now, heh?'

'Father, I don't know that I want to work for the British again –'

'And what will the Husseinis say?' Muammar gasped in horror. He shook his finger in Sulayman's direction. 'I know precisely what they will say. They will say, "Your boy is too irresponsible for us to even consider letting him marry our Leilah!" They will say, "All off!"'

Suddenly Muammar lifted his hand and smacked his son hard on the back of the head.

Sulayman cried ouch! and clasped his skull. Muammar was

not appeased. His blood was up. 'Oh, the *shame* of it all, Sulayman!'

Cross and upset, Sulayman collapsed into a chair, rubbing the sore patch on his head and pulling a face. His father was too angry for regrets. Muammar's bottomless faith in all things British convinced him that regardless of whether his son had actually done anything wrong, Arab incompetence had not matched up to the stainless-steel competence of George VI, Clement Attlee, Fred Perry and fifty million other blue-eyed wonders. He did not think his son had really been negligent. Maybe he was too proud to know when to shut up. That's his mother's Turkish high-horse shenanigans, Muammar nodded. That Diniz, he spat.

Muammar was right about one thing. It was well-known that once you had fallen foul of the British establishment it was very hard to win back their favour. It was all right for his idealistic twentysomething son to say that he didn't mind losing this temporary job. How would he feel when he was forty, fifty, heh? The independence fuckers could be throwing bombs and clucking their tongues for centuries yet. Look at those bloody Irish ingrates, Muammar reflected, nodding to himself. How then would Sulayman feel? A washed-up, underpaid, whinging academic? Sulayman sat, clutching his head where it hurt, knowing the real reason for his dismissal. He had been screwing his boss. Sulayman reflected as he rubbed his new bump, that if Muammar knew quite how much favour he had been currying with Paul Esmond, his argument would be somewhat undermined.

Suddenly, Muammar's face relaxed. The tight, vexed peach-stone eased. Lines softened. Eyes too. He breathed out slowly and almost smiled.

'No,' he began slowly. 'There is only one thing that we can do.'

'What?' Sulayman asked.

'I shall write directly to Mr Esmond and ask him to reinstate you.'

Sulayman looked up in disbelief. He started to shake his head.

'No, Father . . .'

'But it is a splendid idea, Sulayman! *Splendid!*'

Damascus was in the middle of another ordinary day. Tumult, chaos, haggling, shouting, bullshitting, selling, buying, fingers slipping in purses, rent-boys' knives in the backs of white men with hard-ons down alleyways. An army of buses, cars, taxis, carts, motorcycles and pushbikes filled the Street Called Straight, bumped its way up An-Nasr, sped in circles around Al Merjeh. Thousand upon thousand of office workers, businessmen, shoppers in the posh stores, shoppers in the Madhat Pasha Souq, women of quality, women with meat wrapped up on their knees. A gaggle of screaming kids all jostled one another, trying to kick a ball. Vehicles and people of all kinds filled the city's main long street of streets to bursting. And all the time there was noise, noise, noise.

The day was high. Stalls with fish or lamb or chicken on them were starting to smell stale. It would be overpowering by five. The dust and sweat on people's skin, the heat under their veils, their shirts and hats, the bruises on their stamped-on feet, their elbowed ribs, their pushed backs brewing up and up into the odd argument, the raising of a palm in indignation, an angry shriek. Damascus was hot, tired and very, very full.

Sulayman had wandered into the beating heart of Damascus – the Old City – overwhelmed by a sense of doom. His father would write to Paul Esmond, which Sulayman had just been expressly forbidden to do. There was no point in explaining to Muammar that the letter should go to Taylor-Greene anyway, who at least would throw the letter in the bin unreplied-to. And then, of course he was licking his wounds over Paul dumping him so unceremoniously, mulling over how he had let himself be made a fool of.

The Husseinis would get to hear about it, too. Families get nervous in marriage negotiations. Jumpy as hell. The engagement to Leilah would probably never happen now. And of course the loss of such a prize – a full-on tennis-and-piano wife –

would be roundly, permanently and excruciatingly blamed on Sulayman. The sun was going into a red as deep and soft and warm as flesh. Those yellow stones, the thing of citadels and mausoleums, mosques and minarets, were starting to go pink.

The divine city. Pink and ancient as that old sun itself. Sulayman thought of Paul, of the last, happy time at the Alhambra, and wondered what he had done wrong. Cars honked their horns and old traders were calling to one another. The city was starting to shut itself down for another hot summer night.

He hadn't expected to feel this. To feel so much for Paul.

What had Sulayman expected?

A brief affair. A dalliance before marrying Leilah Husseini, before getting his Ph.D. and then a job.

But, as Sulayman stood alone in the middle of the Street Called Straight, alone, he knew he had fallen in love.

DINIZ REMEMBERS THE end of the world.

Ghostly, it stalks her, in her memories.

Night-black in the shadows of her father's house, the women huddled together. The silk of their long dresses rustled as they twitched. New monsters were stalking the city. Christian pigs, with their filthy ways, white men with their evil, flashing blue eyes, had come, they cried. And so the Turkish women muttered darkly about the future, talking Istanbul-style so the servants could not understand.

Turkey has fallen, the British troops yelled out in the street. Diniz remembers being in her father's house for the last time, hearing the damning voices. She remembers how everyone huddled together, terrified, asking what was to be done.

Your time has come, the soldiers shrieked. Rattling their guns, pointing rifle-butts into women's faces, they said everyone had to do what they said now. The old days were gone. Gone.

Diniz's father, Old Erbakan, had shrugged wearily that last time she saw him alive. The two of them sat together in what had been his office, but was now full of documents and money and valuables, stocked up for that moment when the Turkish government sent trucks to bring them home. You see, after all the years in the city, they still thought of Istanbul as home, and trusted in the Sultan to pull them out of the hot water at the last moment. But that moment was come, and wise Old Erbakan knew that the only trucks coming were British. The rumble in those axles spelled out their deaths, not their liberation.

'This is the end of the world, daughter,' her father had sighed sadly.

Diniz had wanted to weep seeing him there, head in his hands, defeated. She could not bear it. She ran from the room, choking on her own desperate tears.

Out in the streets, as she was driven back to the house Muammar had bought with her dowry, the very Arabs who had worked for them for ten, twenty, thirty years jeered and threw rocks at them. She saw a man in Turkish dress being beaten to death by a group of youths with sticks. The driver ignored her demands that they stop and help.

That night, out in every street, came a terrifying order from a British soldier's lips. 'All salaried or stipendary officials of the defeated Sultan's government must report to the Central Square compound before dusk. Failure to do so will result in execution.' Thirty years later, she remembered how good his Turkish had been.

A ghost dances in front of Diniz's older eyes now. There in the shuttered gloom of her bedroom, a nightingale's song drifts. In a half-dark full of scents and memories, the ghost shimmers and hovers, moving like a dance of old. Diniz can barely stand it. She has tried to unhook herself from life, poor Diniz. But she can never escape the ghosts of her past. She remembers the midnight black. She remembers that terrible night of the dead. The loud knock on the door rang through their dowry-bought house.

Muammar went to the door. Diniz had begged him not to. But he ignored her, cautiously opening it. It was his brother, Rashid, come to tell him to hide her away. The British were rounding up any Turk that the Arabs did not kill, he muttered. Shipping them out into the desert. Out into the desert. The Turks took no papers, no belongings. They were not filed in the trucks in any order and no one was keeping a count.

Muammar gasped, put his hand gravely on Rashid's shoulder. Diniz did not understand. Rashid said that Old Erbakan's house had already been raided and emptied. Diniz's father was standing right then in a truck, waiting to be driven out into the freezing desert night. His brown eyes had looked as big and pale as the yellow moon, Rashid said. From a cut on her father's cheek ran blood.

The night of the dead passed. Not one of the Turks in the trucks ever came back or was ever heard of again. For three days, Muammar hid Diniz in the house until a British soldier banged on their door and told him that all Turks and their families must report to Central Square.

He had been sure that they would both be killed. If the Arabs did not stone them to death en route, they too would be driven out into the desert and shot. Only when this didn't happen, when they were sent home and told not to make trouble, did Muammar first bless the British. Turning to his wife of one year, he said:

'You, you fucking Turk, you almost got us both killed, didn't you, heh? You almost got us shot in the back out in the fucking desert! Well, thank God that the British have more sense than the Turks. More sense and more mercy to let us go, heh?'

Diniz let a tear run down her face, thinking of Old Erbakan and all the friends and family she had lost out in the vastness of the desert night. Resting her hand on the bump in her middle, she wondered what the future would hold for her children, here in this crazy city where Arabs and British had so gorged themselves on the blood of Turks on that cold, unhooked night.

MOONLIGHT SHIVERS. MY mother used to tell a story about my birth. 'Paul,' she used to coo, 'have I ever told you the story of your birth?' I never said yes.

She was very poorly after the confinement, unable to get out of bed. Administering the household from under soft, warm covers, she packed my father off to register me, the new baby. My father was one of those men who are so easy-going that it drives those near them to distraction. As I grew up, I realised this unobtrusive behaviour was a selfish behaviour, where his charming easiness tipped easily into gross unreliability, his vague-old-duffer routine was a slow, steady route to getting what he wanted. But when I was young I saw only my mother's sniping impatience, not the disappointment of perpetually being let down.

The name had been a source of friction. Frederick Paul Augustus was her choice. Frederick, after my father. Paul, after hers. Augustus, to mark me out. 'The road to greatness,' she declared portentously, 'starts in a name. Whoever heard of a great man called Stan? Or Wilf?' My father did not want the road to greatness. He was happy teaching English at a crumbling grammar school and watching football. If my mother was oppressive in her over-abundance of ambition for me, my father was just as cruel in his total lack of it. Sending my father off with her long list of names, she issued one warning: 'You mess it up, Fred, and I'll make your life hell!' The bull had duly been shown the red rag.

Hours passed. Mother's eyes fell from her confinement bed down through her bedroom window. Outside was a little garden she kept scrupulously neat. Geraniums and sweet peas tended by her green fingers wooed armies of butterflies and birds. Gazing intently up the winding road on which they lived, she waited and waited for my father to return. When he finally turned up, she was in a bad mood. She could smell beer and cigarettes on him when he at last came into her room. He was tipsy and pink-eyed, determined to make her the ogre. Problem was, she could never resist his provocation.

'So?' she snapped.

'I've done it,' he replied. The alcohol flushed his cheeks.

'What we agreed?'

There was an eerie silence. Just like she imagined what it must be like in the moments before a battle starts. My mother always said that when recalling that day.

'No, Mary, just Paul,' he drunkenly replied. 'Kids in school would have made his life hell if I'd given them your list of bloody names.' She had lost that battle. But the war would be hers. Her final victory – my victory too – came when one day I brought home the pretty and patrician Marina Russell and told them that I was going to marry her.

The moonlight shivers, Sulayman. Now I watch Marina sleep. The moonlight paints the waves in her hair green, blue, silver, white. I can feel the gentle pull and rise of her sleep breathing. She has such a serenity, even in sleep, despite her anger now. I love her, Sulayman. She has withstood each blow I have dealt her. She has not left. She has not abandoned me. And I need her, too. Now she has threatened to leave, Sulayman, and I cannot risk that. I must obey her. I must concede to her. Or I will lose everything. Not just her.

But, Sulayman, I want you.

A mist has descended. White. I no longer see the way forward. Sulayman, I don't know how this can have happened. I don't know how. I tried to keep myself buttoned up, shut down. Usually, men like you – Sulayman – are easily cast off. Easy, say goodbye. Easy, next, please. Easy, say sorry to Marina, even saying to myself never again. But I want you. Your black hair, shiny. Your full lips, splitting. Your quiet calmness. Your mix of modesty and hunger. I'm like Justice, with each of you on a scale. Weighing you up, why I need each of you, why I want – love – each of you. Such different reasons, for such different people, and yet . . . I am laughing, I am not Justice. That's the last thing I am. I cannot choose. And yet I must.

The moonlight shivers, Sulayman. Let me explain.

When Marina woke me the night she realised something was going on, her eyes were on fire. I could see how much pain I was causing her. No, this is not the first time it's happened. It's not the second, and it's not the third either. Now she doesn't cry, or at least she pretends she doesn't. But she used to. She used to weep bitterly, ask me why through her raw tears, shriek that it must all be her fault. You know, the first betrayal is not the worst. The second is. That's when you know that all the promises, all the painful forgiveness, were meaningless. Disappointment is never so bitter third time around. You survive. Don't you?

Now, here in this moonlight, I am afraid. I am pretending to sleep, breathing in the patterns of her breathing, shifting very carefully, so as not to wake her. My throat is dry. My heart pumps the blood around my body at top speed, flushing through my chest, my arteries, my liver, my stomach.

Now, here in this madness, I am terrified. She is pretending to sleep, breathing in the patterns of her fury, shifting very carefully, so as not to lose me. But she knows she – we – cannot go on this way. She knows that, to survive further, to keep going, we cannot keep pretending this is all right. She has turned to me and said, I will leave you. She said, You will have to explain it all away. She has said, in effect, I will withdraw my love for you, and let you get on with it. And I can't risk that. Can I?

Still I want you.

Weeks have passed since I saw you last, since Marina told me to send you away. My desire for you – no, my need for you, my love for you, if that's what you want to call it – is not receding. I am not forgetting you. I am not forgetting your hair, your eyes, your lips, your occasional earnestness, your bursts of humour, the warmth of your skin, the hardness of your limbs.

I want you.

I think I am drowning in my own desire. I feel like a body out of control. This is a time of madess. Inside madness. Outside too.

I don't think I can see you again. I don't think I cannot.

THE HEART
OF MADNESS

A LONG BLACK car was driving through the city. It was very clean. Polished high. Shiny. People on the street watched their faces on the mirrored wings. Eyes caught silver strips along its running-boards. Three weeks had passed since Paul last saw Sulayman.

When the car turned into the university buildings, the well-spoken students sneered. To hide their surprise. They looked at the country-rubbish Arab driver and, in the foolish way that students do, blamed him – him with his little job, which paid him less than their monthly allowances – for what the car repre-sented. You know, in this heat, tensions rise. Arguments flare. A whole city goes about its business but the hot summer wants more. High summer doesn't like courtesy and good manners. No, no. It likes tempers. It likes punches. Women feel too hot in their veils and feel terrible when sweat runs into their secret places. Smart girls in modern dress lift compact mirrors to check their foundation hasn't sweatily separated, that their coiffures aren't wilting. Everywhere, people are swaying makeshift fans – old newspapers, a fallen or snatched palm feather, a sun-wilted cabbage leaf, crumpled-up lecture notes. They all long to undo that button, just for the moment's respite, but can't, for modesty's sake. Good Muslims all, their mothers' warnings not to show too much are ringing in their ears. The whole city sinks into a worse and worse mood. Man, it's hot, they cry! Maaan, it's hot!

'Sulayman!' It was the secretary the History Department loaned

Dr Siddiqi every Tuesday afternoon. 'There is a man here to see you.' She grinned, half in wonder. 'He's in a car. A black Daimler.' Sulayman had been at work for a few hours. Dr Siddiqi, with his usual kindness, was stretching out the few weeks of work into a couple of months.

The secretary knitted her brow. 'Come on, then, Sulayman,' she ordered. 'Get downstairs to see what he wants.'

In his black uniform, the driver Sa'id was sweltering hot. A fine sheen spread across his nicotine-ochre face. Around his hairline beads of sweat glinted in the strong sunlight. When Sulayman appeared through the main faculty door, blinking in the white noon sunlight, Sa'id nodded curtly and stepped towards him.

'Good afternoon, sir,' he said without fuss. It suddenly shocked Sulayman to hear this greeting, given in English. It struck him as absurd and irritating. Absurd that this man was talking like an English servant, in the language of the English master. Irritating that the driver was expected and forced to do this, when his own manners, and, yes, his own language, were as noble and old and every bit as beautiful as theirs. Haroun was not completely wrong, he thought then, watching Sa'id sweat in a black uniform.

An itch is a funny thing, Fatma knew, as she went about her chores, dogged by Diniz and Muammar's endless demands. You hardly notice an itch coming on but, boy, suddenly it's there. You try your best to ignore it. But the itch gets so bad, you can't resist. It drives you crazy! And then it's like you can never, ever stop!

'Salaam aleikum,' Sulayman replied deliberately, that phrase every Muslim everywhere understood. He spoke with that high, proud, earnest tilt to the chin, the one Paul had been missing. But Sa'id wasn't complimented in any way. He just wanted to smash this Turkish boy in the mouth. But instead he calmly added:

'Mr Esmond has sent me to drive you to the government buildings. He wishes to see you, sir.'

'I didn't know if you would come.'

Paul sat at the far side of his office, far from Sulayman, who closed the door behind him. Seated in a high-backed chair, Paul affected an easiness, a charm. Sulayman was not confused. Like Marina, he had learned to spot the cracks. The pale, neat hair had just been patted flat. That starched collar had been straightened only moments before.

'I didn't appear to have much of a choice,' Sulayman replied tersely. 'You don't, as a rule, seem to offer choices.'

Outside the window, a dove was flapping its light wings. Paul and Sulayman avoided eye-contact. A fan was on in the background. Sulayman was no longer as angry or upset as he had been. Paul's guilt had just grown bigger and bigger. Silence.

Sulayman finally broke it.

'What do you want, Paul?'

'To,' Paul began falteringly, 'to see you.'

'Well, now you've seen me.'

'Won't you sit down?' Paul shifted nervously in his seat.

'No,' Sulayman boomed.

'Oh . . .'

'Too blunt?' Sulayman added sarcastically.

'A bit. Why not?'

'In case I have to make a quick exit, Paul. That's why.'

Paul looked up and smiled weakly. Sulayman felt strong. Good almost. Seeing Paul like this, quite unlike he ever had before, made him feel that he could do this. He could face Paul and then just walk away. 'So, explain, Paul. Tell all.'

Paul stared at Sulayman, then down at his hands.

'I'm sorry about sacking you –'

Sulayman belted out one shot of bitter laughter.

'Well, thanks a lot! Thanks a lot! Not that I was really relying on a badly paid job, or anything.'

Their hearts were pounding.

'The reason I sacked you was that Marina began to suspect something was up.'

'Between you and me?'

'She knows it was you. We've . . .' He paused and started to redden guiltily. 'We've been through this before. She and I.'

'I see.'

'You're not shocked?' Paul asked, looking up.

'I'm not surprised.'

'That's funny,' Paul began. 'Sometimes I'm shocked.'

'And sometimes you're not?' Sulayman asked drily.

'No . . .'

'So, how is Marina? How is she, now that she knows about it?'

'She's not to blame,' Paul said indignantly.

'No, Paul, you're damned right she's not. She's the injured party. She's the one to feel sorry for. And I do.'

'And you feel sorry for yourself too?'

'Don't you think I have a right to? I think I do.'

'Marina is my wife, Sulayman. I must think of her.'

Sulayman couldn't believe his ears.

'You never think of her, Paul. Except maybe to indulge your own guilt. You, Paul, think of yourself first, and others later. I'm sure Marina is well used to that by now!'

'She has had a lot to get used to. I owe her a lot after . . .'

'After all you've done to her?' Sulayman interjected angrily. He paused, as if to collect himself. 'How does she bear it, Paul?'

'What do you mean?' Paul looked puzzled.

'Men like you, British men like you, you don't marry for love, you marry for convenience –'

'That's not true!'

'Of course it's true! How can it not be true? How can she bear it, if she loves you, if she married you for love, but now knows that you *never* loved her – not really?'

Paul was aware that their voices were rising. Lifting a hand, they stopped.

'I do love Marina, Sulayman.' Sulayman looked away to his side, towards the gauzy yellow light falling from the window. 'I love her, and I'm not going to hurt her any more than I have to!'

Sulayman couldn't believe what Paul was saying.

'More than you have to?' he hissed accusingly. 'Listen to yourself, Paul! Listen to yourself!'

The doves on the rooftop had lifted into the air and gone. Only the distant sound of street traffic was filtering over the roofs.

'I love her, and she asked me to finish what was going on. I had to comply with her wishes.' Paul spoke as if addressing a meeting. Then he hesitated. 'It really did have nothing to do with you.' Paul was not telling Sulayman the whole truth – that Marina had threatened to leave. Aware that he was not being truthful, he added limply, 'It had nothing to do with your work, either.'

Sulayman burst out laughing. Its sound filled the room. Its force hit Paul, made him jump a little.

'Is that your explanation, Paul?' Sulayman sneered, still laughing.

Paul was embarrassed. However charming, however much fun he was supposed to be, Paul hated being laughed at. Always had.

'Well, yes . . .' he said, irritated.

Sulayman shook his head slowly. He stopped laughing.

'That's pitiful, Paul!' he growled. 'Pitiful!'

'Well, I can't say any more than that.'

'You've called me here to tell me that you love your wife, the one that you deceive with men you pick up in your department?'

'You're young, Sulayman. You don't understand that life is complicated.'

'I *understand* that life is real, Paul! I understand that Marina is real, that I am real, and that you're just playing around with us!'

'No!'

'With *our* lives!'

Paul was becoming agitated. He felt voiceless. Stripped of his voice.

'No, Sulayman, that's not true!'

'And what's worse, Paul, is that we all knew how it would end. Marina would tell you to get rid of me, you'd sack me, and that you and Marina would return to your oh-so-pleasant existence – until next time!'

'You don't understand, Sulayman!'

The two men were standing, shouting.

'What? That I was just somebody you wanted to screw? That I was just someone convenient to provide a suitable sideshow for your marriage?'

And then Paul found his voice.

'She said she would leave me, Sulayman!' His breathing was hard and panicked. 'She told me to get rid of you, or she would leave me!'

Gauzy yellow light. The whirr of a fan. Then they had been silent for a while. Slowly, Paul had sat down again. Sulayman watched him move. His whole body seemed limp, listless.

Moments go. Paul recovered a little, and looked up at Sulayman.

The silence had grown awkward. So Paul spoke.

'I got your father – Mr Ahmed's – letter.'

'Don't you dare sneer, Paul!'

Paul protested, 'I wasn't going to –'

'My father is many things, has many faults, but he is ten times more decent than you!'

Paul waved his hand, to quieten Sulayman down. In case faithful old Joan had her ear pressed to the keyhole.

'I wasn't going to sneer, Sulayman. He said that you might be getting married. Asked me to reinstate you because you losing your job might threaten some negotiations.'

'I didn't *lose* my job, Paul. You sacked me.'

'I'm sorry,' Paul said honestly.

'So, what about it?'

'You never told me you were going to get married.'

'You never told me about Marina finding out. You just sent Taylor-Greene to sack me, without giving me a reason, and humiliate me as much as possible in the process.' Sulayman could feel his anger starting to boil again. 'Do you know how I felt? What sort of contempt did you feel that you could just cast me aside, with no need to explain, no need to say sorry?'

A bright paleness shone through the window.

'I never felt contemptuous of you, Sulayman, you must believe me.'

Sulayman wasn't listening.

'The worst thing, Paul, was not that you humiliated me! I can survive Edmund Taylor-Greene's nastiness. I can survive my father making a fool of himself.

'The *worst* thing, Paul, is the way you were with me . . . Was that you came to me – you came to me, remember – and you wanted me, and made me feel things for you. But when it all became too difficult with your wife, all of a sudden I was just another Arab boy you felt you could discard when things got difficult.'

'That's not true!'

'Yes, it is, Paul! You could throw me away!'

'You can't say that – you don't know! You don't know . . .'

'I know that you conned me, got rid of me when it suited you, and now you've had a pang of guilt and want me to tell you that it's all all right!'

'You're so wrong!'

'At least have the guts to admit it now!'

Paul shot out of his chair and began to shout.

Faithful old Joan shot back from the keyhole, and rushed off to find the other secretaries.

Paul grasped Sulayman's shoulders and was shouting.

'I need you, Sulayman! I do! I want you, I need you, Sulayman! I need you now more than ever before!'

Sulayman pulled away, frightened of Paul, frightened of himself.

'You can't just do this to me, Paul! You can't just–'

'Yes, I can, Sulayman,' Paul was shouting. He was laughing and crying and shouting all at the same time. Madness. 'Yes, I can. Because if you need to hear it, if you need me too, Sulayman, I'll say that I love you, I'll say that I love you and want you back.'

Sulayman was pulling away from Paul, but was pushed towards him too.

'Paul, don't say it!'

Paul grasped Sulayman all the harder, pulled him closer.

'What? That I might love you?' Sulayman's head was swimming madly. He could feel Paul's quick, hard breath on his own face. 'Then I do, Sulayman! Then I love you!'

Blame the heat, dust, the noise, the smells, the Arabs, the British, the French, the this, the that, Diniz would have said from her bed, but cities don't drive people mad. People are mad from the very start. And that's why, even when all the signs and signals warn, 'Run! Hide! Get clear!', one mention of that dreaded, longed-for 'l' word smacks you to the ground, cross-eyed and brainless.

Rumour was, fathia Sadawi was raped. Quite why they arrested her no one really knew. But they did arrest her. Took her off the street just as she was leaving work, piling her into the familiar black Daimler. Dropped her lunchtime-shopping bags as she protested and shouted at the White policemen. An aubergine, plump and purple, bounced at her feet. Her husband waited up all night. Had been to the police station twice before he was told she had been arrested by the Mandate Police. Sending him home, they would only tell him she was being held for questioning.

Rumour was, she was raped. When she returned to her tenement home early next morning, her hair was loose round her face. Wiry black-brown curls bothered her eyes. Too tired to brush them into place. Her husband Mahmoud put his arms round her, without a word, happy she was home. She winced. An anger pricked in his stomach. She did not show him the blood-blue bruises on her stomach and thighs. She never told him about the pain inside her mouth.

Rumour was. Mahmoud told his wife, mother of their four children, to go to bed. To rest. He went to the telephone box to ring the government buildings to say that she was sick. Anger was making his hand shake. He almost dropped the receiver. On a tray he brought her tea to sip and dates to eat. After he left for work, Fathia got up. The tea grew cool. For the longest time she stared into the cracked mirror at her bedside. Then, slow on her stiff, bruised legs, she put on a clean, white dress. Went into the tiny bathroom, closed the door and fixed her loose hair at last. At last. Then, with her husband's razor-blade, she cut her veins open. She was dead hours before her son got home from school and found the bathroom all red.

Damascus reeled with the news of the death of Fathia Sadawi. Rumour was, she was killed and raped and beaten black and blue. Diniz Ahmed, once-upon-a-time Diniz Erbakan, rose from her bed, ignored the nightingales which called her back, put her hand on the door handle to her bedroom, and, for the first time in twenty years, left her bedroom. Life's too short, she was thinking. Life's much too short.

Murder. Rape. Blood-blue bruises. A razor. Children's foot-steps in blood. In the hours and days that followed the death of Fathia Sadawi – mother, wife, secretary, victim and, soon, icon – the city changed. The last winter had been hard. When the British came in early 1945, many Syrians breathed a sigh of relief. The Free French shells had battered the city and left too many dead. On Al Merjeh you could still see the blackened craters in the road and around them, like the points of bright stars, brushstrokes of dark, dried blood. That's why they started to call it Martyrs' Square. Through spring and early summer Damascus was in a trance. A trance of grief and shock. No one wanted to fight any more. No one wanted to recall such images as good men and women fleeing in all directions during the bombardments, right in the middle of the Street Called Straight. Men and women being cut to pieces by shrapnel. One night a light snow fell in Damascus. Shells rained in snow. A crisp, perfect white, patterned with rosebuds of innocent red blood.

So quite why the death of Fathia Sadawi shocked Damascus no one could put a finger on. But suddenly, though many people had been arrested, tortured, bombed, shot by the Mandate authorities, one woman – whose death certificate, after all, quite clearly read 'suicide' – galvanised their spirit. An old memory was awakened as the first of many demonstrations brought central Damascus to a three-hour standstill.

Once, before Fathia's sister Zaynab, herself a widow at the

hands of the Free French shells, led the tense and ghostly ululations of an all-woman protest, the Europeans had said to themselves, 'Ain't no marabouts, ain't no martyrs in this town,' and they were happy. But now, as the brothers of Mahmoud Sadawi raised their fists and cried, 'Justice!', people began to search their heads for a time before the British, before the French, even before the Turks. There was an old word in the world which had become new. The word was Arab.

Change spreads.

Muammar and Sulayman were sitting at the table in the kitchen, eating bread and hummus, but not speaking. Fatma moved around them, bringing water and coffee, clearing plates. An atmosphere gave the room an edge. Only moments earlier, there had been shouting. Reading the pro-Mandate newspaper, Muammar had been loudly agreeing with its obedient editorial, stating that the Sadawi death was self-inflicted, that all this nonsense was useless, just the product of summer heat and insurgent lies. Since forever, whenever Muammar was having a rant, he would look up at his son and at Fatma. Muammar didn't care what their opinion was because Sulayman would always disagree and Fatma would say nothing. But this day, the reverse happened. Sulayman said nothing, avoided his father's eye contact, played with his food, kept his thoughts to himself. And Fatma, she turned from her work, looked Muammar dead in the eye and said: 'Seems to me they killed her, or as good as. Seems to me they killed her, others too, and now only *their* blood will quench people's hunger.' For the first time in the history of the world, Muammar Ahmed was struck mute.

Up in her room, Diniz had heard Muammar's raised voice, and then Fatma's in reply. That had been the last minute of her banishment. The last moment she would accept incarceration. And change spreads around the city. Damascus is being renewed.

Now, just a minute later, she was running through her house. She was barefoot, her light cotton robe floating as she ran. She looked like a ghost. Her breathing was heavy, panicked. She had not been outside that bedroom door for so many years, not when her child was ill, not even to pee. And now, to be out in the world again, to see walls and doors, to tread steps she had not touched in who-knows-how-long, was dizzying. Even as she rushed through corridors and landings, heading for the voices below her, she was not sure whether she had gone completely crazy or whether her craziness had just upped and left her after twenty-odd years.

Marina had been sitting at her desk writing a letter to her brother when the telephone rang. Muhammad, their servant, appeared silently and murmured, 'The telephone, madam. Mr Esmond.'

Paul and Marina's new order had taken effect. He told her that he was no longer seeing The Other. But now he didn't promise never again, and almost mean it. Now he said nothing except that he understood what she had said, what she meant about leaving him. Slowly – so slowly, it sometimes felt – life hauled its broken self back together. Diamonds of light, showered through her house by the afternoon sun. The drift of scents. Lemon, cedar, hibiscus, rose. Marina walked to the telephone, hearing only her heels click against black marble.

She picked up the receiver and said hello tensely.

'Marina, are you planning to go into town today?'

'No,' she replied. It was a little too early for him to be ringing up for errands and favours, she thought. 'Why?'

'Don't go in today. There is a demonstration of sorts in town and it looks as if it might get sticky.'

Marina was intrigued.

'What is it all about?'

'You know that Arab woman who topped herself?'

Marina remembered something about it in the paper.

'Sort of, yes.'

'Well, it looks like the family are crying all sorts of things went on and have called a demonstration about it, the stupid bastards.'

'A riot!' Marina trilled ironically. 'Excitement!'

'Be serious, Mina.'

Paul's tone was condescending and paternal. She hated him. She felt like smacking him in the teeth.

'I'm trying to be serious, Paul,' Marina snarled. 'Can you say the same?'

She slammed the receiver down.

Standing for a moment, thinking, the sound of her foot tapping the marble floor rang through the house. Then she smiled to herself and called Muhammad.

'Muhammad,' she smiled. 'I want the car. I want to go into town and for you to come with me.'

'Very good,' he replied, and left.

Suddenly, magically, Diniz ran as far as her kitchen doorway, where she stopped. You can imagine how shocked Muammar, Sulayman and Fatma were, after all those years.

Diniz looked magnificent and large. Her long hair tumbled around her face and shoulders, loose, wild, streaked with grey. Hollowed-out cheeks were sucked in as she gazed through fiery black eyes down at the three stunned faces.

Her fingers pointed straight, dart-like, out, lightly gripping the door-frame. Her long gown swept down to her visible bare feet, like some gauzy shroud. She was like a ghost risen. Or a witch.

Sulayman thought he was going to faint. Diniz lifted a long, straight finger and pointed straight at her husband of thirty-two years.

'You, man,' Diniz cried at Muammar. 'You, do you know who I am?'

Her husband was open-mouthed and silent. 'Do you?' she demanded again.

'Of course,' he replied, murmuring in disbelief.

Diniz took the biggest breath in the world. Her big, full, middle-aged breasts rose, her opulently fat body puffed out.

'I am Diniz Erbakan!' she screeched at the top of her lungs.

'Diniz Erbakan! And I am risen from the depths, husband! Like the shipwrecked out at sea!'

'Diniz . . .' Muammar hissed in horror, slowly rising to his feet.

'I am the queen of the drowned, Muammar!' Muammar stopped where he was. Because Diniz was terrifying in her magnificence. 'See my hair, Muammar, my old sweetheart? See how loose and wild it is? That's the salty waves, that is, that's the cold green water, husband.'

'Yes, Diniz . . .' he mouthed.

'Husband,' she whispered menacingly, never blinking once, 'I am the queen of the drowned! But I have come back! I have come back from the dead!'

Muammar and Diniz stared at one another, one transfixed, one fearless. Right then Fatma began to laugh. Her laughter was pure and joyous. Three Ahmeds – Muammar, Diniz, Sulayman – turned and stared.

'Welcome back, madam!' Fatma cried. 'Welcome back! Come and sit down here, and let me feed you up!'

Marina wished she had not been so stupid. She wished she'd paid heed to Paul's warning and not done this just to childishly spite him, to show him how things were different and she as not so dependent on him after all.

But the crowd on An-Nasr was huge and heading for Al Merjeh, the square where so many had died when the Free French had shelled Damascus only months earlier.

Marina had not expected this. She had not counted on Paul being right. A vast sea of heads and hands rose high and angry. There were thousands of people. Men, women, young, old. From the car window, she could see them approaching in the distance. Trying to read the banners they held aloft, the slogans, she asked Muhammad what he thought.

'Madam, I think it best if we return to the house now.'

Marina heard the first police whistles and a furious roar rise from the crowd.

'Yes,' she replied. 'I think that would be for the best.'

The driver turned around and they sped back. Looking back, Marina saw the demonstrators set fire to a Daimler. How they cheered. How free and fresh and frightening their anger was.

Marina trembled, wrapping her arms around herself. She prayed her Paul would be all right, that the crowd wouldn't turn on the government buildings. A thousand voices rose, shouting slogans, cheering. Ghostly, thrilling ululations rained around the city.

ALL THE ROOMS at the Alhambra had the old-style showers. Here, in this city of Muslims who never mentioned God if they could help it, every single soul was still an obsessive washer. After the heat, the dust, the push, the shove of Damascus, the first thing everybody did when they got home was wash. That feeling of being barefoot, stepping on to the cold, wet stone of the shower, waiting for the spray to hit your skin. The millions in this city were crazy for it. Muammar and Diniz could remember when the city was finally fully electrified in the late twenties. Electrification had been the great mission of the early Mandate. The Turks had tried in 1916 but ran out of money after only the central district had been strung with lamp-posts. An American company called Refresh turned up a year after the British had done all its wiring, selling the first electric-pump showers. That first shipment – estimated to last five weeks – lasted four. Their second – designed to last six months – lasted three weeks. Man, the craze was on.

One of Sulayman's earliest memories was his first time in the family's new shower. He was four or five. The nurse told him it was a magic waterfall, like those used by djinn and princesses. The showers in the Alhambra were a touch more prosaic by comparison, even if they were the very same model, by then twenty years old. After you turned the handle in an Alhambra shower, you had to wait thirty seconds for the pump motor to clank into action way down in the basement. Sometimes the water was scalding. Sometimes it was freezing. The pump, the basement tank, the showers themselves had seen better days.

After all, the patrons of the Alhambra went there for one thing and one thing only. In that city full of endless ablutions, the most important shower was the post-coital one. In that city full of furtive fumblings, the most worn-out showers of all were the ones at the Alhambra Hotel.

It was quick. Silently breathless, Paul and Sulayman lay in the wide, rented bed. The ceiling fan whirred. The shower-head tapped. A hot afternoon in the Middle East. Sulayman's faithful Muslim nose twitched at a staler, older perspiration on Paul, concealed by the fresher musk of sex.

'I think you could do with a shower,' Sulayman said.

Sulayman lay in bed waiting for the sound of the shower. He counted the seconds from the moment he heard Paul pull the curtain closed. Paul groaned as the water gushed from the shower-head. Only minutes earlier the room had been filled with the sound of laughter. The sound of kisses too.

Well, kisses are deceptions. Paul and Sulayman had started to see one another again regularly. Always, by prior agreement – made at their last meeting, or whispered down a telephone line – they would meet at the Alhambra. There was the Tuesday that Paul had been so funny, telling him the story about the Governor's reception where he had made some comment about a woman's hair. The recipient of the comment had turned out to be her father. There was the Thursday when Paul was late, and wouldn't say why. Sulayman could smell perfume on his jacket and guessed it was Marina's. A Friday when the city would have been at prayer, or eating, or idly losing a couple of hours in the coolness of a café, and the two of them lay silently on the bed, watching the late-afternoon light through the shutters turn blood orange.

But they existed only in this strange, stifling present. There was only that hour or so that they had behind the shutters. Only the glint of strips of afternoon light on a water jug. Blue. It was a Tuesday or a Thursday or a Friday, but, no matter what time of day it was – forget the colour of the light – that was all they had. Paul never mentioned Marina, not even in his own head. And Sulayman never asked about her, not wanting to know, not wanting to think about what might happen. Sulayman knew that he wanted Paul, that he longed for and craved Paul. He would wait for his telephone call, his summons. Not just for sex. But to see him, to touch him, to be with him.

Slow afternoons, with the world shut out. Sometimes they laughed among the kisses. Sometimes they just sat on the bed and smoked cigarettes. Sulayman didn't mention poems any more. They seemed to have lost their importance. And their allure. Paul still patted his hair neat in a small mirror, still asked if his tie was straight. Sulayman watched him do it. He no longer bristled with excitement, but he remembered that Paul had asked, no, begged him to come back. He had talked about love. Used that word. And that word has a power like no other.

Outside the Alhambra, every day, stood a street-boy by the name of Hanif. Hanif was being paid ten piastres a day to stand outside the hotel and watch Paul Esmond come and go. To Hanif ten piastres was a lot. For five he would turn a trick. For ten he would work a whole week in a café or a factory. And all he had to remember was how often Paul Esmond came to the hotel, when, for how long he stayed, and with whom he had been there. That last part was easy, Hanif thought. He only ever came with Sulayman Ahmed, he explained to the man with the piastres. Edmund Taylor-Greene.

DINIZ THOUGHT SHE had forgotten how the world worked.

Now, each morning, each afternoon, she watched silent Fatma cut vegetables, slice meat, light lamps, beat rugs. Diniz marvelled how fast the days passed. She used to think that life was so long. But now, since Fathia died – everyone was on first-name terms these days – her life was speeding past. Twenty-four hours, one thousand, four hundred and forty minutes, eighty-six thousand and four hundred seconds. It's nothing at all. Time swept by and she could barely catch her breath. Sometimes the pace of life made her dizzy, almost made her sick. She looked at her beloved son as he toyed with his food and asked him questions about the day ahead. His half-answers made her feel warm. She wanted so much to put her fingers through his hair, to lay her hand on his smooth forehead, in blessing.

Later that day, her Suli would return from whatever he was doing. He'd come for her. You see, Sulayman had ordered a taxi to come to the house. It would take them into the warrens of the city. Diniz was frightened. Of heat, of dust, of the million people in Damascus, their elbows and faces in hers, the honking of the car horns. She was frightened too of all the years she had lost, let slip away. Cos she and the city had been intimate strangers for too, too long. Muammar had grimaced, 'Don't you come to the shop, woman.' But Diniz had no desire to go and see Muammar. Turkish princesses don't go to bloody printing shops. All Diniz wanted was to feel the pulse of this crazy city. To count it out. One. Two. Three. She wanted to look these bloody Arabs in the eye and screech, 'Hey, you Arab murderers, I'm still alive, you know! We Erbakans are still up and jiggling! You never got to me, you country-rubbish pigs!'

Diniz had forgotten how the world worked.

'Fatma, heh,' she called. 'Which end of this carrot do I start cleaning from, then?' Even these simple tasks had left her. Now she was relearning them. Fatma smiled with a small, quiet affection. She quite liked Diniz up and breathing, you see.

Sulayman laughed loudly, then stood up.

'I've got to go now, Mother,' he said. 'Things to do.'

'What are you doing first, son?' Diniz asked lovingly.

Sulayman slipped three books into his bag.

'Meeting Haroun for tea.'

Diniz clapped her hands, the unpeeled carrot squashed between them.

'Haroun, heh? I haven't heard his name for a while!'

'Oh, well, you know,' Sulayman blushed.

His mother walked towards him, carrot still with her, and brushed her free hand over his shirt. It was some attempt to make him look smarter.

'Well, you say hello for me, now. I haven't seen Haroun for such a long time. You ask him how his mother is for me.'

'Okay! Okay!' Sulayman cried with a smile. Then he breezed out of the kitchen, towards the front door.

Walking in the morning sunlight, Sulayman felt excited and happy. The sun was not too warm yet. Here and there, glinting rivers of water trickled from faulty pipes. Café owners were dragging stacks of seats out on to the pavement. Grocers were balancing lettuces on one another, oranges, lemons, garlic, tomatoes too. The first of the office workers were out, in shirts, ties and smart dresses. Briefcases and open-toed sandals marched the length of the Street Called Straight. The beep of car horns and the neighing of horses and market mules filled the street. There had been a murder in a coffee shop the week before – people said the resistance executed an informant – so the police had closed the place and boarded up the windows. A week later, the people of the city barely glanced at the shop. No one read the police notice. Pity, it offered a big cash reward. In this most secular of Muslim cities, everyone is up for a buck.

Salaam aleikum, friends cried when they saw friends. Wa-aleikum asalaam, flew the replies. Marhaba. Hello. In the distance Sulayman could see his old friend, who raised a hand in greeting. Haroun stood in front of the Jewel Tea Stall. The tea-boy was there as usual, pulling pipes, squirting hot black tea, calling 'Penny, please, penny, please,' to his patrons.

They drank tea and chatted idly.

'You know, my mother has gone completely crazy. She's got up out of bed! And started cooking and cleaning and things!'

'No!' Haroun gasped in surprise.

'She has. She really has. She got up one day, unannounced, left her bedroom and came down to the kitchen.'

'No! What happened?' Haroun's broad, happy, shocked grin signalled a thaw. Soon the old friends were laughing loudly, slapping thighs.

'We were all in the kitchen one day. We were arguing about, you know,' Sulayman looked shiftily around them, 'Fathia Sadawi.' Haroun nodded just as shiftily. 'My father was being a big jerk as usual. Then, suddenly, the world went crazy! Fatma started shouting at my father.' Haroun went wide-eyed. 'And then, moments later, there was my mother, standing in the kitchen doorway! Like some wildwoman!' Haroun laughed, shook his head. 'Didn't she just tell my father what she thought! Didn't she, heh?' Haroun was shaking his head and laughing no, no, no. 'And now she spends all day trying her best to cook me banquets and talking about going shopping, buying American gadgets and "some lovely shoes"!'

Sulayman laughed too, then they glugged down the rest of their tea.

FATHIA SADAWI. NEVER had a ghost been so persistent. Never had a ghost so thrilled the city. Feeling their veins and arteries constrict, their blood pump faster and faster, people took to the streets, lifting fists, raising voices. Ululations blended with shouted slogans, echoing in the age-old architecture. Rocks were thrown at car windows. Fires were started. Paint got daubed on walls and doors, naming traitors, enemies, calling for action. Fathia Sadawi's brother and husband got arrested in the middle of one demonstration. Five others were taken, too. Yusuf and Aadam, two street-boys along for the ride, got knocked down by a police car as it raced to the scene of a small vigil. Aadam died of his injuries. Yusuf lost his sight. A woman walked into a Whites-only shop and fired a pistol. She missed, hitting a mirror. Screaming White women's summer dresses stained with spots of blood as shattering glass rained around them. Danger breeds bravery. The worse things got, the harder the response, the further the people were prepared to go. Sulayman was astonished when his mother rolled down a taxi window and cried to a group of students with banners, 'God bless you!', as the police bustled them into the back of a van. Haroun was told he would lose his job unless he stopped agitating. His father told him he would be thrown out of the house. Haroun didn't care, collecting money for the Sadawis inside his office. People gave generously. Haroun got sacked. A stone was thrown through the window of Muammar's shop. Suspicion was falling on those reticent in the new patriotism, the new Arab nationalism. Finally, the French and the British had pushed Damascus too far.

*

Heh, Fathia, do you see the trouble you've caused?

Diniz said to Fatma one day, apropos of nothing, this world is changing fast. Thank God, Fatma replied with a glint in her eye. It needs it. Haroun appeared one day at Siddiqi's office, banging on the door, rushing in uninvited. Inside, he saw Sulayman alone, poring over books.

'Come on, you have to come with me!' Haroun cried out loud, like Sulayman was a hundred, not two, metres away.

'What's the matter, Haroun?' Sulayman asked, concerned.

His friend rushed over, grabbed Sulayman's wrist and pulled. Sulayman dropped the pen in his hand and cried out.

'Aiy!'

'Come on!' Haroun yelled impatiently. 'Let's go! There is a huge demonstration! There are hundreds of people there. Soon there'll be thousands. Thousands! And we have to be a part of it, Sulayman! This is the first blow!'

A sea of heads filled the main street of Damascus, from An-Nasr at one end, down Madhat Pasha Souq, into the Street Called Straight. From the steps of cafés on the right-hand side to shuttered windows of shops on the left, Damascus was just people. The city had risen. Got up, stood up, strapped on their toughest pair of shoes and gone out to greet the future. These were ordinary people. They were like you or me. Factory workers and clerks. Students and nurses. Housewives stood alongside the doctors who treated their kids. Teachers put down their chalk, closed their classes, and joined round-bellied café owners and butcher's boys. They spoke together in Arabic. Or rather, Arabics. Uppity city Arabic, country-rubbish Arabic, the far-north, the down-south accents, in Syrian or Lebanese dialects, with Turkish twangs, Persian spices. The human swarm, running into thousands by the time Haroun and Sulayman joined them, were not there just to protest, they were there to celebrate too. Because, after the longest time – so long they could barely stand to count the years – the city had woken from a deep, deep sleep. Ululations rang thrillingly from the older women, who held their hands modestly to their mouths as they cried out. The city was together. The city was one. Haroun and Sulayman, swept along in the tide of people, raised their voices, calling on the British to get out. The two friends could barely speak to each other because conversation became impossible. Sulayman could not believe what he was shouting, what he was demanding. But he wanted to shout it. He wanted to demand it. British out! French out! Syria for the Arabs!

For the longest time, they marched forward, waiting for the French police or British soldiers to appear. Such tension made the occasion especially electric. Sparks flew from tongues. Fists were raised like torches. Bright and brave. But eventually word began to race through the crowd. The Europeans were not going to come. They were holding back, hoping the demonstration would fizzle out. This was a self-fulfilling prophecy. Suddenly this first blow became so good-natured, so celebratory, it slowly, happily, peacefully dispersed. No one got hurt, except for the odd stamped-on toe.

For Sulayman the world was split in two. One half was Paul. Paul who said he loved Sulayman. Paul who brought Sulayman such real pleasure. The other half was Fathia, and all that was contained in her cremated ashes. Damascus. Syria. The Arab world. Islam. The fissure was clean.

Between these two halves stood Sulayman, considering both, compelled towards both. Yes, he went on that march that day. Yes, he raised his fist. Yes, he shouted 'British out!' and called for a free Syria.

But he loved Paul.

No matter what, Sulayman loved Paul.

CLOSE TO MIDNIGHT. Marina left the heat of the floor, asking her smiling dance partner if he would excuse her. Through open French windows she sailed into silver moonlight. The city sky, in its nightly war with the desert cold, was black and turbulently breezy. She could smell the large, floral garden beyond. The last of the cicada song drifted over the honeysuckle creepers dropping around her. Her hands gripped the cold veranda rail and she breathed in deeply. The air was cool on her neck and shoulders. So cool in fact that after a minute or two, she pulled her silk shawl higher, holding midnight's fingers at bay.

It was a party to celebrate the engagement of Colonel Jack Foulkes's daughter Patricia to a young officer she had met only a few months earlier attending a tennis match. The couple looked happy as their friends, and the friends of Jack and Cicely Foulkes, milled around them. An eight-piece band – piano, bass, drums and horns – pumped out lively dance music all night. Champagne and cocktails appeared magically on trays for four or five hours. Paul was inside somewhere, turning on the charm. Marina was happy. He would come to her later, in the warmth of their bed, with the titbits of gossip and funny anecdotes he had gathered. It would make her laugh, too.

Now Marina had done her duty. Danced with his colleagues, chatted politely with their dull wives, been kind to cross-eyed children. A clock on the wall had crept round to twelve. Away from the happy, dancing throng, a light breeze slinked along Marina's throat, out among the moonlit creepers. She pulled her shawl a little higher. Closing her eyes, she could almost see herself back in England, standing on the sea-front at Brighton. The cold breeze was the same, she thought. Ozone – she was sure she could taste the ozone spray of a winter stroll along the stretch of pebble beach from Hove to Brighton Pier. The moonlight on the garden looked a little like the English Channel, with its silver sky and silver rain. It was then Marina said it to herself, 'I want to go home.'

Suddenly a man behind her coughed theatrically. She swung round, gasping. In the shadows stood Edmund Taylor-Greene. Stepping forward, he moved into the light falling from the open window. Marina barely knew Taylor-Greene. Paul had disliked him from their first contact. Paul said that the dislike was mutual, too. So, out of loyalty, she supposed, Marina had decided not to like him, either. But she smiled politely.

'Hello, there.' Taylor-Greene stood perfectly still for a moment and said nothing.

'Are you enjoying the party?' she asked.

Suddenly, Taylor-Greene lurched towards her. He was obviously drunk. Then he stopped just as suddenly in front of her.

'Very much,' Taylor-Greene slurred brightly. 'Very much,' he repeated.

Marina smiled but felt uncomfortable.

'Have you seen Paul inside?' she asked, already running out of things to say.

'Oh, yes, I've seen old Esmond,' Taylor-Greene grinned. He paused, turning his eyes puckishly towards the moon. Even in its silver light, the whites of his eyes looked alcoholically pink. 'Charming the ladies and making the fellows jealous.' He looked at Marina again. 'Or is it the other way around?'

Marina's throat constricted. She felt sick. Yes, the implication was clear. All night she had watched Paul out of one eye. She was sure that if they got back to London, things would be all right. She had been sure. Now she wanted to leave.

'You'll have to excuse me,' she said brusquely.

Taylor-Greene moved to stop her leaving, thrusting his arm in front of her.

'Don't go!'

Marina could smell the alcohol on his breath.

'Let me pass,' she demanded.

'Oh,' he giggled, 'don't you want to stay here with me?'

His face was close to hers. Marina couldn't meet his gaze. She could think only of what he had said. Charming the fellows.

'No, I don't.'

'But I want you to stay.' His voice remained light and merry. It was disconcerting.

'Let me go, or I shall tell Paul,' she hissed.

She could feel her panic rising. He giggled again.

'Can I call you Marina?' he asked, ignoring, as drunks do, the last thing that was said.

'Call me whatever you wish,' she replied tersely, 'just let me pass.'

But he did not move his hand. He did not let her pass.

Moonlight painted silver puddles along the verandah. Green leaves twinkled on the trees like stars in the night sky. Marina suddenly returned Taylor-Greene's gaze.

'What do you want?'

He stared at her for a full second. She dropped her gaze, looking out over the garden.

'Do you ever wonder, *Marina*, why Fathia Sadawi got arrested?'

Marina did not understand. 'I mean, do you ever wonder, *Marina*, why that secretary gets arrested and roughed up so badly she goes home and kills herself?'

'I expect,' Marina stammered, 'she was suspected of some kind of crime. Spying, or something.'

Taylor-Greene laughed. He shook his head and smirked. Suddenly he seemed less drunk than he had before.

'You know, for the longest time, I've been watching the goings-on in the Special Envoy's office.'

Marina watched Taylor-Greene speak slowly. And so she was

hooked. When Taylor-Greene dropped his arm from in front of her, she was free to go.

She did not.

'And?' she asked.

'I – me – sent a memo to the Governor about agitators, suspects in the department.'

'So?' Marina laughed thinly. She was trying to sound like she didn't care really. But she did care, and Taylor-Greene knew it.

'I sent the memo because I wanted to settle a score I have,' he growled. 'Fathia – poor bitch – got mixed up in it almost by mistake.'

'So what does that have to do with me?'

'You don't seem unduly bothered, Marina, that a woman is dead.' Taylor-Greene's drunkenness was lending itself to remorse.

'It's not that . . .' Marina said, suddenly ashamed at how harsh she must have sounded.

'The woman did nothing wrong. She was never my target.'

'Target?'

'That's right. I needed a list of names to write to the Governor with. Suspects. Those who might be dissidents, traitors. I just made the list up. I put a few known malcontents and a few people who would never be seriously suspected. Who would be exonerated immediately if there was any action taken against them.'

Marina was confused. And frightened too.

'Then who was your target?'

Taylor-Greene came closer to her face.

'Sulayman Ahmed.'

She felt the familiar chill.

'What's your point?'

'Sulayman Ahmed *is* my point, Marina.'

The desert air had grown colder. Inside the house the music had died down. Somewhere in her head Marina could hear the bandmaster bidding the dancers good night. Peals of merry laughter floated on the midnight breeze.

'Sulayman Ahmed and your husband, to be more precise,' he added.

'What about them?'

'I think you know.'

Marina glanced up at him. His small, black eyes. Mean.

She studied him for a moment, thinking about how they could have, if they chose, extended the game, drawn it out.

She could have asked him to explain. She could have tried to bluff him out. But why would she? That burning in her throat, the pounding in her chest, the acid pain in her thighs, her stomach, inside her skull all meant one thing. This was it. The end.

In a moment, Marina fled from Taylor-Greene. She ran across the veranda, out into the blackness of the garden.

She was running on the lawn, her heel turning on the soft soil. No louder than the beating of wings, she reached the fringe of bushes. The leafy branches, black and silver in the moonlight, enveloped her.

The night garden took Marina and hid her from the world.

The silence and the stillness bewitched her. A silver Damascus. Moonlight strummed the petals.

In the distance she could hear happy, merry voices. She could hear Taylor-Greene softly, desperately calling her name. Languages. Different, foreign languages.

A cicada cricketed to her, off in the long grass.

Her hands were freezing, her shoulders too. The leaves were tickling her throat, catching her hair.

The moonlight, so diaphanous. The soft mesh of her blue gown. Her hands, freezing.

This was it, Marina's brain kept telling her. The end.

MARINA'S RUNNING.

Running through the streets, out of the house where she'd been to a party. Running in the streets with the night on fire.

On a road that leads into the heart of the city, she runs. Her heels clatter on the pavement. Same tempo as her breathing. Fast and hard and desperate.

This desert night. Winds work up from outside the city. Little storms are raging out over the sand and the scrub. But inside the city – where it's safe, Marina, where it's safe – warm, loud breezes pour over the millions. The black cypresses rustle their leaves, rustle like a Spanish dancer shaking out her skirts. Above, Marina can hear the pine cones clicking together like maracas. And at that very moment she cannot think, she cannot speak, or stop herself from running.

Suddenly Marina hears a car.

She turns around, looking behind her. Two lights in the distance, coming towards her. Fast and desperate. If you'd seen Marina there, caught in the headlamps, if you'd seen the yellow spotlight thrown on her, you'd have seen a woman terrified. Her eyes, haunted and huge, ringed with black mascara, just starting to run. Strands of brown hair fall mad and wild across her face. Her colour high, her cheeks red from running. The car screeches to a halt.

'Marina, what the fuck are you doing?' he cries as he flings open the door, and starts to get out.

She recoils from him. Like an animal. Like the madwomen who live out in the desert, the ones Arab mothers tell their children about, how they will come in the night to claim the naughty ones.

'Paul . . .' she hisses. 'Is it true?'

'Is what true?' he shouts back, scared by her like this. Never seen it before. Will never want to again.

'Is it true? Is it true?' She can feel herself shivering. Hear herself jabbering. Talk so fast. 'You know what I mean!' So fast.

'Marina, I was looking for you at the party! You were gone! What the fuck's going on?' He's cottoning on to 'somehow . . .' He's working out 'got to be . . .'

'You haven't answered me!' she says. Her voice is quiet. It feels like a howl. In the throat. In the blood and the bones.

'I want you to come home now,' he says. She hears a tremble in his voice. A hole into the truth.

'I want! I want!' she sneers. 'What about what I want, Paul? What about that?'

'I don't understand you,' he protests weakly.

'You're sleeping with him again, aren't you?'

'Marina . . .'

'Answer me!'

But he does not know how.

Now that the headlamps are looking down the street, not at her, Marina could look how she wanted to. The night is kind to women past the first flush of youth, those glossy magazines say. Marina is not even nearly old, it's true, hardly middle-aged. But tonight she feels like an ancient.

Such a blue light gives Marina the strength not to feel like an animal, like a madwoman. If Paul has killed her, then the night resurrects her. Her hair is no longer wild. Her eyes are no longer tear-smudged with mascara. She is beautiful. She is alive.

Two straight lines of light point down the road. She blinks. The moment is here.

'I think, Paul, I think that I'm leaving you.' Marina's voice is faltering. She can barely believe what she is saying. But now that she's saying it, now that the night is on her, and she's speaking the words, she feels like she might just make it.

'What?'

She feels surer. Paul's terror, Paul's shock is her sustenance. Because he didn't dismiss her, didn't say, 'Don't be stupid!', or 'I've had enough!', she thinks she can go through with her old threat. When he just said, in that horrified voice, 'What?' she knew that he was afraid of her.

'I'm leaving you, Paul.'

He steps towards her and grabs her elbow. Wants to pull her into the back of the car, but, in his heart, he knows he has lost.

'Come home!'

'Come home . . .' She mimics him, but not to hurt. Merely to point out the pathetic tone which their lives have taken.

The wind is high in the black cypresses. The desert is restless.

'Marina, please . . .'

She looks up into his eyes. Quaking blue pools, lighter than the depths of midnight in the Middle East.

'No more,' she says. There's a terrible hush in her voice. A hush. 'No more,' she says again, meaning it.

She shakes Paul free and gets in the car herself. 'I'll come home with you now, Paul – I'll get in the car – but it doesn't change a thing. Not a thing.'

Silence in the car. The blue night, kind to women of a certain age. Desert winds, stories told to children about madwomen, a rhythm section of pine cones, the hemlines of the black cypresses fluttering. Paul does not want to speak in front of the driver. Sa'id keeps his eyes on the road. (He will be dead in just over a year, not a martyr to his beliefs, not a victim of imperialism, but killed in the crazy Damascene traffic by a man driving a van full of goats to the butcher, who turned right at the wrong moment.) Paul sits in the back of the car, with his face in his hands, unable to think straight. He knows that she must have found out. Treacherous voices, he thinks. Treachery, he cries to himself, not recognising that he is the traitor, not her, not Sulayman, and not whoever told her the truth.

Finally, after five minutes of silence, he asks quietly:

'Don't you love me any more, Marina?'

His words come out of the blue. No hint. No warning. She looks at him in disbelief. As if to say, you fool! You damn fool!

'What?'

'Well, don't you love me any more? Are you prepared to throw it all away – your life, our life – just because of this?'

'What?' she repeats. But the surprise is fading.

Because until now – until this very moment here now – Marina would have said yes. Yes, yes, *yes*, of course I love you. I love you more than I love life, Paul. More than my own life. But now, here in this madness, for the very first time, she questions whether she does love him. (And the answer is yes, it's as much yes as it's ever been. What she's mulling over is not the answer, it's the question that he has asked. She finds the question has become irrelevant. The saddest thing.)

'How can you ask me that, Paul? After all I've had to put up with?' She can feel the tears under her eyelids, rising hard.

'Because you've just said you're going to leave me!' There is a slight, desperate yelp in his voice. It both frightens and reassures her. Because, after all, she had thought her world was laid out in a plan where Paul was strong and she was weaker, where she needed Paul more than he needed her. And now she can hear the flood of his panic, the way its very noise drowns out the thoughts in his head.

'This is not my doing, Paul!' she replies firmly, without spite. 'All of this – the lies, the affairs, the deceptions – are yours.

'*Your* lies, *your* affairs, *your* deceptions!'

'And this marriage is ours! And you're deciding to end it, to just walk off. So easy, isn't it?'

Marina thinks for a moment. She cannot believe that he could turn around and blame her for what might happen next. Like he was some innocent bystander left with blood on his shoes from an accident. Poor Paul, with blood on his shoes. And she is about to say, how can you, how dare you, you don't know, you can't say, when she stops. She stops and looks at her husband. Pale eyes, pale hair. Pale in the blue-black midnight. Moonlit. Eight years, lost.

And all she says is:

'I am not Sulayman, Paul.'

Suddenly – such a fire-bright moment – the fury, the bitterness of her humiliation seems to disperse. Up into the stars it flies, past the black cypresses, silver-lit by the moon, past the heaven-high minarets, toppling the muezzin off their perches. And what is Marina left with? Not the death of love, but the death of the possibilities of love.

'I am not Sulayman,' she says, meaning I can never be, I would never want to be, I never could even try to be. Meaning I am Marina and you've never accepted that. That small but crucial fact.

Silence returns to them. And in that silence – without the anaesthesia of fury, without the blindness of recrimination – they both know.

Everything changes.

Muhammad let the car through the gates. The high screen of cedars swayed in the breeze. They looked like impossibly tall trumpeters in a band, idly swinging when their part was over. Marina let her eyes follow their shape to the very tops. Into black brushstrokes and stars.

She and Paul did not speak at all, not until they were in the house. Standing in the room where she kept her piano, they both sighed heavily. Marina was tired. She slipped off her high heels and unclipped her earrings. Paul loosened his tie and poured each of them a drink. Marina never touched hers.

Black brushstrokes and stars.

Fingers sweep along a piano lid. A clock on a writing desk shudders towards one o'clock. Paul turns to look at his wife.

'What do you want me to say?' he asks quietly.

'Maybe that you're sorry,' she half laughs.

'And if I did, would it change anything?'

She walks towards him, away from the piano. He can see her reflection getting smaller in the high black veneer. Like they're ghosts, or just memory sketches, shrinking helplessly from the real world.

Marina stands before her husband. She lifts her fingers to his stomach, and softly presses the tips against his shirt. There are tears in her eyes, and in his too. She can feel his body, hard and warm. But it feels like it's no longer hers, and now, of course, she wonders if it ever was.

'No,' she whispers sadly.

'Not even if . . . Not even if I were to agree to anything, to anything that you wanted, Mina?'

Her hand is flat against his stomach. She can feel the blood pulse beneath his skin. A human heart.

'You've already made promises, Paul.'

A human heart.

'Yes, but then I didn't know . . . I didn't understand . . .'

She sighs and shakes her head. Release me, she thinks in her bones. Let go, in the blood.

'Could you agree to never fall in love again, Paul? Could you agree to never want someone again, like you want Sulayman?'

He does not answer.

A few minutes pass in silence. Marina lets her head fall against Paul's chest. An arm loops around his back, under his jacket. There's such sadness in the world. Such sadness and disappointment, more than a bow on a violin, a mournful little song, a poem could ever articulate.

Their moment of failure. Lost in it, deep, deep down in it, there are no words to make things better, no chords to softly press on her fancy piano, no wistful melody to be half-sung. This is their moment of defeat.

Sulayman is real. The other is here. Corporeal, flesh, sensual, composed of and by the senses. Now she knows the colour of the other's eyes. Now she knows the way his voice sounds. She can hear him talking about poetry, about his father's business, about his life at the university. Poor, stupid Paul. All he can understand is the terror of what she says – I am leaving you – and not the enormity of her reason for saying it – I am not Sulayman.

They can hear Muhammad going to bed. The last noises of the house in the blackness before dawn. Marina, the night says, this is it, goodbye. Paul, the night murmurs, this is it. Good-bye.

'What will you do?' Paul asks. He wants to call her Mina – their special, private name – but finds that he cannot.

She shrugs.

'I could move into a hotel.'

'I don't want you to. You don't need to. You can stay here, in a different room.'

'So that we can fester?'

'No.'

'So that we can grow to hate one another?' Marina's head is perfectly clear. In this single moment, with the desert all wind, with the night on fire and her eyes ringed in black, she is sure of what she has to do. 'No, Paul.'

'When will you go?'

'Straight away. In the morning.'

And they are silent for a moment.

'You know, I do . . .' he begins to say, but falters.

Love you, that's what he wants to say. Love you, that's all she ever wanted to be true. Love you, that phrase so often said, so often meant, but so rarely considered in all its terrifying complications, in all its complexities and responsibilities.

'Yes, Paul . . . I know you do. In your way.'

'Then why?'

She smiles sadly. She is thinking of eight years gone in a flash. November 1937: the sight of early-morning snow on the city streets, the scent of yesterday's cake, the delicate brushstrokes of lovemaking on her skin, in her hair. January 1945: an Egyptian airport is still hot in winter, so much hotter than London had been, or the places she had stopped off – Portugal, Tangiers. She is thinking of their marriage. Gone in a flash.

'Then why?' he asks, and she considers the question with that sad smile.

'Because love is not always enough, Paul.' He looks at her like he cannot understand what she is saying, but, in reality, he is starting to know what she means. 'You can't always survive on knowing that someone loves you.'

MARINA WROTE A letter.

Paul,

I will contact you in a couple of days. I know you can find me easily if you try, but don't try. I need to clear my head. I feel like I'm ill (*that sentence crossed out, but still visible*). I feel like I've been ill, and that I need some time away.

I think I must leave you. I HAVE NO CHOICE. I wish it was all so easy. Just a click of the fingers.

I love you. That hasn't changed. But these days I barely seem able to remember my own name, let alone WHY I LOVE YOU. And why you love me.

I wish I could sign myself Mina. But I can't.

Love,

Marina X X

She slipped the note under Paul's bedroom door. What had been, until yesterday, her bedroom door.

Muhammad called a cab, as she asked, obeying her request to make as little noise as possible.

She looked at the clock. Seven o'clock. She could hear the taxi's motor running outside.

HOW BRAVE THE night. When Marina stood, trapped like a wild animal, between the headlights of Paul's car, she suddenly felt that she had nothing to fear. She felt she had looked into the heart of their madness and saw that she could survive. Walking away from Paul that night, through the cool, dark corridors of their house, to sleep alone, she could see into the future and it looked all right.

Hers had been a life of survivals. Surviving her parents' disappointment with her: the man she chose, living without him in his threadbare flat throughout the war, leaving London to go to him in the Middle East. Surviving the life that her husband had chosen for her: out here in the heat, among the suburban and provincial horrors, as they all breathed in the final gasps of the old times. And surviving Paul. That night – alone with the stars watching her through the bedroom window – she was sure she could survive again. She packed a few cases at first light and told Muhammad that she would be gone for a while. And when the taxi came she did not look back. She did not see Paul watching her from a high window, watching the car move away from behind a screen of cedar branches and pale sunlight.

The night is brave, yes. But the next day is followed by another, and that by another, and that one, too. Marina sat in her hotel room.

Marina had taken an expensive room on the top floor that looked out over the city, over that drama of Damascus, of architectures, of domes and spires and minarets. That age-old palimpsest of the age-old writers. For hours on end she sat in a straight-backed white cane chair looking out over the city, sipping lemonade, or chilled Chablis, not eating a sandwich or grapes, not reading the book and the magazines she had brought with her. She just sat in a straight-backed white cane chair, thinking. In the bravery of the night, before she had cleaned the tear-smudged mascara off, before she had delicately, perfectly reapplied more, before she had touched up her lipstick and pinned up her hair, she had not anticipated such fear.

A single, clear drop of white wine felt cold on Marina's lower lip. She licked it away, tasting it dry and flowery. Her eyes fell to her lap. Her wedding band glinted in the heavy golden light of a late afternoon in the Middle East. She could smell the sweetness, and the greenness too, of the trees outside. Just a hint of the well-tended flower-beds that ringed the hotel. She had asked for a clock to be removed, and she had taken off her watch. But Marina could not escape time. Knowing the colour of light – how it changed during the course of the day, how it changed season to season – and seeing the big grey or black cars, the knee-length skirts the women wore in the street, the way they dressed their hair, Marina knew where she was. This was 1945. It was all very well escaping time, refusing to take Paul's phone calls (yes, of course he'd called, ignoring her request that he should give her some time alone. To Paul, the day was always less frightening than the night), pretending to be the big girl. But this was 1945.

She had said that she had survived her parents' disapproval. She had said she had survived the move from England. She had said that she had survived Paul. But, wedding band or no, she knew that all of these survivals had depended on Paul, on being his wife. Sure, her parents had disliked Paul, thought him beneath Marina, sure, they had squirmed when she told them what his parents had been. But then again, he was a perfectly decent enough chap – that's what her father had said – and that he did appear to have very sound prospects in the Civil Service –

so her mother had sighed, finally accepting it. 'And at least you are married,' they had both said when she lived alone in that crumbling flat in Sussex Gardens whilst German bombs flattened the city. 'At least everyone can see that ring on your finger.' And when she had come out to Syria, hadn't it been to be with her husband? Even when Paul had strayed, she had been able to stand it because she was his wife. She could look around at all she enjoyed in her life – all that Paul gave her, as well as took from her – and say, I must accept it, I am his wife.

And now she had said to Paul, I don't want to be your wife any more. To the world, she would have to say, I don't want to be a wife any more. Had enough of that. Got burned, badly burned. Time to move on. She would have to return to London alone. To sit in an aeroplane seat alone, and not say, 'Oh, I'm going to be with my husband', 'Oh, yes, he works for the Empire Office, in Syria.' She would have to tell her parents that she had left Paul, that she was going to divorce him. (Yes, divorce him.) At the very best they would say, we told you so, admit you were quite wrong, Marina, marrying that sort. (In a way, they *were* right, but they meant class, and Marina didn't.) At worst they would hide her away, shamed by her failure, or even worse, quickly find some 'suitable' numbskull to marry her off to. ('Don't you dare say no! After all, what choice do you have? And look at the mess you made of your life when you could have bagged Alfie Villiers!') In one fell swoop, her battle for freedom – that freedom which, ironically, came from being married to Paul – would have been futile all along. She would have to face the whispers and the slights. She would be forced to live with her parents in the Chelsea house, not allowed to get a job. After all this struggle to be herself, to be Marina (which Paul allowed, never questioned), she would, after all, be nothing more than a well-bred womb (and hardly a young one, at that).

Marina needed someone to throw her a line. A lifebelt.

Finally, after much thought, Marina sent her brother a telegram. She went down to the hotel desk and asked the Arab receptionist where she had to go. A pencil and paper in a little booth. It was sandalwood, the booth, and smelled delicious.

DARLING
COMING BACK TO LONDON FOR A WHILE WITHOUT PAUL. NEED A
HOLIDAY. DON'T TELL THE OLDS YET. WILL TELL YOU WHEN.
KISSES, MARINA.

Soft and sad and silent, but with a little hope.

She started to make plans then.

A flight back to London, eyes on the crisp blue waves of the Mediterranean. Slow circular movements, learning to swim, as she returned to London, even to her parents' house in Chelsea. Wait. Breathe. Come back to life.

She knew that her family would not be pleased about a divorce. At the worst they would allow her to come back to cool her head. They'd say, 'Go back when you've cooled your head.'

Slow, circular movements. Once she was home, she could get a job, live quietly, wait a while before returning to life.

She waited for her brother James's response.

M
YOU STAY PUT. MUMMY AND PAPA WILL STOP ANY NONSENSE. SORT
OUT PROBLEMS WITH P, THEN COME HOME.
ALL BEST, JAMES

Marina crumpled the telegram up in her hand and started to cry. She whispered something to herself, but who would have heard? The cedars? The bees? Through a veil of tears, she had murmured, 'Oh, Paul . . .'

Marina could feel her body recoil in her horror. Blood, bones, liver, heart, ovaries, kidneys, tightening, bruising in deep, terrible shock. James had said no. Don't come back. Don't breathe. Don't wait a while. She felt her panic rising.

So Marina wrote another letter.

Clem,
I am in such a mess. Come quickly. Please! Please! The name and room number at the hotel where I am is below. Come quickly. Tell no one, especially not Paul.
Please . . .
Love, Marina

She paid the bellboy to take the letter to a taxi-driver, and gave him further money to pay for that too. She returned to her room, and for the first time genuinely and bitterly wept.

TAYLOR-GREENE WAS not apologetic. Not at all.

'What do you mean, how dare I do this?' Taylor-Greene was standing, staring at Paul, like he was crazy. 'The question, Mr Esmond, is how you can endanger this mission in Syria in such a sordid way?'

Paul could feel his skin a hot red. He was furious. Furious that Marina had been told, that Taylor-Greene had done the telling, that Taylor-Greene had found out at all. He slammed his hand hard down against the desk. Every paper on it, all the pens, even the keys on the typewriter momentarily lifted from the veneered surface.

'I have not endangered anything!' Paul shrieked. 'I have done nothing wrong – this is all rubbish!'

But Paul had lost control as soon as he had decided to come here. That was the moment when things could not be rescued. 'I have done nothing wrong. Your nasty little insinuations are absolutely groundless.'

Paul liked to think he was a survivor. A charmer. Had he kept a cool head, he could have gone to the British consul in Damascus and simply despatched Taylor-Greene to some god-forsaken place, never having to talk to the little toad about anything. (Let panic in.) By the time Taylor-Greene had started to make his accusations, huffing loudly as he was told to go to some new outpost, even Sulayman's fingerprints could have been erased from Paul's life. (Let panic in.) Paul could have just said, the man's resentful, and brushed it all aside.

But no. Paul lost his temper. And so he lost control.

'Groundless? Oh, I think not!'

'Yes, they are!' Paul cried, banging the desk again. A second impact is always less of a shock. 'You have no proof,' Paul attempted to laugh dismissively, 'except for the gossip of secretaries!'

'Oh, but you're quite wrong, Mr Esmond. Quite wrong.'

Taylor-Greene's calmness unnerved Paul.

He had come here expecting he didn't know what. Contrition. Denial. Apologies, written in blood.

The second time Paul had rung Marina – the first time she had refused to come to the phone – they talked about the same old things. Why and how she could do it. What she would do to survive. When she would do it.

'Oh, Paul,' she had cried down the receiver. 'What does any of that matter?'

'Then, just tell me who told you.'

'What's the point, Paul? What does any of that matter to us?'

Marina didn't understand the sort of politics in which Paul was involved.

'Just tell me Marina! Please . . . !'

On that last, black night together – that night of goodbyes – it had not occurred to Paul to ask this most obvious question. And yet he had to ask it. Paul had a position. He had power. And someone wanted to damage him with the information. Marina had asked what it had to do with them. Marina was not brought up to fight battles, which might explain why it took her so long to learn how. But Paul knew that he had two fights on. One for Marina and one for the rest of the world.

That fraught phone call had only been an hour earlier. Now Paul was standing in Taylor-Greene's office, banging desks, shouting the odds.

'What do you mean, wrong?' Paul asked, lifting his head high.

'There is no confusion, there is no misunderstanding.' Taylor-Greene tapped his finger lightly on the desk, like the tick-tock of a distant clock. Paul's heart was beating fast. 'There was no confusion. Not when you were seen entering the Alhambra Hotel – that well-known homosexual haunt – on a number of occasions with Sulayman Ahmed.'

The air stopped dead in Paul's throat.

'There was no confusion when you sent him notes via your secretary, about meetings in gardens, in that hotel, elsewhere too.

'There was no confusion when you spent two or three hours, or sometimes twenty minutes, with him in rented rooms and emerged in the middle of the afternoon to go back to work. Not when he would emerge five minutes later.'

Paul slid down into a chair, literally breathless. The air itself, stone dead.

'There is no confusion, Paul.' Taylor-Greene emphasised the name. Paaaaul. 'You have been conducting an affair with this Arab. You are here in Syria to conduct government business, and you've been finding . . . diversions with one, possibly more, of, well, the natives,' he sneered.

Suppose Paul had got up there and then and punched him right in the mouth. Blame – and the truth – would be written all over Paul when Taylor-Greene was questioned about his bruises.

Suppose he had gone to the British consul. He would have to admit that Taylor-Greene was saying these things and, in turn, would suggest that these things might be true.

Suppose Paul was asked, well, bring on the little wife, bring on this Arab boy. Surely she can settle this . . . Paul breathed in. He suddenly felt that those games were over. He suddenly felt as if he really, deeply owed them both something more than pangs of guilt, outbursts of remorse.

The bottom line was this. If the affair with Sulayman was exposed – no, if the affair with Sulayman was even seriously suspected – it would mean the end of Paul's career. He would lose his job, and any hope of future responsibility. He would lose his friends, who would not wish to be tainted by 'that sort'. And he would lose all of them. Every one. He would have no role either in the Middle East or in London and, unlike those well-connected painters and poets who were ferried between the two worlds, he had no means to support himself independently. Even if he did not lose Marina – which he could – he would lose, for him and for her, any social connections, advantages or dignity she had. In London he would be a middle-aged pervert with no hope of realising the goals he had set himself in life. To be better than his parents. To have things. To have power. Anywhere else he would be a nobody, a drifter – a life for which he had no experience and no appetite. If the affair was exposed, if it was even seriously suspected, his life would be as good as over. *Paul Esmond would cease to exist.*

Paul suddenly sat up straight, the last straw still free for grabbing.

'But what proof do you have, then?'

Taylor-Greene started to stand up and began to laugh thinly.

'I don't need proof, Paaaaaul. Your wife has left you. I have eyewitness testimony about these sordid goings-on – from men that the British have used before. I could bring in your driver for questioning. Or Marina. Even Sulayman Ahmed.'

'You wouldn't. It would all fall apart, then,' Paul sneered.

Taylor-Greene laughed again, but his laughter concealed his anger and irritation. That Paul continued even now to deny the truth was like an insult. Like Paul was saying to him, don't bother me with your little accusations.

'Oh, but I would!' Taylor-Greene cried out. 'Nothing would give me greater pleasure than to haul in your little black bender and get someone to smash his fingers to pieces!'

The introduction of the savagely personal.

'You evil little –'

'Now, now, Paul, you'd better shut your mouth! Don't you dare talk to me like that! Not when you owe me so much!'

Paul did shut up, too. The boldness of Taylor-Greene's anger shocked him. 'As I said not when you owe me so much . . .'

'What do I owe you?'

'Isn't that obvious? You don't want either Marina or Sulayman questioned, do you? Especially when my silence has such a small price, Paul.'

Looking down, Paul could see the veins on the backs of his hands. Blue and round. Sulayman loved them. He said they were like irrigation canals, pumping through a flat, colourless landscape. Blue in the flat.

'What is this price, then?'

Taylor-Greene was standing above Paul. His chest was rising.

'My price is quite simple.' He paused, to emphasise the drama of the moment. 'I want your job, Paul. That's all.'

Paul had seen it coming, of course, but still it shocked him to hear it. Taylor-Greene didn't want his money. Paul had none to give. No, he wanted his job. A diplomatic success had been pulled off in Syria. The British had fished the Free French out of trouble. Now they were going to force the French to give Syria up. Lebanon too. London would have a chain of grateful Arab countries stretching from the Persian Gulf to the Mediterranean Sea. Paul was one of several men who were due big brownie points. Taylor-Greene wanted those points badly.

Taylor-Greene made it clear he was about to go.

'Your choice is really very simple, Paul.

'You can resign your job immediately. Get your wife and ship out. Go back to London, go to Cairo, go off with your little black bender if you really want him. Just leave Damascus. Tell the consul that you want me to replace you. That you trust me with the work in hand, that I know the territory. Or, if that sticks in your throat, that there is simply not enough time to find someone else. And that will be the end of the matter, as far as I am concerned.

'Or I can go now to the consul, tell him what a dirty queer you are. He probably won't mind that so much. But you have brought this Arab boy into your confidence, flashing your disgusting little affair all around town, so that even your wife couldn't stomach it any more.'

'You'd do that, just to get my job? Just to get one step further up the ladder.'

Taylor-Greene came close to Paul, clearly annoyed by the sudden high tone.

'I'd do a damn sight more than that.

'Fuckers like you cruised along through the war and came out on top, in nice jobs, with your careers mapped out in front of you. Cleaning up the messes left behind by the war. Cleaning up on the damn honours too!'

'It's just a little job in the middle of nowhere, man! It's not exactly Foreign Minister!' Paul cried.

'Well, I've worked twenty years for a job like this, Paul! Twenty years and it's got me almost nowhere! To see you march in and take it without a care in the world . . .'

Taylor-Greene's voice fell away in a distressed screech. He looked at Paul, composing a sneer. 'Well, what is your reply?'

Paul met Taylor-Greene's gaze. Those small, mean, black eyes. So filled with hate and envy. Paul thought of other eyes. Marina's, great and glassy blue. Sulayman, dark brown with yellow whites. Such innocent, hopeful eyes, his and hers, spoiled. Spoiled by ambition and greed. And by a misplaced sureness of always being able to have whatever one wants.

'I don't have much of a choice, do I?'

Taylor-Greene shrugged.

'Of course you have choices.' His voice quavered. 'You had a choice when you decided to fuck Sulayman Ahmed!'

Paul felt a heavy dread pulling in his stomach. Choices – the choices he had made – had been narrowing down and down. Until here he was with no choice at all. *Paul Esmond, you will cease to exist.* And Paul – survivor, charmer, success story – hadn't even guessed what was going on.

'All right, then,' Paul said quietly, after a moment. 'I'll resign.'

LOVE. DOWN THE telephone Sulayman had immediately sensed the urgency, the alarm in Paul's voice. The quick, curt instruction that he meet him in the garden of Azem Palace sent an electric shock through Sulayman. Trouble, it's here. Loud as bells. Ringing in the bones. Sulayman caught the bus through a hot and angry Damascus.

Hot, that's the summer. Angry, that's the time. 1945. The Free French have become the Old French. The British are back, still talking about independence the way they had a quarter-century before. Dark eyes lift from the daily work – from under veils, away from which oranges and which lamb to buy, away from typewriters, eyes up off the road they're driving along – to watch a city as it boils over.

Azem Palace is in the heart of the Old City, just south of the Omayyad Mosque. It was built in 1749 by a Turkish pasha. A well of peace, slap bang in the innards of Damascus. A moment of stillness. An eye in all that ancient noise. Black basalt runs in long lines against pale limestone, so that it looks like a huge cake, layers of cream against layers of dark fruit. But it's the gardens that people come for. Still and elegant, they stretch out around the palace. A haven. Birds, bees and butterflies tend a rainbow of flower-heads. Little workers, keeping the flora perfect. Perfect for the governors of old. Perfect for office workers nibbling lunches. Perfect for ageing couples strolling, just looking at the flowers. Lift a purple or gold-yellow blossom to your nose. Shade yourself under a high, aromatic cedar, away from the midday heat. Breathe. You can breathe in the city, here at the Azem.

Paul was sitting on a stone bench near a bed of pale-blue daisies. Sulayman stopped his brisk pace and, for a split second, watched him. Paul looked agitated and upset. Sweat glistened around his hairline. He slipped a finger under his shirt collar, then blew out, hot and impatient. Sulayman felt terror rising. He knew whatever news Paul had it was not good.

Paul turned and saw Sulayman. He was about to rise from his seat in anticipation, but stopped himself.

'Come here,' he said sharply, lifting a finger.

'What's the matter?' Sulayman replied anxiously, sitting down beside him.

Paul knows that it must end. There is no choice. There is no time.

Marina is hiding away in her hotel, barely able to speak to him on the phone. Taylor-Greene holds him by the throat, shouting demands. And here is Sulayman.

Paul has to finish it. It is better, and easier, for Sulayman to hate Paul, then. Let him hate me, Paul was thinking, if he must. Hate me and get on with the rest of his life.

Soon, he knew, if Marina would take him back, he would leave Damascus for ever. They would fly away and never come back. Sulayman could not come, too. Nor could Paul stay here with him. He could not leave Marina. He could not live here, a parasite on the heart of a young man full of hopes and plans for the future. Soon Sulayman would be married and in a proper job. Better to finish it quickly, Paul thought, knowing that he himself would not be able to bear to string it out much further.

'Look, I'm sorry,' Paul began. 'I'm really sorry, Sulayman, but I'm going to have to stop all this.' He was waving his hands around, starting to babble. Didn't look Sulayman in the eye. Kept his eyes on the flowers, that floating mist of honeybees. 'Somebody's found out. Marina knows. Look, I know it's hard, I do . . .'

'What?'

'Yes . . .' Paul lifted his fingers as if to touch Sulayman, but then stopped himself. 'I can't see any other way, Sulayman. I'm sorry.'

Sulayman dropped his head. Hiding any tears that might start to rise. Suppressing any desire to smack Paul in the mouth.

Seconds passed without a word. Paul's mouth was dry. His throat burning.

'Say something!' he cried, his voice rising. Paul was aware they were being watched. People around them – people who probably spoke little or no English – were having their tranquillity spoiled. 'Marina has left me,' Paul repeated, this time quietly. 'Somebody in the consulate has found out. I can't say who. I . . . I don't know what to say, Sulayman.'

Sulayman understood better than Marina what this discovery meant. Sulayman came from a university, where academics searched for dirt about other academics. He came from a family where the father longed for ammunition against the mother. And he came from a city where Arabs were forever dodging the white man's bullet. Bullets real and metaphorical.

'I can't believe this, Paul,' Sulayman sighed angrily. 'I can't believe that here I am again, getting dumped again, getting pushed off you because of Marina.'

Paul saw Sulayman's face screw up in disappointment. He felt his heart sink watching confusion, then anger, pass over those dark eyes.

'But it's Marina I have to think about . . . Don't you see that? Don't you see that I have a responsibility to her?'

Sulayman jumped to his feet and cried:

'Yes, I do, Paul! You've had a responsibility to Marina all along, but you've chosen to ignore it except on any occasion she found out! You've always had a responsibility to her, Paul! Always.' Sulayman stopped and sighed aloud. When he continued speaking, his voice was quieter. 'But I don't, Paul. Marina is *your* wife. She is not *my* responsibility, and yet my life seems to be dictated by you and her. You, her and the fucking British consulate!'

Sulayman stormed off into the heart of the gardens, that rich, sharp afternoon soup of pollen, buzzing wings, murmured voices. Paul followed him at once. Like he never wanted to let him out of his sight. Like now that the last moment was here Paul could barely stand it.

'Suli, stop!' he shouted. 'Stop!'

Sulayman swung round.

'I know exactly what's coming, Paul! You don't have to say it!'

Azem Palace, midday or just after. Beauty and stillness in all the heat of the Old City in the summer. In the distance, beneath the music of birds and bees, of stifled laughter, of the exchange of gossip, or tips on getting the best bloom, you hear the sound of traffic.

'What – *what* – do you think I'm going to say?'

' "I love Marina . . . I must respect her wishes . . . It's really nothing to do with you . . ." '

'Well,' Paul whispered, 'is that so very wrong – to love your wife? To want what's best for her?'

'But, Paul,' Sulayman cried, shaking his head, 'don't you *ever* think that maybe I would like it to be "something to do with me"? That I want you to actually think about me as well? To think about what I might want?'

Yes, Paul was thinking, yes.

But his words were merely rasps. He could hardly breathe, let alone speak.

'But I do! I . . .'

'Don't you dare say it, Paul!'

'What, that I could . . . love you too? That it's possible to love two people? To love them for different reasons, but to love them all the same?'

'Don't, Paul, because it's not true! You don't – you can't love me too. Not if you behave this way. Not when you treat me like a toy to be discarded!'

'I've never thought of you that way. I've always wanted to be with you. No matter what. It's just . . .'

'I know, poor old Marina.'

'It's not her fault.'

'I know that! Poor old Marina is your excuse. But she's a big girl, Paul. She can make her own choices. It seems that everybody except me is allowed to make choices. I have choices *made* for me! I'm just some damn Arab you think you can push around.'

'No, Sulayman . . . I have loved you . . . I do love you . . .'

'Just don't say it any more, Paul.'

'Why not?'

'Because it's not true. Because we've been here before. And yet you're still going to dump me, aren't you?'

'I have no choice, Sulayman. It's not just Marina, is it?'

'Thank goodness!' Sulayman cried. 'Thank goodness we can now get to the heart of the matter!'

'If this was to get out, if there was to be a scandal . . .' Paul paused for a second, as if to stress the importance of what he was saying. 'If people were to know, it would be disastrous.'

'For whom?'

'For me, for you!'

'No, for you, Paul! That's what you mean! It would be disastrous for you!'

'And for you . . .'

'I would not lose my job – I've already lost my job. I would not be disgraced – no one would remember it for a day here. No, Paul, you would be the one who would lose his job, who would be sent home ashamed, the subject of gossip.'

'Is that what you want for me, Sulayman?'

'Is *this* what *you* want for me?'

Sulayman rubbed his eyes. He didn't want to weep. Maybe he could say the pollen was pricking.

'But that doesn't mean that I don't love you, that what I feel isn't real. That I should stop saying it.'

'Then don't say it because I don't want you to.'

'But why?'

'Because I am not worth more to you than a job, Paul.'

Paul sighed unhappily.

'My life is much less simple than that, Sulayman. If only my life was as simple as being in love, as simple as a job I could give up.'

'Then explain it to me, Paul. You still haven't explained a thing to me, except that you love Marina, except that you might lose your job. How is it more complex than that?'

'I come from a different world, Sulayman. I'm not from this world. I'm beginning to see that I – none of us – belong here. Me, Marina, our friends, Taylor-Greene, the Free French, none of us.'

Sulayman shook his head slowly and sadly.

'I don't understand you, Paul.'

Damascus. The afternoon was hot. And there is nothing, and so, so much, to understand.

'The world – the planet – that I'm from doesn't give me the freedoms you have. Men like me – dare I say, like us – are not free to live as they please. We are monsters, queers, ogres.

'And those who do live as they please are ostracised. They are reduced to figures of ridicule and abuse and violence. The people in my world would never understand you, or me with you. They would not forgive us. They would destroy us.' Paul shook his head and blushed a little. 'They would destroy me.'

Sulayman looked into Paul's eyes.

'So is that what I'm worth less than? Your world?'

Paul smiled bleakly.

'No, Sulayman, my world is not worthy of you.' The smile faded. 'And neither am I.'

Paul could see what he had done. He had taken this young man – with all that hope, all that innocent, happy desire of youth – and stripped him bare. Looking at Sulayman now, he saw for the first time an older, sadder man. And Paul realised that he had done that to Sulayman. For what felt like the first time ever, Paul knew true, terrible shame.

Waves break on a shore. The pollen lifts and lands. The blue sea. A sea of colour in the flowers. Rippling, cold water on warm skin. A hot breeze makes every stem and petal and leaf sway this way and that. All Sulayman had wanted was a fling before he had to marry Leilah Husseini and leave university. A good wife, a great job, a slow death: Sulayman just wanted some fun before all that. Warmer, bluer, sleepier. The sound the waves make. The taste of salt on dry lips. Sulayman hadn't bargained for the 'l' word.

LOVE.

Hard and unforgiving. Soft and all-encompassing. Violent and destructive. Calm and nurturing. Love! What a word, to be able to save or kill as it pleases! A half-hour passed with few words. Sitting in the sun, in that oasis of the Old City, just the songs of birds, murmured Arabic, the distant drone of cars and the souqs.

Paul looked up, seeing the brown sparrows up in the trees. Through the leaves, the sunlight was soaked green. Even the sand in the sparrows' feathers glinted gold and green.

'I wish it could be different.'

Sulayman turned at Paul's soft, sad voice. Maybe he was about to shout, to sneer, but he stopped himself. Now there seemed little point. Even the green sunlight seemed to agree. This really was the end. Sulayman could sense a change in Paul, but even if Paul returned to him the next day, saying it had all been a mistake, Sulayman would not take him back. Sulayman was tired of this affair. The exciting fling he had wanted had turned sour. Suddenly he just wanted to read his poems again, to think about Leilah Husseini's hips, and the rest of his life.

'I'm sorry, too, Paul,' Sulayman replied. The sun was warm and strong, but under the red-barked cedars, they felt cool, almost relaxed.

'But, you know, what you said isn't true.'

Sulayman looked puzzled.

'About what?'

'About love.'

The two men were looking at one another. Suddenly, outside

the palace, a car backfired. The sparrows lifted from the trees, frightened by the bang. The garden-admiring Damascenes, months from a winter of bloodshed, jumped too. Then they smiled and laughed nervously when they realised it was only an engine, not a gun.

About love . . . Sulayman felt the tug at his heart.

'Don't, Paul . . .'

'You're more to me than . . .' Paul fell quiet.

He was going to say 'than the others', or even 'than anyone else', but he lost his nerve.

Suddenly, their intimacy – that right to say what one wanted, what one felt – was gone from them. They were no longer in love. Paul had finally made too many demands on love. This little love that was born out of old-fashioned desire, a mutual need to touch and be touched. This little love that was never meant to be a battleground.

Sulayman did not want to stay any longer. He suddenly wanted to get away. Didn't want to hear excuses or explanations. He got up from the grass, walking out from beneath the shade of the cedars.

Paul lifted his hand above his eyes. The Syrian sun was so strong.

'What are you doing?' Paul asked.

Sulayman was reduced to a silhouette. A black shape receding into the bright white.

'I think I'll go now, Paul.' Sulayman tried to smile.

A panic raced through Paul's body. He felt he had so much left to say. So much left to explain. Once, part of him would have felt that he had not given Sulayman permission to leave, to go, to be away from him. But not now. Maybe that part of him had finally learned that people are free to do what they want. With their own hearts, at least. To give or remove love. To choose when to stop loving. To leave. Maybe Sulayman and Marina had taught him something then. About hearts.

After a second, Paul said:

'I have loved you, Sulayman, you know.' Two men. Barely

smiling. In sunlight. Green, gold, white. 'For what it's worth,' Paul added.

Sulayman managed that smile.

'It was worth more than you'll ever realise, Paul.'

'You must hate me, Sulayman.'

'Is that what you want, Paul? For me to hate you?'

'I think it's what you will need.'

Sulayman broke into a warm, gentle smile. Like a little bit of happiness was left in him, had burst into bloom.

'I don't hate you, Paul. Well, maybe just a bit around the edges.'

'Around the edges. Quite.'

'I'm not a child, Paul. That was your problem all along. You thought I was a child when I'm an adult. I made my own mistakes.'

'Sulayman Ahmed . . .' Paul was whispering.

'And not all of it was a mistake. It might have gone wrong, but I don't think it was a mistake.'

'Nor do I, Sulayman Ahmed.'

'I don't hate you, Paul. You have – once or twice – made me very happy.'

'Will you forgive us, then? Marina and me?'

Sulayman laughed out loud, stepping backwards, further into that white sunlight. Vanishing.

'I don't need to forgive either of you, Paul. You said something about responsibilities, Paul. Neither of you are responsible for me. I am responsible for myself, Paul.'

Love, what a word.

Dizzying. Foolish. Maddening. Exciting.

Sulayman raised his hand slightly and smiled. Then he turned and left. In moments he was gone, vanishing into the bright white light. Under the shade of the cedars, Paul was unable to follow his shape as it receded.

Suddenly, Paul rushed out from under the tree. One last attempt to see him. Sulayman. But as he span around and around, Paul realised that Sulayman had really, finally gone.

What a dizzying, maddening word.

The greatest thing of all, the poets write, is love. The love between two people. Romantic love. A love of intimacy, of privacy, of the secret knowledge of one another's soul. To share one's love between two people, then, is not love at all. Merely desire. Merely passion. But put down your pens, you poets, and admit this one fact. Paul did love Sulayman. And he loved Marina, too.

THE AFTERNOON HEAT. Perspiration sticks clothes to the chest, between the thighs. Men and women look up at the sun, craving relief. Down in the souq, over mountains of fruit or dried fish, from behind shawerma or shish kebab stalls, dark-eyed matrons fan themselves with palm leaves. Up on hotel or club terraces, white ladies in couture sip chilled lemonade and breathe out. Somewhere in the heart of the city, a clock is ticking. Everyone knows it. Everyone hears it.

Independence, a time bomb.

Clem stood in front of the hotel steps and sighed. Her cream cotton dress and wide-brimmed hat gave her no peace in the heat. She always said to George that she was too fat to live in the Middle East. Climbing the low hotel steps, a handsome Arab boy in uniform bowed, pulling the door for her. Inside the lobby it was dark and cool. Electric fans hummed like moths in the darkness. Air moved in quick, cooling circles, like great, diaphanous wings were flapping above them. Clem sighed again and walked towards the mahogany counter.

The receptionist buzzed Marina's room. Another Arab boy showed Clem the way. In the heat, beneath his red-and-gold uniform, this boy seemed so plump and odorous compared to his sleek and lovely predecessor. It made Clem smile. We're two of a kind, she thought to herself, you and me. Too fat for the hot Middle East, but stuck here all the same. Then she wondered, with a private chuckle, if he, looking at the sheen of perspiration across her forehead, her heat-pink cheeks, was thinking the same thing.

Room 405. A grand door, decorated in plaster shapes, painted white, edged in gilt.

The bellboy knocked on the door. They heard Marina's voice summoning them in. The door swung slowly back, revealing a long, dark corridor to the main room of the suite. At the end of the corridor, swathed in atmospheric white light, stood Marina. As soon as she saw Clem, she started to sob.

'Oh, Clem!' she cried. Clem rushed forward and took her friend in her arms.

Women's parts in these dramas are so practised. Compared to the panic, the resentment, the annoyance men feel at sudden, overwhelming displays of emotion, women respond with the precision and expertise of surgeons.

A strong arm across the back, the right word softly murmured into an upset ear, even a clean, scented handkerchief pulled magically from a handbag. What a medicine! What a cure for heavy hearts! Clem and Marina began this age-old routine. Heart surgeon and patient.

'Come on, now, darling . . . Come on . . . Take this . . .'

Marina curled herself up into her white cane chair. She dabbed her eyes with Clem's clean hankie, sniffing into it from time to time. Clem pulled a stool close to her friend and, lightly and comfortingly, was rubbing Marina's shoulder.

'Oh, Clem . . .'

'What on earth's wrong, Marina?'

Marina sniffed again and began to speak, in that loose, shuddering speech of the heartbroken. Clem knew it well. She knew how to nod her head, how to look, which words to say. Woman to woman, friend to friend.

'Oh, bloody hell . . . Oh, Clem, everything is just so . . . *fucked*!'

Clem pulled her stool closer again, knitting her brow, sure she had another handkerchief in her bag, if they needed it.

'What do you mean, Marina? What's the matter? Has Paul done something, darling?'

Marina laughed wearily to herself.

'I've sat here for what feels like weeks. It's barely two days, really, and I've been trying to think what to do . . .'

'But why?'

Marina, eyes ringed in smudged mascara, looked down across the polished white marble floor.

'I've left Paul, Clem. I've left him.'

Clem raised her eyebrows, startled.

'Not left him properly?'

'Well, I do think that I have, actually.'

'My God, Marina!'

'I don't think I can go back, Clem. I don't think I can.' Marina paused for a moment, swimming in her own fear. 'But I've got nowhere to go. Nowhere . . .'

There was a silence. Clem was shocked and scared by what she knew she was about to hear. For one, Clem knew that the life of women who left husbands was so very, very hard. George had told her stories of American friends who got divorced at the drop of a hat, but this wasn't Los Angeles, it wasn't New York. Clem was British. She knew that, divorced, Marina would be dead socially. She would be snubbed in the street. Passed over for parties or dinner invitations. Left off the guest-list of concerts and recitals. Ignored in restaurants. Women like Marina (and like herself too) had been raised solely to be socially acceptable. To face total ostracism was to face being totally obsolete.

After a moment, Clem said:

'What has happened? Tell me, Marina.'

Marina coughed, pushing a loose strand of hair behind her ear. As she spoke she kept her eyes on her hands. They played with the crumpled, smudged handkerchief. Clem watched her intently. A light warm breeze drifted through the open balcony window. The bleached gauze nets danced lightly. White waves of sunlight.

'Paul has been unfaithful, Clem . . .'

Clem felt a terror in her gut. The terror of the familiar and the concealed.

'Oh, Marina,' she said slowly.

A little sympathy buoyed Marina. She began to speak more quickly.

'I don't mean it's a one-off, or anything. He's been having an affair for a long time.'

'Oh, darling . . .'

'And it's not the first time. It's not the first time.' Marina screwed up her nose in discomfort. 'But this one, this one, is different. I lost him, Clem. I lost a part of Paul this time . . .'

Clem lifted from her stool until she was sloped around Marina's back, her arm stretching from one shoulder to the other.

'What do you mean?'

Marina was shaking her head and sobbing.

'He used to have these little affairs. They never lasted long. Sometimes – once or twice – I found out about one or other, but there must have been more.

'But they never meant anything, not really. Yes, it used to hurt. It used to hurt badly, but Paul . . . Paul is a wonderful man, Clem. He gives me so much. He gives me this freedom to do what I want, to think what I want, to be . . . To be me. That's rare, isn't it? When you look around, isn't that rare?'

Clem smiled a little.

'Haven't we said as much time and time again?'

'If I found out, I would tell him to stop it. He used to make some vague promise about it never happening again, but I've come to expect that it would happen. I tried not to think about it, and I found, after a while, that I could survive.

'Because it wasn't so much the fact that he was with someone else. Rather it was the fact he could lie to me about it. I hated that most of all, him not being honest with me. Me and him, we've got this . . . pact, almost. A pact to be straight with one another. Not to play games. And when he does lie, that's the worst, Clem . . . That's the worst.'

A skylark landed on the balcony. It began to sing sweetly. Clem was reminded by its high, pure voice of the street children she had encountered all over the Middle East. The little dirty angels of Algiers, of Teheran and Cairo, of Damascus too, who would sing the most beautiful songs for a coin or two. But these same children would go with the pink-burned white men too, for a few coins more. Clem looked at Marina telling this story of her husband's infidelity with a sense of dread. Infidelity among Europeans in the Middle East, it often seemed, was never a tale of some man fucking his secretary. Clem shuddered at her own history, and the histories of all those men and women she knew in these hot, crazy cities, where White people had too much power, too much money, too much time.

'With whom did he have this affair, then?'

Marina started to cry again, but Clem felt compelled to know. She repeated the question, this time more forcibly.

Marina began to speak through tears of release and regret. She felt that she was betraying Paul. That she was admitting her own defeat, her own failure.

She, like Clem, had been brought up to be this wonderful wife. Beautiful, elegant, cultured, uncomplaining, accepting. In making such revelations, wasn't she betraying that? Wasn't she forcing it to breaking point?

'A man!' Marina cried out, so loud that her voice echoed in the chairs, in mirrors, in tables. 'A boy! A boy in his department. A man who worked for him, who came to our house, who came to our house and made me like him!'

'Oh, my poor thing . . .'

'Yes! Terrible, isn't it?' Marina let out a bitter laugh. 'Well, it's heartbreaking, let me tell you, Clem . . .'

'Oh, darling, I know it is . . .'

'And the worst thing of all, Clem, is not that he slept with this man – this nice, intelligent, decent young chap – but that I can't hate Paul for it. And, believe me, I want to hate him more than anything.'

'No, Marina . . .'

'Yes! Yes . . . I want to hate him. I want my love for him to be dead. Dead!'

'Oh, my poor darling . . .'

'I wish . . . I wish I could wake up and my love for him would be gone.'

'But it's not that easy, is it?'

'No, Clem, it's not easy at all . . .'

'What does Paul say, darling?'

'He wants me home. He wants me to forgive him and to go back. My brother wired me to tell me not to come home, to stick it out.' Marina sighs to herself. Such burning unhappiness in the world. Such heartbreak. 'So my family will not accept me, or at least will make my life nigh on impossible.'

'So what will you do?'

'I don't know . . . What can I do?'

'Do you want to go back?'

'I don't want things to stay the same for ever. And what guarantee do I have that things can change? They haven't yet, have they?'

'But do you *want* them to change?'

Marina finally looked up. Into friendly eyes. Dark eyes and pale, a sunrise. Her friend was watching her so intently, like the whole of the world depended on that very moment. Like if they so much as took a breath, the whole future of the world would be irrevocably, maybe dangerously, changed.

But do you *want* them to change? The question had slipped out so easily. But answers . . .

What did Marina want? She wanted Paul. She wanted Paul to be hers, to love her, to be with her. Babies or no babies. London or Damascus. Today, tomorrow, for ever, she wanted Paul to give himself to her. To place his life in her hand and say, take it, keep it. Be mine. I'll be yours.

Marina looked at her friend hard. Clem never flinched. Not once.

'I can't imagine life without him, Clem. I can't imagine myself – my self – without him.'

The girl in the clamshell grew up. Standing against the white nets, Clem looked like some forgotten, middle-aged Botticelli. Pale and soft, older, less wide-eyed.

But the gentle, pure light is just as peach-kind on her skin, just as gilding on her downy hair. When she told Marina she had something to tell her, Clem took a gulp and closed her eyes, beginning to speak.

'Marina, I'm going to tell you something. Something just like you've told me. This happened to me in Teheran. Except it was a bit different.'

Marina sniffed again and widened her eyes. Oh, not you too, she was thinking. Not you, Clem, have been hurt this way. Have been so injured by the man you love.

'Oh, Clem . . .'

Clem turned and looked straight at her friend. She began to speak clearly and deliberately, but her voice was threaded with sadness.

'Marina, I had an affair in Teheran. I had an affair in Teheran, and George found out.

'A MAN NAMED Ruholla. A man with funny big hands and beautiful green eyes. Crooked teeth and dark, wavy hair. He worked at the oil company. He was tall and kind, odd-looking, and he made you laugh. He had this strange, husky Persian voice and spoke this Dickensian English. And every time I met him, my heart leapt, my brains started swimming, I lost control of myself.

'The first time I saw him he was on a telephone. He looked up and smiled at me, as I knocked at his office door and asked if he knew where George was. That first time, when I waited at his door for a minute, and I think we exchanged eight or nine words, I wanted him then. Put it to the back of my mind – where I dreamed of him. The back of my mind – where his face stayed every time I talked to George.

'And then one day, after a week or two, we met again by chance. He was looking for a present for his little daughter, he said. Her name was Farah. He adored her. We went for a coffee – his suggestion – and then, somehow, to a cinema – mine. The seats were big and covered in that fuzzy, itchy material.

'It was so dark. It was a Bette Davis film. Was it *Now, Voyager*, maybe? And it was in Persian! All of it – in Farsi. I sat there, not understanding a word. This awful silence between us, and this babble of Farsi going on up on the screen! And then I let him kiss me. He asked, and I let him, like it was all his idea.'

Marina watched her friend reveal herself. Slow. Lives unfold.

'You said that you did not know what to do, Marina. That you wanted change.'

Clem turned briefly to look through a window.

'For four months I kept seeing Ruholla. Each time, after I had seen him, I was filled with remorse. I would watch George eat or dress, I would listen to him speak, or ask him about his work, and I would think to myself, no more, never again, how can I do this?

'But then to glimpse Ruholla in the oil company offices, or to hear his voice when he phoned me during George's working day, and I would just melt. I never felt so much excitement. Every part of me was alive. Every part of me was thrilling with him, with the possibility of, yes, how sex could be, when I'd forgotten what it was like to be kissed, to be touched, to be held so tight that you feel you're going to have the air squeezed right out of you.

'And then one day Ruholla left the oil company. No warning. He never rang me. I couldn't find him. I couldn't trace him through the phone company. He was gone. I started to go crazy. So crazy in fact that eventually, when I could stand it no longer, I asked George, in a matter-of-fact way, whatever happened to that nice Persian man in his office.

'But the way George looked at me just then. The look in his eyes. Like I had slashed him open. Like I'd taken a knife and slashed him open with my bare hands. He told me that he had had a record of phone calls made from his office and discovered Ruholla had been ringing me four or five times a week. George sacked him, without even confronting him. He said Ruholla left without complaint. Couldn't look George in the eye when he told him to clear his desk.

'George had been waiting for me to ask. He knew I would, he said. Knew me so well, you see. And when he asked me if I still loved him . . .'

Clem could take no more. Lifting her hands to her face, she started to cry, like this is the first time she has ever admitted how much she hurt George. Marina got up and it was she who now put her arms around a friend. It was she who whispered words of comfort and said, there, there.

'That's why we left Teheran, Marina. That's why. Geoge said

that he could not face a divorce. That we had to put up with it, that we had to pretend that nothing had happened.

'We came here. George is always in demand. People seem to think he can just magic oil up wherever he goes. We never mention what happened. He is the perfect gentleman, and pretends as if everything is all right. But it's not, Marina. It's not at all all right.

'When we're in company, we laugh and joke and everyone thinks we're so happy together. But when the company is gone, we stay silent most of the time. We are polite, we share the daily routine, but we are two halves now. Separate. We aren't a team any more.

'Only once has he ever discussed it with me. Just after we arrived here – before I'd met you – we got home from some reception. We were both a little drunk and we were laughing about something somebody had said. He leaned forward, as if he was going to kiss me. For a moment he had forgotten about Ruholla and me. But he stopped. He stopped doing it, and said he was going to go to bed. So then I asked him, "Why did you not leave me?" Straight out, Marina. "Why did you not leave me?" '

Marina was close to her friend, touching her friend, engrossed, horrified by what she was hearing. Clem was like Paul. George was like Marina. And yet they were different too. Until now, there had been no distance between Marina and Paul. His affairs were a source of pain, conflict, unhappiness. But they felt like the two of them were still a team. Paul had been unfaithful several times, probably more than Marina knew about. But Marina's problem was that she could *not* separate herself from Paul. Whereas George's was that he felt *too* separate.

'He turned and looked at me and without any bitterness or side, he said: "What else could we do, Clem? To separate – to tell the world – would have destroyed us both. At least this way, our lives are easy, comfortable. Maybe one day they'll be happy again too, but separation? It would have destroyed us both."

'It's not much, is it? Not when you expected him to say,

because I still love you. Because I still need you. And this man –
this man that I have so badly, terribly hurt that he can hardly
bring himself to kiss me now – can only say that the alternative to
staying together is even worse.'

Clem cleaned her face in the bathroom mirror. Marina gave her
some powder and lipstick. Separated for those few minutes – in
different rooms – they quietly reflected on how much each had
revealed during that afternoon. Each felt differently about the
other now. Closer, but alienated. Knowing too much about each
other, but caring deeply about what they knew. Lonely, unhappy
women, far from home, with husbands from whom, one way or
another, they had been cut off. Both of them were chilled by such
isolation. But the prospect of being alone – of being alone,
outcast, failing — chilled them even more.

Clem returned from the bathroom, smiling.

'You can come and stay with me until you get a flight home,
Marina.'

Marina smiled gratefully. Both knew that would be impossible
now. Marina knew too much. About Clem. About George. She
shook her head and said thank you.

'There's no need, though,' Marina began. 'Paul will pay for
this room, and I am happier alone just at the moment.'

Clem picked up her wide-brimmed hat and said she would call
a taxi from the hotel lobby.

'What will you do?' she asked.

Marina smiled sadly and stood up.

'I don't honestly know. I don't have many options. My family
look as if they won't want me home. I can't go and get a job here,
can I? Can you imagine who would employ me?'

Clem laughed a little. These women were like beached whales
once the house, the husband, the round of parties were gone. So
few ever really came close to seeing what life alone would be like.
Those who did were so terrified by that prospect that they would
accept almost any kind of marriage. So many accepted much
worse than Marina had.

'What if it happens again?'

Marina smiled.

'Oh, I'd survive. I've survived so far, haven't I?'

'But at what price, Marina?'

'I don't know, Clem. Everything has a price, doesn't it?'

They were silent for a moment. The breeze billowed in the white nets.

'Will you go back to Paul?'

'Will George stay with you?'

Clem thought for a moment, slightly hurt by the question.

'I can't say, Marina. I've hurt him so badly that I don't seem to have any rights any more. But that's my doing. I want George. Even when I was with Ruholla, I wanted George. But I gave up any claim I had on him. But there are no more guarantees. I hope he stays with me. Life without him – in so many ways – would be unbearable.'

Marina had not answered Clem's question. They kissed goodbye at the door to her room and each stood quietly for a second, looking at the other. This person who knew so much about them. This person whom they had trusted. Clem turned and walked away.

The girls in the clamshells had grown up.

As SHE BRUSHED her hair that last day at her hotel, she wasn't sure that she was going to do these two things. Then speaking to Paul convinced her. Dabbing on pale lipstick, checking her handbag for a handkerchief, she became surer about two things she had to do. She had already told Paul the first thing. The Arab receptionist, who she liked and whose name she never knew, said he would phone straight away for her taxi. 'I want to go to the university,' she added. To do the second thing.

Paul had told her where Sulayman was working as soon as she asked him. Paul had rung three times in three days to ask her to return. This third time, Marina felt a pull towards him that had been absent before. She had wanted to hate him before, to hate the sound of his voice, the way he used sentences, what he meant in the way that he phrased familiar words. But this time, she realised that she did not. His voice was familiar and soothing, not provoking. She was pulled into its tide, warming waters around her body, caressing her.

'I love you,' he said.

'Don't, Paul . . . Don't force it,' she replied, feeling anxious.

'I'm just saying.'

'I know . . .' she whispered down the line. She realised that she no longer wished that were untrue. And maybe in the last days it had even been untrue. She had not truly known that he loved her. Or at least she had not known what it meant, this love of his. A love which could include her and others. Her and Sulayman.

A silence then.

Silences to Paul and Marina had never been awkward before. They had enjoyed a wordless intimacy. A privacy of silence. But now a friction existed in the empty telephone wire, ringing out how much each one missed the other's presence. They were not Clem and George, two people occupying one loneliness. Separation to Paul and Marina was painful, not a release or a relief. Marina missed Paul in a real, physical sense. She had told Clem she wanted to be alone in the hotel, but she did not. That was a lie. She knew it even as she said it. What Marina wanted was Paul with her, by her, beside her, in her. The friction down the telephone wire electrified their separation. Each felt emptied by it.

When Marina finally asked the question, she had nothing planned. Seeds in the memory, getting planted and watered by this isolation.

'Have you seen him, Paul?'

She could hear him breathing slowly, nervously.

'Only once. To tell him it was over.'

Trust glimmers. Marina believed Paul. It's over, he'd said. There was a nakedness in his voice, in which she could hear the truth being told.

'What is he doing now?'

The name was not used. Not Sulayman. Reducing to pronouns, that tack of surviving infidelity. He. She. Them. It.

'He is working up at the university, doing whatever he did before . . .'

Marina felt sick. And then she felt the double edge. She could forgive him or not forgive him. She could go back or not go back. But their history was real. It had happened. Whatever Marina chose to do, she – and he – would have to live with it, deal with it.

'Before what, Paul?' she snapped.

'Before he came to work at the consulate.'

She could hear him breathing.

'Poems,' she whispered, half to herself.

Hush.

'Will you come back, Mina?' he asked softly, after a moment.

Mina, come back . . . Mina, be mine . . . Marina could feel her heart, her stomach, her thighs, her arms, her whole weight dropping, falling, letting go. Be mine. She was thinking hard about how to respond, about what to say. This was the rest of her life. She looked ahead at it, a life on which she must gamble for real. Drop, fall, let go, Paul was saying. Come back. This was her moment to decide which course she should take. Either way, she had to risk all.

She could leave Paul, go back to London, risk everything she had if she couldn't live with what he had done to her. Life would be hard and lonely – and she would not have Paul. And that more than anything terrified her. She would not have Paul. Or she could go back to him. She could take her pride, her dignity, her independence – all of which she had now finally asserted – and say to Paul, I give these things to you, I entrust them to you, only to have them thrown back at her by some new affair.

Paul was losing his nerve. She could hear him starting to hesitate as he said again:

'Come back, Mina . . .'

Marina felt like weeping. She forced her tears back. She took her tears and suppressed them. Stay brave, she thought, become the stronger one.

'I don't know. I might.'

Paul started to laugh, letting in a delicate happiness.

'Oh, Marina, I promise . . . !'

Marina cut him dead.

'Don't promise me anything, Paul! No more promises!' She sighed heavily. 'If I come back, *if* I come back, I don't want to exchange promises. They don't mean anything any more!

'I'll stay as long as I want to, as long as I'm happy being with you. Don't promise me anything, Paul, and I won't promise you. All that is over! I am not your colonial wife, Paul. I never was. You forgot that. You forgot that I am free to do what I want, Paul! That I am free to leave you. To go!'

Marina was thinking of Sulayman sitting in his university,

poring over poetry, scribbling pencil annotations. And here they were, Paul and Marina, fighting for their lives.

'All that is over, Paul,' she repeated. 'If I come back, I can leave again. You can no longer assume that I am yours for ever, no matter what, Paul. You can do as you please, behave as you like, but, remember, Paul, I am free too. Free to stay or go. Free to not accept second-best from you any more.'

Marina was standing in front of a full-length mirror in her hotel room. A black Bakelite receiver was held to her ear. Her soft brown hair fell in waves over it, around the hand which held it, down to the sleeve of her cream silk blouse. She was breathing slow.

Through the open windows to her balcony she could hear larks singing in the high trees. Black cypresses moved in the wind. A scent of yew and lime trees. Damascus was about to be reborn, about to be rewritten again. Soon Paul and Marina, the British, the French, would become another lost veil in the ancient palimpsest. Marina could feel that moment upon her. She could smell change as sensually and as tangibly as she could smell cypress, yew, lime.

'There is one thing, Paul,' she said.

'Anything,' he replied.

'I want to go home.'

Paul laughed to himself. Marina heard him laugh and asked why.

'Taylor-Greene is trying to blackmail me into leaving . . .'

'The little shit,' Marina said.

'But if you want to go, that would solve that problem, wouldn't it?'

Marina sighed. Paul could hear her breath against the phone.

'Give him what he wants, then. It's not so very much, is it?'

Paul became quiet.

The telephone wires hummed.

'No, it's not so very much, Mina. You're right.'

THE NEW CITY

AUGUST 1945. FARAWAY bombs turn the world red for a whole autumn. Cities are flattened in the blast. Human bodies don't even leave a dust. A war ends. All killing will now stop, they say. Sixty million bodies in battles, death camps, bomb-sites, along tropical dirt tracks, strewn across autobahns. The murdered and the raped of the world.

August 1945. The French, under pressure from the British, surrender control of the Syrian army to the Arab population. Agreement is reached for withdrawal from Syria and Lebanon for the New Year, 1946. Old India and unborn Pakistan are yet to writhe in orgies of bloodletting. The British are yet to drive ordinary Kenyans to slit the throats of white ladies in the dead black night. The Americans are yet to carpet-bomb Vietnam and Cambodia into still greater slaughter. The French are yet to kill and be killed by Algerians, or to conceal the dumping of the bodies of Arab immigrants in the Seine.

Marina's taxi slipped through the city. People rushed through the streets. Fireworks were being let off. Everywhere men and women were smiling and laughing. The plans for independence had finally been unveiled. Marina saw a people letting the last veil lift. Their dark eyes, their brown skins, their black hair, their clothes, even the way they walk or speak with their hands. She saw them all anew.

Damascus was new again. But Marina, Paul, Clem, George, Taylor-Greene, would not be part of it. They too had been consigned to the history books and the architecture, along with the Turks and the Romans.

Up in the university, groups of students were starting to cluster. Voices were being raised. Hands too. Women in veils and women in high heels raced through the precincts, torn between the rush home and the desire to lift their fists, to shout, to cry their freedom.

On arriving in the university, Marina stepped out of the car and was hit by the late-summer heat. London might be awash with rain now. It might be filling the gutters, she thought. Leaves would be tumbling in the gushing waters, blocking up drains. Or maybe it was sticky and hot there. Children might be licking their ice-creams, running through play-pools.

Marina felt betrayed by her freckled skin, her blue eyes, her light-brown hair. In her bag was a pale green scarf. Tying it around her head, she avoided the worst of the students' fire-bright glances.

She moved quickly through the university precincts. Her heart was beating at a terrifying rate.

A man of about sixty, with a kind face and a scrawny beard, was opening a glass door. Reading-glasses were perched book-ishly on the end of his nose. He peered intently through them as Marina dashed towards him.

'Excuse me. Do you speak English?' she said loudly.

The man smiled.

'Of course, miss.'

Marina stopped in front of him. She was thinking, I must smile, be nice. The edgy curl on her lips did not fool old Siddiqi.

'Do you know where the Islamic Department is?' she said.

Dr Siddiqi grinned.

'Of course,' he said. 'It's my department.'

He thought she had the biggest blue eyes he had ever seen. He thought he could just stand there, forever looking into them.

Then, remembering his manners, he extended his hand. 'Oh, my name is Siddiqi. Hello, Mrs –?'

Marina offered her hand back, but told a lie.

'My name is Marina . . . Russell,' she murmured. 'I'm a friend of Sulayman Ahmed's. He is in your department, I believe.'

'Why, yes.'

Marina smiled at Siddiqi politely then. The doctor did not miss the sudden switch from edginess to sweetness.

'I need to see him with some urgency,' Marina added.

The two of them climbed Siddiqi's tower. Marina talked endlessly to Siddiqi in her sweet-edgy voice.

Rambling across subjects – she could not tell if she was saying these words, or merely thinking them – the architecture of the university buildings, how her footsteps reminded her of a Mozart piano sonata, she did not know which one, the echo of the plunging white keys, the traffic down in the Old City, and Sulayman, Sulayman, always Sulayman.

Here she was, the murderess! The avenging angel!

But her bag concealed no knife, it was hiding no gun. Still she felt like a ganster in a film noir. She felt like Jimmy Cagney.

Siddiqi asked her how she knew Sulayman, but Marina did not answer. Everything had a stinging electricity, even their few bits of low talk, even her sonata of footsteps in C.

They hit a landing with a single door.

'This is it,' Siddiqi said, as he came to a stop.

She looked up at him and said impatiently:

'Well, shall we go in, then?'

Siddiqi placed his hand on the door handle.

'You didn't say how you knew Sulayman?'

Marina smiled, then added her hand to the door handle, and turned it. Pushing the door open, Marina said deliberately:

'Through my husband.'

Sulayman looked up, watching the door swing back.

Marina was pulling the green scarf from her head. Her brown hair tumbled loosely around her face. It was only the second time they had met.

Old enemies, all the same. His face – long, angular, composed rather than handsome – was instantly and terribly familiar to Marina.

You see, she knew it so well. It had been lying with her in bed these months. It had shared the secrets that she had confided in her husband. It had even taken part in their lovemaking.

Seeing the terror flashing in his black eyes, Marina had not expected to feel such anger, such hate. She was shaking with it.

All the time she had expected to be able to speak to him calmly and coolly. She thought she would make her point. But now she realised she didn't even have a point. Now she knew she had come for a fight.

She had come to be Marina again.

She lunged forward, raising her arm high. Later, she recalled it all as slow motion. Sulayman watched her mouth starting to shout. His eyes dropped in time to see her throw her handbag to the floor. Gunless.

The green scarf slipped from her shoulders. Billowed in mid-air. Sulayman threw up his hands. Started to tumble backwards.

'You fucking little shit! You fucking little shit!'

Her hand slapped hard against the side of Sulayman's face. The stinging force with which she hit him rang through Marina, so much so that she hurt her own shoulder striking him.

His whole body reeled backwards. A horrible, painful yelp whistled out of Sulayman as he smacked back against a bookshelf, and slim volumes tumbled around his slumped body.

Siddiqi rushed forward to restrain Marina, who stood trembling, too angry to cry, in the middle of a stranger's office in a place she had never been to before, swimming in her anger.

Dazed, Sulayman got to his feet. Siddiqi was gripping Marina's arm hard enough to hurt her.

'Mrs Russell, what is this?'

'Let go of me, please,' she insisted.

Marina felt both foolish and indignant. Fury had tipped out of her in that blow. A tide of hate spilled out of her eyes, her mouth, her nostrils, into the world. Siddiqi and Sulayman stood there, staring at her in disbelief and outrage.

'This is madness,' Siddiqi cried, shaking his head.

'Mrs Russell?' Sulayman said, not understanding. The red raw mark on his face was burning hot. He lifted his fingers to his face but stared at Marina in disgust.

Siddiqi was becoming angry. This gentle old man, locked away in an ivory tower of study and deciphering, had his own fury.

'Mrs Russell, haven't you heard?' he snarled. 'The days of *nice* white ladies slapping Arabs as they please are over! You can't walk into an Arab university any more and abuse whomever you please!'

Marina felt ashamed of her anger.

'No, that's not it *at all*,' she began to say, her voice trailing away.

Sulayman pointed at her.

'This woman is not called Mrs Russell, Doctor. She is called Mrs Esmond. She is Paul Esmond's wife.'

Siddiqi poked his spectacles up the bridge of his nose.

'I see . . .'

'She has come to upbraid me, no doubt.'

Marina and Sulayman. A pair of foes. Marina and Sulayman. Each hating the other for what he or she has done to the other. Each knowing that any hate is misplaced but that, at that moment, feels real.

'Shouldn't I upbraid you?' Marina asked. 'Shouldn't I scratch your damn eyes out, for what you have done?'

'What *I* have done? What *I* have done?'

'Yes, that's right. Behaving like some rent-boy!'

Siddiqi stepped forward.

'Mrs Esmond!'

'Well, it might be all right here, this sort of carry-on. But it's not all right with me!'

'Mrs Esmond, if you cannot keep a civil tongue in your head, I shall ask you to leave.'

'I won't leave, not until I have had an apology, an explanation!'

'Then I shall throw you in the street myself!' Siddiqi cried, putting his hands on the top of his head, to stop his brains exploding.

Marina turned and stared at the old man. She nearly said, 'How dare you?', but stopped. White ladies in pretty dresses no longer existed in Damascus. The city had a new veil. Marina's day – the time of white ladies being spoken to respectfully – had passed in Damascus. She was now the *interloper. Invader. Occupant.*

Get out! the city cries. Be gone! the people cheer.

'And what,' Sulayman began, 'am I supposed to apologise for? Or to explain?'

The rawness of the blow to his cheek looked like it was fading. Or bruising. Out of the window in that high tower there was the noise of all Damascus. The voice of the city. And it was shouting loud. Freedom, it was saying. Justice. Change.

'I want you to explain to me how you just walked into my life – into Paul's life – and turned everything upside-down. How you think you can just walk away now.'

'But isn't that precisely what you and Paul want? For me to disappear? To forget about you both, pretend all this has never happened?'

'Let's all be friends?' Siddiqi sneered, thinking of other matters.

'No, that is not what I want! I want you to take responsibility for what you have done!'

Sulayman stepped forward, closer to Marina. Her leg muscles flinched for a moment, as if she was frightened of physical retaliation. She had no need to be.

'Responsibility? I am *not* responsible for you, Marina. I am not responsible for Paul's behaviour. If you have a husband that likes men, that is not my problem. It's yours!

'It was yours when you married him. It was yours when you first forgave him and thought that you could change him. And the second time too!

'And what a presumption, to believe you can change what is not broken, Marina. What cannot be changed! If Paul cheats on you, and you can't live with it, it becomes your responsibility that you have never left, that you have never made him see what he was doing was not acceptable!

'You are not a child, Marina! And neither is Paul!'

A sudden burst of pale yellow light entered the room.

A sea of academic dust was illuminated by it. Shifting, sparkling, sublime. The three of them there – Sulayman, Marina, Siddiqi – became one with the afternoon. They became part of the sunlight. Every bit as transitory and imagined as the colour of the sunlight in that room.

Marina pointed a finger accusingly at Sulayman.

'You have no right to question my marriage.'

'And you, Marina, have no right to question my relationship with Paul.'

'Oh, don't I?'

'No. If you want to ask questions, ask Paul about why he's been unfaithful. Ask him why he does this to you. Or don't. But leave me out of it, all right? My life is none of your business!'

'But you having an affair with Paul is my business!'

'No, it's not. You having an unfaithful husband is your business. If you want to change that, you must talk to him, not to me.'

'So I should forgive and forget, is that it?' Marina laughed.

She felt so terribly weak. Damascus was once a city where White ladies in pretty dresses were never questioned. Even if Marina hated colonial society, its presumptions, its patronising privilege, she was guilty of being shocked that these Arab men should so forcibly question her right to go there and start shouting.

They shouted back. They told her to get out. Their responses disabled her. She felt capable only of limp questions that were no match for Sulayman's angry, articulate answers.

'Hate me. Don't hate me. You choose, Marina. But you have nothing to forgive me for. Your fight is with Paul, not with me!'

She could not respond. Her voice ached to be heard, but it was lost somewhere in her, in her own past, the past of the White ladies.

'I see that Paul is not with you. Hiding away, is he? Afraid of dealing with you and me together?'

'He doesn't know I'm here.'

'So this is just a single-pronged attack, then? A little raiding party? Sent to trample on the fact that I have nothing, whereas you get to pick and choose, to say whether or not you forgive Paul, whether you'll let him back into your life!'

Marina stared at Sulayman for a second. A tear brimmed in her eye. She knew her mascara would run. She knew it.

Here he was, The Other. That evil, selfish, destructive Other, come to claim Paul from her, come to wreck her marriage and her happiness. Here he was, pointing out that Paul had already made decisions about him, the same decisions that Marina now had the privilege to make.

What decisions had Sulayman been allowed to make? Paul had dropped Sulayman. He had said, I don't love you enough. I don't love you any more. And Marina knew that this wasn't even true. Paul had dropped Sulayman because Marina had left him no other option. And Taylor-Greene had not left him any option. Sulayman was here, alone, abandoned. Do Arabs get no options, then? Are they not in on the luxuries of life? To him, she suddenly saw, her presence was just gloating. To him, *she* was The Other.

And he was right too. None of this was his doing. If she had a fight to pick, it should be with Paul. But she had already made up her mind about Paul. She was here merely to vent her anger on somebody, half-knowing that the person who deserved her anger was not Sulayman.

Marina wiped the tear from her eye. A trail of mascara smudged beneath her eyelid.

'I think I'd better go,' she said quietly.

'Yes,' murmured Siddiqi, who had been standing silent and embarrassed in the corner of the room.

But Sulayman cried:

'Wait! Don't go yet!'

Sulayman started to madly scan a bookshelf, filled to the point of bursting with ancient paperbacks and dog-eared wood-pulp files. Siddiqi watched him, Marina too, wondering what on earth he was doing, spinning round and round. Sulayman pulled a book from the lowest shelf.

A blue hardback with a red spine. Marina recognised it at once. It was the book of poems she had given him the night that they first met. When Paul had left him that day at Azem, he had brought it to the university, intending to give it to the library's Literature section.

'*An Anthology of Modern British Verse*,' Sulayman said. 'It's a very good book, you know.' And then he smiled. 'Don't you remember, Marina?'

'You came to dinner,' she replied quietly.

'You gave me a glass of wine. It made me drunk, you know.'

She had not forgotten that she had once liked Sulayman. She had allowed the irrationality of her hate to consume her memory of him.

'He was mine, Sulayman,' Marina murmured. 'He *is* mine. My husband. He wasn't yours to take.'

She took the book from him.

'Well, now I have nothing of yours. You've had it all back.'

Sulayman's sad, brittle voice trailed away. The echo of his words – now I have nothing of yours – struck Marina as a tragedy for both of them. Marina looked at him. He was so young, she thought, when he was really only eight or nine years her junior. And, she thought to herself, maybe we're not so different, me and you. Not so different at all.

'That's not true, Sulayman. You had a part of him that I never had. That I never will.'

They were silent for a moment. It was time for her to go. They had nothing more to say to one another. The burst of sunlight had suddenly and dramatically changed. There was rain in Damascus. A rare storm in late summer, a whisper of winter. Large spots of rain sped through the open window, splashing on the papers all over Siddiqi's desk. Years of scholarship soaked into round, blue circles of wet ink. Progressing through the wood pulp, icicle fingers in blue. The doctor rushed to close the window. In the commotion, their silence was broken.

Marina pulled her green scarf over her head and tried to smile.

'Will you go back to him?' Sulayman asked.

Marina looked at the floor. It was covered in old dusty footprints. A few spots of rainwater, and they were now drawing muddy patterns.

'Yes,' she replied.

That was the first time she had said it out loud. She put the poetry book under her arm.

'Why?'

'What else is there?'

'A lot, Marina.'

'I still love him.'

'He is a homosexual, Marina. You'll never change that.'

She picked up her bag from the floor, where she had thrown it.

'He does love me, Sulayman, in his way. It's a real love.'

'Yes.'

'I love him and want to be married to him, and he wants to be married to me. But from now on these are his decisions. He can be faithful to me and keep me. Or he can have affairs and run the risk of losing me. I can't be the ogre who makes demands any more. I have my own life to lead now.'

Sulayman smiled at her, looking into her big, blue eyes.

'Then live with your decision, Marina. Live with your decision and try to be happy.'

'And what about you?' Marina asked.

'Me?' Sulayman looked surprised.

'Do you still love him?'

Huge spots of rain were pelting the glass windows now. Sulayman walked to the office door, and held it wide for her. It was a signal for Marina to go.

'It doesn't matter, does it? He wants you, not me. I can't change that, even if I wanted to.'

Marina tied her green scarf and left. Sulayman watched her walk away. Her footsteps echoed in the cold stone corridor. Like the last tremble of the piano wires, heard from another room.

MARINA AND PAUL drove through the city in the back of a rusty, imported cab. Holes in the road made it jump and creak. The leather seats had grown hot, even though the late-summer sun had grown noticeably weaker in the last days. An afternoon of rain was tipping the city off. Winter's coming. Damascus didn't mind. This was the greatest winter of four thousand years of history. It would be the winter of their independence.

Paul didn't mind, either. Back to London soon, he thought. But he would miss the rough-and-ready bumps-in-the-road craziness of Damascus. And he would miss Sulayman.

This crazy old city, he thought. The rush, the push, the pull, people, cars and motorcycles, it was all there. In your face. Hands, feet, elbows, mouths kept the commotion going. You see, the population itself was the city's powerhouse. In fact, the people were the city. All around you could hear the singing, jumping, squawking tones of Arabic. Salaams, marhabas, Gods-will-be-dones. Ma sha' Allah, its people sigh. Oh, and the scents. The cloak of petrol, yes. Underneath, there were the delicate, delicious perfumes of the washed. The sweet, heavy drift of coffee, tea, tobacco. Kif from the open-fronted cafés. The tart corrosion of fruit and meat and confectionery left too long on market stalls. Drifting from the stoves and pots of the shawerma and kebab sellers. It was a song and a faith, this crazy old city. Mystical, powerful, serious, joyful, secular, fluffy and light.

The great man said Damascus was a palimpsest. You remember that, don't you, from your history books? Because it's true.

From his taxi window, Paul watched the men and women all around him. Yes, their minds were on new troubles, on politics and religion, on desperate measures, and on the Holy Quran. The pork eaters were putting away their hams and trotters. The boozers were putting away their arak moonshine.

The French sighed that a great city was passing. The British welcomed a new republic, with which they could be big pals. And the Arabs hailed a golden age. Syria – old as time but never given the chance to grow up – would at last stand on her own two feet. Damascus, the oldest city in the world, would be free.

And all the while the people of the city kept rushing back and forth, to work, to shop, to meet a friend, to ruffle a grandchild's hair, to catch a glimpse of the one they loved, their minds were also on the latest show in town, the latest Hollywood hit, wedding negotiations, entrance exams, jobs they were losing, jobs they were getting, what their wife had meant when she said, what their new *amour* meant when he refused that cigarette, and what the hell the kids were going to eat tonight.

Falafels and Arab nationalism. *American Vogue* and Islam. *Mildred Pierce* – in Arabic – and independence. This is one crazy city, Paul laughed to himself wearily, as he watched it from the back of a taxi.

Muammar wakes Sulayman from his first deep sleep since Paul told him the news in the gardens at Azem. From sleep's black, still silence, Sulayman could hear the excitement in his father's voice.

'Son, Firdaus Husseini is downstairs! Old Firdaus has come to call on us! She says that Leilah is waiting outside in the car. She wants to know if we will receive her in the house!'

'What?' Sulayman mutters sleepily.

'Come on, son! You know what this means! You will be married in six months! You will be married to Leilah before spring, son!'

Down in the kitchen, Diniz and Fatma were in a whirl of excited preparations. Fatma was brewing coffee the way only she knew how. Diniz was chopping the sherbet to make a cold lime drink for the magical princess sitting in an imported black car.

Ululations! When Sulayman appeared, both women cried aloud happily. Diniz rushed over, raised her hand to his head and blessed him in the traditional way. As soon as she removed her hand, she spat in her palm and flattened down a lick of black hair standing up on his head.

Sulayman could hear his father talking animatedly with Mother Firdaus about how exciting it would all be, this independence business. And Firdaus was agreeing that it was a great time to be a Syrian. And to be an Arab, Muammar added gleefully. Sulayman and Diniz smiled knowingly at each other. Fatma tutted loudly as she shuffled around her bubbling pots. Muammar was a survivor. And what else is age-old Syria, Diniz might have said, but a survivor?

Diniz looked at her son with adoring eyes.

'Oh, my beautiful son, great things are ahead. Many changes. In a year, you mark my words, the man that you will become will barely recognise the boy that you are today.'

Suddenly, Muammar was at the kitchen door, clucking and waving his arms. Diniz, Fatma and Sulayman all swung round.

'Come on, you bunch of goats!' he hissed so as not to be heard. 'Firdaus has gone to get Leilah from the car!'

A whirlwind of excitement swept through the kitchen. This was the future.

Marina sits in her plane seat. She's doing up the buckle on her seat-belt. An air stewardess comes by and asks her if she wants a magazine. Marina says no. She has a book of poems in her bag. She might read it during the flight. But she might not.

Paul asks her if she is all right. Touches her hand lightly. Neither of them know what he will do when they get back to London. The Civil Service probably wouldn't re-employ him now. But she doesn't worry about it. There are other jobs. Other lives to be led.

Through her window, Marina looks out at Damascus Airport.

In the distance they are pulling down a row of black cypresses to build a modern terminal. The old one was badly damaged during the shelling by the Free French. She turns and looks at her husband.

She has always wanted Paul. That has never changed. Sitting with him now, in the dry, blazing heat of Damascus Airport, she looks at their lives ahead.

Propellers start to spin. Seat-belts get fastened. The cabin is full of clicking mechanisms and nervous, flight-wary chatter. Silent, Marina turns to look out of the window. Diggers move slowly around the new terminal. Black cypresses fall to the ground, one by one.

Out there is the desert. And the city too. The air feels hot, even though the warm rain spots on sandy roads whisper softly of winter. Marina feels impossibly small, dwarfed by Damascus, by its colour, by its commotion, by the enormity of its history.

She knows that the city is out there, and that its people, those cosmopolitan, ageless, self-absorbed Damascenes, will soon forget her face, her name, the sound of her voice. Suddenly Paul touches her hand and she turns her face away from the window to look at him. He smiles gently, making her look down, towards her hands, folded in her lap.

Outside, the diggers keep moving. And the black cypresses keep falling. And the city keeps whispering. Damascus is swapping faces again, Marina, and those words, the ones which recorded your presence, are already being written over.